THE ACTAEON TIDE

Tom Anderson

Tom Anderson was born in Watford and grew up in Porthcawl. He worked as a private investigator for a range of clients after studying at the University of Glamorgan, before developing a travel-writing career using journeys taken as a surfer. *The Actaeon Tide* is his fictional debut.

Also by this author:
Riding the Magic Carpet
Chasing Dean
Grey Skies, Green Waves

surfers may be weirdos but they are weird in wonderfully unpredictable ways.' – *The Daily Telegraph*

'Something as seemingly mundane as the weather is impressively transformed by Anderson into a source of compelling interest... he has a beat sensibility.' – *Babylon Wales*

'Great writing...' – *New Welsh Review*

THE
ACTAEON TIDE

Tom Anderson

Parthian, Cardigan SA43 1ED
www.parthianbooks.com
First published in 2014
© Tom Anderson 2014
ISBN 978-1-909844-81-0
Editor: Susie Wild
Cover design by www.theundercard.co.uk
Typeset by Elaine Sharples
Printed and bound by Gomer Press, Llandysul, Wales
Published with the financial support of the Welsh Books Council
British Library Cataloguing in Publication Data
A cataloguing record for this book is available from the British Library.

For Del

Hindsight will prove fate and destiny responsible for Actaeon's misfortune, rather than his own wrongdoing. For it is perfectly acceptable to lose your way from time to time...

Ovid, Metamorphoses

Zero

If low water ever comes at midnight, we'll get the biggest tide possible. Simple science. Gravity's game. It's the laws of nature.

Mind you, that has to be midnight on the dot, and not necessarily what it says on the clocks. I'm talking about 'midnight' as in the furthest you can get from day in either direction; night-time's halfway mark; the point when this side of the planet is dipped as far into freezing space as it gets before being pulled back around to the sun. Match that exact moment with the turning tide – not a second or a nanosecond either way, and, well, it's almost too rare to reckon on. But it does happen, once in an Actaeon moon.

Midnight, and she's going through it again. Noise everywhere. Whatever she doesn't want to hear – worst fears, deepest regrets, hidden fantasies. They're pouring through the air around her.

She's seen the figure sitting on her lawn. No chance of it being a shadow. This time she's going out to meet it. What's the worst it can be? Not even pain.

Midnight. If it ever happens, then surely it happens like this: rushing at the emptiness, outdoors, her hair flailing in the freezing night. No witnesses beyond the stardust of the Milky Way overhead.

The figure rises to meet her.

And it is everything she could have feared, and more.

If someone's leaving this world, does it matter what they go through on the way out? Does how you meet your end shape anything at all?

There's the cooling of the heart, fainting, draining of sense while bleeding dry. It's as if she's always known this feeling from somewhere. No time to think of the injustice of it, the barbarity – what if it's worse than she's imagined?

Furthest moments away from daylight. Something else that no longer matters. She won't see the sunrise anyway.

And then, just as it's nearly done, right when that tide is turning to come in again, there comes the pain.

WINTER

1

The instruction

The job that changed everything first came onto my radar about a month ago. How do I know it changed everything? You just do, don't you? Funny, when something major like that happens, things just kind of... stand out.

I can see that whole day over in my mind, and probably always will:

I'm wandering around, lunchtime, trying not to succumb to buying chips again on the first of those really dark days, when the sun comes up for such a short time you feel as if you're never really awake.

Almost out of ideas, I make it back to the office with a baguette instead – don't ask why, it's not even fresh, either, by the look of things. Starsky's sitting opposite me playing with some kind of security camera and a box of Kleenex. A pretty compromising combination – if you didn't know what he's actually doing with them. The camera's going to go inside that box, concealed. Then he'll leave the whole package on the back shelf of a car outside some unsuspecting fool's front door. Starsky is bad news. Although the worst bit is that you'll probably never know his role in your downfall. Unless you go to court, in which case he'll tuck you up even tighter.

But speak as you find, I reckon, and right now I find a living through this joker.

'Alright Noah,' he croaks at me. He's got that Londoner's

way of smoothing out the hard bits of a word while making the smooth bits hard in their places: *Aw-roii*.

'Aye, not bad,' I reply. He sucks you into his ways. I almost sound like him these days – which given that I'm half his age and smoke twenty a year to his twenty a day isn't anything to wish for. 'So who's the box of tissues for, then?'

'Just testing it,' he says, and slides it my way – lens first. My face comes up, filling a screen on his desk. I aim a middle-finger-salute at the box and my fingernail swells into the fisheye image.

'Top quality pic on that, eh?' He looks pleased with himself, which can only be bad for someone else.

We go quiet for a minute, and then he croaks:

'Job's come up, matey. And I've got a feelin about this one.'

When he says that, he's always right. He may have left the police for 'reasons unknown', but fifteen years' experience working in murder squads still means his hunches get to border on the psychic.

'Bring your lunch, Noah,' he adds, just as I'm about to bite down on that baguette. 'I'm meeting this client in an hour. I wanna drive around where she lives first. Get a decent recce – in case it all goes to pot.' He's already pulling his jacket on and reaching for a scarf. Each slight gust from the coldest ocean of the year gets through whatever you wear, anyway – sharp-edged breezes, able to spread the greyness across the town's walls, pavements and the soaking, dark sand of the seafront a few streets away.

We wind our way out of the Crawl, engine lurching, lurid green screenwash sloshing away the dried salt and rubber fragments of a half-frozen road. It's been such a rotten day that dusk has been on us for the last two hours at least. Starsky flicks the fog lamps on and starts to tell me more.

'So this bird phones the 0800 line about ten this morning,' he explains. 'Says her name's Michelle Lovell.' He talks; I write – makes it look like I'm going to be some use.

'She starts asking about what kind of work we do, so I tell her. You know, start off cagey and all. Recovery, serving people, reporting, tracing.'

It sounds more glamorous than it is. These days 'recovery' is what we get the most of by a mile.

'She just listened for a bit,' Starsky explains. 'Listened without saying anything. Which I wasn't really liking. Made me think this is someone who's after something, you know, er... untoward.'

'Without saying *anything*?'

'Well, the odd "yes" maybe. But then she calmly comes out with it: "Can you search a place for bugs?" And I'm like... Er, well, in theory, yeah, we can. Depends who's asking and why...'

'And can we?'

'Well, I have done. About three hundred times. So yeah. Mate of mine's company in Northampton has even got some equipment for it too. So unless the stuff being used is like, the bollocks, then yeah, I can have a pretty good go. It's easy work if you know what you're doing. I've been asking around the last hour or two about how much to charge these days.'

We push out into the overtaking lane as our car hits the dual carriageways past Bridgend. At a roundabout I just make out, through fading twilight, dry bits of the road that are still a pinky white from salt thrown down last week. Bare trees and thinned hedges want to become silhouettes. I give my thoughts to the journey, staring at tail-lights of cars in front which shrink away from us as the country roads rise and dip. We're well into the Vale when he pulls over and starts peering at the damp, ten-year-old RAC road-map he keeps under the driver's seat. It's covered in little ink dots – each one represents a person who almost certainly didn't want a visit. This by-appointment stuff is rare.

'Roads we need aren't on here,' Starsky muses, reaching for a printout he's folded in his coat pocket. 'Got a fair idea, though. Went to this bit of the Vale once before, bout two years ago. Had to serve some wife beater in one of the farms.'

It's not quite dark yet, but day has certainly lost any of the weak hold it had as we're winding through the smallest lanes. We pass houses I never knew existed in South Wales. Already you get the sense you can't see well enough.

'Biiiig old houses around here, matey,' he tells me. 'We're gonna do alright out of this if she turns out to be *compus mentas*, like.'

I won't forget the first sighting of her as long as I'm *compus mentas*, that's for sure. Mrs Lovell, as Starsky was already insisting we call her, lives at the end of a street that shows up like some kind of oasis. A narrow road, unpaved, with lumps of grass and hibernating weeds growing out of its middle, goes for at least a mile before the bumpy surface breaks back to Tarmac and ends on a T-junction. A short street – dead end to the left but on the right a rise up to several houses. It's all there in my mind whenever I want to go back. And so is she.

Separate gravel driveways lead to three clean, pin-edged houses, each at least six-bedrooms, and then another bigger one still, much older, that sits on top of the incline at the end of the road. The other three probably used to be its grounds, Starsky's voice is there telling me, forever. Probably sold off to raise some cash when the family needed it, he goes on.

Since an unknown car showing up here is probably a pretty rare event, Mrs Lovell is already at the gate on foot, waiting for us. Must have seen our lights a way off.

Her face looks haunted by some sort of glow, that you pick up easily even from a distance. It's not really something you can see as much as something you just know. She's got dark hair that's held in half curls which wave a little in the evening breeze, along with her long dress. It's freezing but she looks totally tough to it – as if her essence has retreated to deep inside her body where it's completely safe from the elements. A pale face shows off sharp features. No need for makeup. She's at least forty, but will look like this forever. Her cheekbones are dainty and prominent. Wide eyes, almost too big for the sparse flesh that surrounds them, pull everything inwards. She walks with folded arms towards the back door of the car and gets in without waving, without making any kind of gesture.

'Can we drive?' she says.

Got to warn you here – whoever you are – before we go further in. It's been in the back of my mind the whole time so it's only fair I share it, right?

We're getting on board here, aren't we? I mean getting on board with *her*? And with whoever else is floating through this next rise of the tide. Thing is, what if you end up with that little crosshair over your forehead too? Marked out to play a role against your will, you know – just for being there with us when we hear it?

It's probably too late for me. But if you're also peering in, sharing the guilt, the blame, the responsibility or whatever else it might be, then... oh I don't know. Who cares? It's just that we might *all* end up pulled in by that current.

Long as you're OK with it. That's all. Only saying. So that you can't cry foul when midnight comes and we're all in for the haul.

If midnight comes, perhaps I should say, coz you never can guarantee it, right?

'Don't worry, I'll know when to get out,' I say to myself, or anyone else who's listening.

Of course you will. Of course.

Starsky said before we got here that this Mrs Lovell would be blunt, but nothing readies me for the stuff we're about to hear next:

'I really mean it,' she says. 'Not a word until it's safe. We need to drive. Now.'

We oblige, and Starsky fires us through the lanes again, until we get back towards the real world. At a roundabout we pass the same exit three times before going on, and then stop at the edge of a busy road – one of the ones feeding in towards Cowbridge again. Lots of movement around us – and I know why he's chosen here. We can't be listened to, and we can't be watched or tailed without someone having to make a tit of themselves in the passing traffic.

'I'm sorry for the fuss,' she says, 'but we do need to be away from the house and sure that nobody followed us. It's filled with bugs and cameras. I know my husband is involved, with intent, and strategy, and I'm pretty sure it goes to the top.' She thinks about every word, as if she's rehearsed this a thousand times before meeting us. But all of a sudden she's done, and tails off mumbling something like, 'Or elements of it.'

I can feel my face going prickly and hoping she can't tell as I try and act as if I've heard this shit many times before. Starsky doesn't need to act though, and I'm following his cues.

'OK,' he says, calm as. 'I'm happy with this spot. I reckon you can talk now. So tell me how you've come by that idea.'

She says nothing for two minutes that are so heavy you can chew them, then gently prises a piece of folded lined paper from the side elastic of her dress, and looks over it without expression.

And then she talks. Slow, careful, sucking emotion back in at every relevant break.

There's one thing about her I can't ever call to memory, by the way. It's her voice. I know her story, I know how she says it – the pace, the pauses – but I can't hear her voice.

The words though. The content of it. It's inescapable.

'OK, thanks for coming at such short notice,' Mrs Lovell starts. 'It's very welcome. I am at... at a point where if something is not done... If something isn't... I am, well, it's getting beyond what I can cope with.' Suddenly this supremely confident woman is trying to get reassurance. She doesn't want to say something yet knows she needs to. She thinks we won't be interested. But we are. Who couldn't be?

Starsky treads softly: 'That's OK. What's bothering you?'

'It's so much. There are so many things.' She pauses, as if she's running it all through again, to check she really does need to tell us this. After fishing for that piece of paper it looks as if she's no intention of using it. And then, still in control, still breathing calm and regular:

'I am awoken every morning, at four a.m., by things I shouldn't have to deal with. Every day, and I mean *every* day, I get woken by... by the sound – pre-recorded, I sincerely hope – of a man.' She pauses. 'A man, or at least a male voice, *climaxing*, from within the walls.' The way she just floats through the words means you almost miss it.

'OK,' Starsky coughs. How he handles these delicate moments will define whether we hear more.

'It's being played to me, I know. But in real time. It's the most horrid noise – the voice has relish. It's different every morning. And if I try to sleep again after that, it starts back up within a minute. But that's only one of the sounds.'

Now, most of my life I've kind of relied on being sharper than most people – getting a read on a situation, but as this stuff carries on I know already that I'm miles behind Starsky. He's taking this stuff seriously. He's tuning into it straight away, and I'm only getting the tells second-hand.

She's taking breath between each bit – but the need to break and pull herself together is getting less. 'My entire house is talking to me, Mr White,' she says, her back and neck held straight and true – body language that knows he's listening: 'When I walk down the stairs there are the sounds of rocks falling from above – each of my steps being echoed in rhythm – from the ceiling of my own home. I try to make breakfast and a motorbike engine starts up around me. I turn the hob up, it changes gear. When I use the hoover a wild, high-pitched alarm sounds. It's a, a… a fire alarm, I suppose? That would best describe it. If I boil an egg then there's this subsonic hum that fills the kitchen. Someone's watching me, aren't they?'

At this she stops; her breathing is about to get heavier. Composure is threatened again, which she can't allow. She wants to see what we think.

I'm obviously made of something other than Starsky, because I want to tell the woman she's gone in the head – and I mean *gone*. But then pity kind of washes over that, before intrigue swallows it all and makes me want to hear more.

Starsky just says, 'Fine. I've heard worse. You're doing the right thing talking to someone professional about this.' She looks as if that's what she wanted to hear. 'I suppose there are several very obvious questions,' he adds, 'but first why don't you make sure you've got the hard bit done? We'll need to know what else. Noah Lloyd here can make a few notes – and in a minute I'll sketch your house, or a plan of it at least. So are these the only noises?'

'No,' she says, immediately, ready again. 'There's too many to list to you now, but I've started to keep a log of times and, well I suppose, the things that trigger them.'

Starsky nods. 'Well done. That's what I was gonna suggest next.'

'Well, I've got it, but I'm scared to take it out and show it to someone. I'm worried what it would mean for them.' She swallows, and gets her breath in order again, before adding, 'I would, of course, understand if you did not want to get involved with this.'

Get involved with what? I'm bursting to say – but the way Starsky's giving this so much time and respect is binding me.

He keeps his voice soft, still soothing, cajoling. Arms flat on his lap, neutral, Starsky reassures: 'I can see why you'd say that. It's thoughtful of you, Mrs Lovell. I mean it though, I've heard worse. I can vouch you that. And Noah here is more than up to something like this. He knows right from wrong.'

She looks at me – the first time she's caught me straight on, eye-to-eye. It hurts. There's a world behind there that I'm just grateful is not mine. And this is only the back-seat. Starsky's sitting almost square to her in the front – though he is looking around constantly. Poor guy never rests like that. Probably looks the sun in the eye more than he would most people anyway.

She goes on: 'It happens in the shower too. And when I undress. There's applause if it's in my bedroom. There's sound effects... that I suppose are best described as taken from a cartoon. The bangs, the clangs, the whistles and scurries. There are rumbles, whirs, rattles, canned laughter. There's birdsong at night – all coming from *inside* the walls of my house – but with this... acoustic clarity that makes it feel as if it's all around you. It always seems to be the most... inappropriate noise to what I'm doing, too.'

'Which you think means you're being watched,' Starsky adds quickly.

That momentum she needs to talk about this stuff has arrived now. It's like being sick – she seems to think this is the heave that's going to get it all out:

'Being watched.' She nods. 'Well – I must be, isn't that right, Mr White? Somebody is picking up on my movements and creating these sounds to go along with them. Either that, or I'm losing my mind. And that, by the way, is what makes this more frightening. The fear I had at first – you've seen my house – when these, these, *hauntings* – man-made, I know, but they are hauntings – started. That was… extraordinary. I thought I'd be killed. I mean, we don't live our lives expecting to hear voices or things go bump in the night, do we?'

We both shake our heads. *No Mrs Lovell, you're OK.*

'Of course we don't,' says Starsky. 'But that doesn't sound likely to be what's happening here.'

'No. I've never thought that. I can't.' The pressure drops in the car again. 'I'm glad to hear someone say it, though. It's comforting already to think this is something you consider to be… Well, not all in a day's work I'm sure, but, I suppose… credible?'

'Yeah. It is, Mrs Lovell. Completely credible.'

'Good,' she says, nodding. 'Thank you. It didn't take me very long to realise there's a cause for what's happening. But that was what scared me more. A *person* is doing this. Somewhere, this is being… controlled.' Here she does almost falter for a second – but it's reined in at the speed of light. Toughness, composure – they come back over her immediately. 'I'm lucky if I'm sleeping more than a few unbroken hours a week. That's what they do when they torture people isn't it? Sleep deprivation, Mr White. Someone wants me to be driven mad, completely, and I… That's why I think it's my husband.'

'Er – yeah. You're just ahead of me there, Mrs Lovell. I was gonna ask you about that. How does this stuff happen when your husband is around? He hears it as well?'

'No. That's what gives him away. It only happens when he isn't at home.'

At this I can feel Starsky's inclination to believe her drying up a bit. And so can she. Which doesn't work for me as this is the only thing she's said that makes sense in my mind. A flash, a short shock-wave of panic passes in the deeps somewhere behind those eyes of hers.

'Oh, God,' she groans. 'This is the bit where everyone stops believing me. This is why I'm so alone, Mr White.'

'Alone? People say that a lot more than they should, Mrs Lovell. What makes you think that then? Have you spoken to anyone else about this?'

'Of course I have. My sister has stayed in the house with me. Several times.'

'And?'

'Nothing. No noises. And when my husband comes home on the weekends, it's the same. No noises.'

'So have you suggested that your sister comes to stay for longer?'

'Of course I have. That's the logical thing to do isn't it? Well, she will. But only if I agree to go and see a psychiatrist with her first. I don't want to do that, Mr White. It's so important to me. Do you know what it's like to be asked to see a psychiatrist when you know nothing's wrong with you?'

'I can imagine,' says Starsky. Again the doubt is in his voice. It's here to stay.

'I've said already, you don't have to take this work. I am sure of what's going on though. I know what's behind this, Mr White. My husband has, well, more than a vested interest in my losing control.'

Midnight never really happens anyway. We only imagine the things it tells us, don't we? Washed out by daylight, pulled back under by the rushing tide, all that matters is the now.

And whenever the now gets too much for me, there's the other Noah that I can call on. Small, unimportant me, sat listening to things I wish didn't exist, and then it'll all become alright when my mind drifts back to the sea. And its waves. Riding waves is why I live where I live; even why I do what I do. The Crawl sits on the edge of the sea, backed up by hills. That's the right place for me to be – either right at the ocean, or as high from it as you can get. I'll often welcome in the winter dusk on a shoreline anyway – loving the size and stillness of the water that will rise and take all our houses one day, whether Starsky's lot lay hands on them or not. A bit of Swansea cityscape usually hibernates across the misty, salty currents to the west. Ocean winds push hair across my face – reminder of summer, which will come, sure as anything I do or don't try.

Someone keeps telling me to look out for a green flash when the sun goes down. I forget though, coz I'm normally too busy thinking about how that same ball of life and deep red promise is busy heating the waters of Florida or the Caribbean at the same time as it's dropping off the edge of Wales's world.

Must be something to do with me, that I never see that flip of colour. Maybe I'm blind to it. Or perhaps it doesn't want to reveal itself. Either way, it feels like another one of those things I'll never quite reach.

Let's choose a time… Three-thirty in the Crawl. How about that? That's mid morning in Puerto Rico. I wouldn't have to spend so much hope if I was somewhere like that instead. The doorstep would be enough of a change.

Few more years, I always think. Couple of big jobs. Like this one, even. Save a wedge. See a few people right, then outta here. Even the idea is usually enough to put a skip in my walk. It's a means, I remind myself – to an end. No… To a *beginning*.

She knows her version, that's for sure. Inside out. Husband is a money man – works in London. But he merely makes money – whereas she *is* money. So he's married her because of the family name. That way, if he ever gets served or if his eye-for-an-eye world catches him in the wallet, he can fall back on this magnificent upper-class bride, on whom wealth grows like – oh I don't know – wisteria.

But then she's telling Starsky how she never trusted hubby from the start – why do these people marry in the first place? – and got some sort of pre-nup knocked together. One that meant he got sod-all if she died first, and less than sod-all if he ever did anything that caused a divorce.

There is still a way around their blissful little wedding-day contract though. And this is her theory. Mr Lovell *can* get his hands on her real 'everything' in one event – namely her getting sectioned. *Lasting Powers of Attorney, Mental Capacity Act, 2005.* Someone has to look after the estate if she goes round the twist. If she starts hearing noises in the night. Ouch.

This man of hers, we're told, is running a big-budget plot to send his missus nuts so he can get control of the reserves of money held up in that piece of paper he probably never wanted in the first place.

Either that – or she *is* mad. Which means the prick has power of attorney anyway and she might as well give me and Starsky a wedge of her money anyhow. That would be the easier option in many ways, I reckon.

'I'll give you everything you need to know, Mr White,' she's saying.

'OK,' says Starsky, 'and I can ensure confidentiality, professionalism.' He's telling her about his past – locking up bent coppers, murderers, the vilest of the vile. 'We know right from wrong,' he keeps repeating. 'I won't work for bad people, Mrs Lovell. Now tell me more about your husband. Where's he based?'

'He's in the City. Investments, trade. I can give you the details. This is why you must be beyond circumspect. I think he's got friends who are very rich, short-term rich. They're terrible people, Mr White. These people see something, want it and take it. They move such a fine line between crooked and clear. He could arrange this kind of thing, easily.'

'Watching his wife with a hundred hidden cameras?' It comes out with more of a wobble than he means to show. Starsky's self aware though and slows, thinks for a moment, slight evidence of a nod moving through his neck muscles. 'I can see it happening,' he reassures. 'You don't have to pitch it to me. Trust me, in my time... I ain't surprised easy.'

He fires off a rapid row of questions to establish the basics of what we're about to get into. How long have you lived here? *Five years*. Could this stuff have been installed before? *Maybe*. Have they redecorated at any point? *No*. Longest she's been away in one go? Month – with hubby the whole time.

He presses to the limit: 'And no signs of plaster moved about – no odd textures in the paint?'

Nothing. No. Never. None.

How d'you tell your husband you think he's doing a stunt like this, and that you're onto him? Some life to live, this. I start wondering if she sleeps with him and gazes into his eyes when they're together on weekends, despite believing this preposterous shit about him. Imagine the intensity of going to bed with this woman when half a second of catching her glance makes your fingertips prickle. Something's been left by that stare – in the air around us – in the cockpit of this car. There's a well dropping downwards, opening where she is and sinking away. I'm peering over – and Starsky's already halfway down and asking for more rope.

'Mr White,' she adds with a voice that suggests this first meeting's end is moments away. 'I have just warned you. My husband is involved with very powerful people. I'd imagine this to go to the top.'

Of what? I think. Starsky doesn't flinch though. Tell him things that would shit most people up, and all it'll do is get this guy keener to take on the job.

'So this instruction,' he announces. 'I'll need it in written form from yourself with the address named on it. You'll have a copy too – although probably a good idea to keep it somewhere discreet.' He delays briefly, her eye contact full and sustained, before going on. 'It's gonna need to be done with the right people around me, who I'll trust, or with no one. Either I can make the decisions I think are right with this job, or it doesn't get done by Whiteout. We can solve this, Miss, we can, but it's gonna be about twenty-five grand.'

'Fine,' she says immediately, as if she's been expecting it to cost twice that.

'Er, OK...' You can see Starsky kicking himself for going in too low, although he still tries to take what little advantage he can of this client's absolute willingness to throw money at her problems: 'Yeah, twenty-five,' he says 'and I'm afraid I will need half of that up front.'

'No problem,' she says. 'Would you like cash?'

My *other* other place. If it can't be the sea. Let's go there, drift quick, just for a power-up. So that I can get through the next bits:

Closed eyes, Starsky's voice retreats, the interior of his car and the small print of the deal he's making lose their grip over me. I push my floating mind across the country and head for the hills. When I find the place I'm looking for and stop, we're the furthest up I can get from the low-water mark. It's the summit of the biggest hill behind the Crawl and I climb here to remind myself not to care. D'you ever get that burning, that upwelling – a sense you're banging your head against a wall? There's so much I want to be, to do, and most of it can't be up to me. Some people are born to pull strings, and others are born puppets. But up here I get it.

Slopes drop away. The Bristol Channel pans out, the Crawl, the Vale, its linking roads and segmented fields, all bare and humble beyond squares of miles of miniature land. Look the other way and I can see the curve of the horizon, above a dark triangle of shadow where the rock I'm on cuts out the light. From down there the sun has already set. To the west more reddening peaks scratch the belly of the clouds, like waves themselves, but rising out of an even angrier ocean of supreme scale. My size feels great. A puppet – but right now, for once, looking down on my own show.

Wind running from the north whips up into my face. It hurts, and I like it. The evening's going to be biting cold.

I can go back when I want. Or not.

She's got history. Perfect. Already, there's a dilemma. It's taken Starsky one hands-free call to a crooked administrator he used to work with – straight away forking out expenses on this case – to find out. I've seen him push boundaries, but it's the first time to my knowledge he's fished for info like this since going civilian. Worth it, mind. Fifteen years back – turns out she had a spell under the watch of a psychiatric team after being convinced someone was perving on her in the bath. This was before hubby even came on to the scene – when she went by her maiden name, 'Clare'. Michelle Clare. Not much more detail than that, but it's there forever in a database accessible only to those who know what they're looking for. Three weeks under close watch. Thought there was a man climbing the branches outside her window to peer in at bath time. Cut the tree down herself – badly, so that it fell back and crushed a car. Volunteered for 'minor medication' and has behaved ever since. So says our still-serving, so-called confidant, anyway.

Still on the way back to the Crawl, Starsky tells me what he thinks. But not before bashing the wheel and throwing out every expletive in his pretty extensive profanisaurus.

'Fuck. Shit to get into. Arseholes. City arseholes. Mad, mad, old fuckin...'

I ask him if he's taking it serious.

'The things she describes, for sure,' he says.

'No – her *previous*.'

'Irrelevant. She's been alright ever since – we have to assume that now – this is our client, and an instruction's an instruction.'

So what is it, then? The story. That's what's bothering him. He's come across this *kind* of thing before, but there's something else that's rattling him here and he doesn't know what. Right now his only evidence is instinct. And it's enough to send Christopher 'Starsky' White, calmest man in the northern hemisphere, off the handle for a second.

'It's not what someone says, see matey,' he muses. 'It's the way they say it.'

'What d'you mean?' I ask again.

'Noah, if I knew, I'd fuckin tell ya.'

When we get home I've promised to meet Mum and my little sis Josie for a bit of dinner – kids eat free with two mains – in the sizzler up the street. She's twenty years younger than me. Josie, that is. They both live round the corner. That's how far I've flown.

'Busy day?' I ask them.

'For Josie,' my mum replies, 'yes. She's been pushing the trundle wheel in school. Maths lessons, wasn't it, Josie? Metres and feet? Measured the distance from every classroom to the toilet.'

'Great,' I say. 'Nice work.'

Little sis adds only a proud grin for now.

'Her class is nearest – to the toilet. Explains the smell, doesn't it Josie?'

'Yep,' she's forced to acknowledge.

'Was a secret project too. She was only meant to measure the corridor.'

'Secret, eh?' I raise an eyebrow at her. 'Keeping secrets at your age?'

She grins again. My mum carries on:

'Josie, tell Noah what you're meant to measure for homework.'

'Hill,' says my little sis.

'Really?'

'Yes.'

'They've let her take the wheel home,' says my mum. 'She's been telling her teachers how her big brother takes her to hills. Maybe she can get some photos next time?'

'OK,' I say. 'Whatever she needs to do.'

I don't tell them anything of where I've been that evening. Nothing of the Vale, of the houses I only knew existed tonight, nothing of work. In fact, I'm no use to anyone. Josie starts chatting about some friend who doesn't have a TV which Mum is telling her, unconvincingly, is a good thing. Means the friend will be brainy when she grows up. But Noah isn't in the room. His eyes are on the walls, even of this ten-year-old pub – rough plaster over thick, fake stone; what secrets might they hold? What stories do we all need to share, really, when our souls are laid out? This isn't the world you think it is, Josie. Even your mother can only scratch the surface. And me? I've got nothing to offer. I'm a passenger – yeah, all I ever promised.

'Long drive.'

'Eh?' I glance up from my menu card.

'Long drive.'

'What, me?'

'No. *I* had a long drive today,' says my mum. 'Bedford. I'm back there next week again too. Up and down in a day – like today. That's why I thought we could grab dinner out.' She says it as if it's not something that happens often.

I float through the next hour of idle chat and then walk the long way round to get back to my place. More than just a beer and burger to walk off along the soaking beach. At the shoreline, light jumps off the ground, flicked back up at me from water between the low-tide sand-wrinkles. We haven't seen the sky in the Crawl for a fortnight. Behind me, smothering, glaring streetlamps prevent being able to connect to the loneliness. I can't hide, even here.

Vapour in the air is chilled by the turning northerly winds as I find the pavement again. There's no salt now, apart from on the roads. Freezing drizzle, night after night, never enough even to wash the grit into the gutters. Indoors is the place to be – unless you're Mrs Lovell.

It is almost lonely at home, though. Sleep is late and meagre, but it does arrive. I settle, knowing I'm part of something, take comfort that the course will stay set. Closed eyelids; I'll let someone else direct. There's peace in that – that and the rhythms of the sea again, and its frequencies.

2

The source, and what
isn't inside the house

So there's me, Minor Threat playing on my car stereo, and, when fate affords, bringing my world up those golden driveways to the doors of the rich and powerful. Most of my days are filled with winding-up petitions and bankruptcy notices, discreet asset enquiries or recovery reports. And can you see why it's perfect for me? If money and influence are your things then what use is it trying to find empathy from a punk-pumped, late twentysomething whose only care in the world is hanging out in a nothing town and making the time to do sod-all once in a while?

It all suits me, the man at the centre, fine. I'm not even joking when I boast that there's only one external force that Noah allows to alter his plans – and that's the sea. No amount of cash or petty personal power can stand up to that master.

It doesn't work for some – my mum just thinks it leaves you never sticking to anything. Change your mood with the sea, and like all the other surfers in this town you'll be about as constant as the swells you wait on. Except the sea is older than any of us, and will last longer.

There I go again. I'm changing my mind even as I talk.

Any season though, whatever the temperature, when tide and time are right, this is the ritual that sorts me out.

Park up in the streets behind the beach, board waxed and then quickly whip jeans and shoes off. Wet neoprene wrapped around my ankles, then a grimace and it's pulled up to the waist. I've got the act down – top half on with minimum skin exposure to the biting northerlies. This time of year, frost crunches under my booted feet as I round the bracken to see lines of unbroken ocean pulse wrapping in from the Atlantic.

Yeah, I'm in love with the whole thing. Even the way your head shrinks around your skull as you push underwater for the first time. Brain-freeze; the 'ice cream headache'. You know you're earning something from this kind of pain. But then, once I get out behind the breaking waves, it's all release. Shore is just a model now – a different realm, left behind. Things make meaning and take shape as I stroke into a lined-up little peeler that stands up to me, its folding crest holding my eyes. Body weight isn't mine anymore, as I rise to the top of a strip of thin, wind-groomed water, edge tilted to the outside rail and drop back in. The sea's pulse moves through me. Confession, absolution. I'm shaking off a burden, rinsing away things that I don't need. Nobody can stop anyone doing this.

Two more waves, forgiveness in the bag, and I'm into the replenishment. Storms thousands of miles away charge me up. Good for anything once a few more of these frequencies have tapped through my life-force. Anything.

When decisions lie on the horizon, this has always been where Noah gets his counselling. Cut off too long from the sea, not riding waves, things lose their shape. And when I'm tuned in, it all works out.

'Wait for dark, Noah, matey, and tonight... you and me are in that fuckin house.'

'You what?' The waves sink straight to the back of my thoughts as my boss announces the rest of today's schedule.

'I've thought on it… a lot.' Starsky stands up and steps to the window. 'You know I ain't a good sleeper, and my best ideas are always the late ones, so I know this is the right thing to do. We're going in for a look. Let me get the feel of the place – see if it fits. That's how to be sure we don't get dragged along with a rich bird losing her marbles. Thirty seconds inside that place and I'll tell ya if she's with it or not. You'll be able to see if that's the house of some nutcase – there'll be something about it. Trust me. We get to know for sure this way.'

'Bullshit.'

'I wish it was, mate. But that is what we're doing. Unless you wanna drop out of a job that could earn ya a coupla grand for half a day's work?'

'Bullshit. How're we going to get inside there, then? Without the whole thing going…'

'Easy. We'll walk in.'

Now I'm sure this is a wind-up, but Starsky keeps insisting:

'Go on then. Don't believe me. I can do it myself if you ain't up for it.'

'That's not what I'm saying.'

'Course not. Here we go, matey. Remembering that cash eh?' He grins at me, rubbing fingers together. 'Yeah, that wedge ya keep tellin me you're gonna save up. Well it ain't gonna come from serving papers or chasing credit card overspenders. If you're really serious you want to piss off out of here and become some surf bum with whatever you're lucky enough to have left on the clocking-in card once the Whiteout years are through…'

'No. I know…'

'Yeah, well you'll have to grow a pair then, won't ya? This is what the bigger jobs are about. Come on Noah, coupla grand minimum in it for you here, matey.'

And he wants to get into Mrs Lovell's place, tonight. 'Just one minute with a torch in my hand and I'll know if her story is for real or not,' he says, as if to reassure himself. Or me. Or anyone else who's got sense to know it has to be harder than that.

And as for how to actually do this, his big plan is... not to have one.

'You what?' I say again.

'Sometimes you have to just walk on through, Noah,' he tells me. 'Glance sideways or hesitate and you're done. No indecision. Can't prep for everything.'

'Yeah, but...'

He cuts off any dissent. 'But nothing, matey. We walk through the unknown all the time. Happens every now and then. You'll only know what to do when you're there. Ready in half hour. We'll get close to the place, then wait for dusk from nearby.'

➜

Leafless trees flick strobe-flashes through the windows of his car. We're flying through the lanes, forty, fifty miles an hour. Once is enough for Starsky to know any road. It's bright, and dry, and he's taking his determination out on the accelerator. A low winter sun slouches behind rows of barren branches that mask the fields and hills beyond. It's gently heating my face through the glass. Winter at its most admirable. There's colour in the landscape – almost – and yet a greyness, a freshness, a gloom, is everywhere.

'See, Noah, I've told ya this before. Best way to do something sketchy is to just do it. Don't look about yourself, don't look back. Don't look like you think you're doing anything wrong. People spot the ones who look around all nervous.'

He's actually serious. This really is how we're going to execute our plan that isn't. Walk straight in the front entrance just after dark, look around for a minute, and walk back out.

'What if it's locked?'

'Won't be, mate. She won't have it locked till bedtime.'

'You seem pretty sure?'

'I am. I'll *promise* that door is open. How's that sound?'

Starsky's a man who needs to be in control. That's how he drifts around so expertly in this seedy world of greed and dishonesty. It's how he solved child murders and built files on terror cells in his past life. He's an organised person. Starsky would recce just about any job before taking it on. I've been up to council estates with him dressed in tracksuits, to walk around the block just so we know how many exits some benefit fraudster has from their bedsit the next morning.

When he goes balls to the wall though, he goes balls to the wall.

I've been watching the sun's daily arc descend. I do every year, as autumn loses out. It's still got to be close, now, to as low as it gets – solstice less than a month behind us. Shadows are long, the pavements back in the Crawl don't see direct light any more. If I look low out the window here then it's slush-mud and water that's been frozen over and over. A brook drops in and out of view through a bush, clear water jumping around on smooth stones, moving just enough to survive.

Hedgerows start to look cared for, then the track turns to gravel. You can feel it underneath, and hear it grinding too, as the tyres of the car bump on to the rough surface. Less trees around now, and the lane is dry enough to throw up dust.

I was here twenty-four hours ago, nearly to the minute. We're too early. Starsky wants to let dusk finish filling in.

This means we wait. I get out and sit on the bonnet. The land has flattened out completely. You wouldn't ever think there was this much empty space hidden away in the Vale, but here we are. A row of clouds miles to the west, deep-grey and blue – probably where the sea starts – sits just low enough over the horizon to stop there being a sunset. But enough light's been left in the atmosphere for day to last another fifteen minutes at least. Behind us, where the arc will start again tomorrow morning, the land rises a bit, and I can see two lights. One is a house on a hill, the other a single, constant dot in the sky above it. Has to be a planet. Venus or Jupiter – low and watchful.

Once we're in the post-dusk, Starsky drives again, fog lamps only. I don't get to see the bit where that freshly tarmacked road starts again but it can be felt, and heard, rolling underneath us, scooping us up and pulling us inward to what's at the centre of this void in the Vale. Her street.

Two of the newbuilds have a light on. Hers doesn't. 'No sign of life,' Starsky is saying, as we park up close to the little pathway. He gets out. I follow.

'Believe, Noah.'

And we march, brisk, lightfooted but sure, up to Mrs Lovell's front door. Starsky tweaks his thumb-sized torch on, and pushes the door ajar. He's kept his promise. It wafts open easily. Inside there's a little porch, cement-floored with a flannel of loose carpet. Behind that is another door, also open.

Less than three hours after being in the sea, I'm in her hallway, and immediately neither me nor Starsky like it, not one bit.

'No-oooaaaaahhhh!' Little Josie always flies at me like this. Bursting with ideas to tell me in return. Stick out a palm for high-five and then the warmth comes over me. Whatever our purpose in this corner of the universe, one thing we must create is *meaning*, and between me and Mum we're doing a good job of feeding this kid's appetite for the world.

'What's happenin Josie?'

'Dressing up.'

'Tidy.'

'What as?'

'Frog.'

I was wondering what the wings and wand were about. Not stuff that's adorned the few frogs I've come across, but her take doesn't tend to be the usual. When she gets closer there's a silver sticker on her nose too. Mum follows a few steps behind, and then Scarface – my dog technically, though I'm not much use to him.

I shove sister and dog around for a few seconds before slumping into the old couch's darker end; my inevitable response to their energy. Neither really understand what it's like to be Noah, of course. Both probably have idealised versions of the experience in their imagination, but they'd be fools to swap places. I kind of like the idea of Josie staying right here for ever, in this age, in this guise.

'It's too cold right now to be a frog,' I tell her. 'Ponds are all frozen.'

'Are you having food?' my mum interrupts. The world's easiest ice-breaker.

'Yeah, go on then. Josie going anywhere this afternoon?'

'Not unless you're thinking of something, Noah.'

'OK.'

'OK what?'

'OK. Just OK.'

'Well, *are* you thinking of something?'

'The hill!' Josie yells out. I don't want to disappoint her:

'I hadn't planned on it.'

My mum's already left for the kitchen. Josie runs after her, and is back in seconds with a can of Coke already open for me.

'The beach?' I suggest, giving in, slightly. 'Gonna get dark too early for the hill. And anyway, Scarface can come then too – if we go to the beach.'

She's in, of course. The smallest, most knowing smile in my world creeps across her face. She pulls the elastic wings up over her short black hair and runs off looking for a coat. Scarface goes nuts within seconds, and then I hear Mum yelling at the pair of them from the kitchen.

Must be a pain when you're busy like my mother is. Accounts to see out, orders to make, time on the road to plan. These little fragments when I can take Josie off her must help – and it's not as if the kid's dad's gonna do much.

The beach. OK, twist my arm. Come on then, sis. You can ask me about the tide, and I can tell a just-so story. Maybe it's the queen of the seas pulling her duvet about as she sleeps – or it could even be the moon. If we want then Time can still be a clock ticking away and fish can still be fish, surfers surfers and boats, well, they're adventures waiting to happen.

'So is Mr White telling you to take days off again now?' Mum starts down the stairs from her desk as we head for the door. I want to say that no one tells any of us to take anything – but she sees through bullshit if it's coming from me.

'No – we've had loads of big jobs lately, that's all. Best to take it easy here and there. Did sixteen hours sitting in the back of a van on Tuesday.'

'Frisbee?' says Josie. There's no reply from Mum.

'Alright then. You'll lose though. Frisbee in winter. Are you alright in the head?'

'Yeah.'

'OK. Never say never. Come on.'

At the bottom of the street is a hole in the fence that has always been there. Through it you can be straight on the edge of the big dune, where it comes down to the marina.

Brown Bristol Channel wind-chop drives its way along the outside of the harbour walls where, beyond the deep-water lane, the sea's march goes on. Boats roll gently over the faintest

31

remnants of it back in their moorings. We head for the other side and thin, stone stairs to the shore. Mid tide: easy.

So why do we live by the sea Noah? she starts. There's so much land, why are we only on its edges? Why are we in the Crawl? Who put the Crawl here? Why Wales? Why's the dog want to run when he sees sand? Does he even know he's a dog? Why don't we ever walk on the beach in the dark?

You know, you get this clarity of mind when you can't tell kids things in words. Not needing to explain, even if you could. They get it anyway.

Because, Josie, *because*.

'Because of what?'

'Just because.' Your favourite answer.

'Why does the Frisbee bend at the last bit, Noah?'

'Dunno – cool though innit?'

'Is it the wind?'

'No. Otherwise why does it still bend on a calm day.'

She thinks – but not for long. 'Why can Scarface catch it every time?'

'Coz he's a scally.'

'Why can't he go on the beaches in May?'

'Coz he'll bite the yoga people.'

She laughs with the memory.

'Why can't we go to the hill?'

It's not as if we see anything straight off in this house that gives us the willies – far from it. If you're thinking we walk into some chamber of horrors you're miles off. That would be a situation Starsky White would revel in. He'd be seizing control – he'd have all the schemas for it, having been there plenty of times.

What's wrong with this place isn't anything you can snap in

a photo or record in a notebook. It's just that the air is sort of heavy as soon as you pass through that porch. Mrs Lovell – or someone else – has painted the wall on each side of the hall a different colour. Starsky's little circle of torchlight shows it up real obvious. On our left it's a dark green – as lifeless an interpretation of green as you're ever going to see. It's a green straight out of that roadside ditch at dusk. And the right appears to be an even deeper rendition of red. Maybe a coat that's been slapped on over the same midnight green.

I'm wearing a pair of daps, but still my steps can be heard – every-single part of my shoeprint sticking to the parquet floor, and then peeling back off it. Maybe it's just my ears overcompensating, but I can almost *hear* the patterns on my soles. As for Starsky, the poor fucker's got much harder shoes on, and the clip-clop of his steps is echoing all the way down this hall.

We were wrong about so much from outside. First, there is a sign of life in here – at the end of that hall, where Starsky's echoing footfalls meet light that's coming from round a corner. My mind fills in gaps, tells me the story of that light… A lamp? Mrs Lovell reading under it… no… Mrs Lovell, waiting to sink a foot-long carving knife into the intruders that have come to a space she undoubtedly owns outright. Or even Mrs Lovell and her husband, ready to say *glad you've come, we've been waiting for you*.

The air in here has everything. It's dry *and* damp, warm and cold, fresh and foul. It's older than the air outside. The thought of those neat, angular, surveyor-approved, red-brick houses existing on the same plot of land as anything that once belonged to this edifice sends a chill down your back – which stops right in the stomach. Those people, the families, or couples or innocent commuters that live in them, they haven't a clue what sort of star their wagons have been hitched to.

And aside to all that, you can't compute space properly in here – as if there's more room inside the building than there should be. The ceiling's too high and the back wall is way further off than it's meant to be. The porch seems to be dropping away from us, so that I almost turn and chase after it – except all my concentration is on making sure I don't make any more noise than I can possibly help.

This is when we both think, only for a second, that there's a third set of footsteps right with us. Only for a second. But it's long enough. Someone watching us?

The sound is crisp, and ordered. Clop. Clop. Clop. Clop. Heel going down first, someone with a good sized stride. And yes, they have to be right here, between the two of us. We stop. I look at Starsky. He's throwing the thought straight back: *This isn't right.*

No sign of anyone though. Except us. The light up ahead trembles a moment – so it must be a flame. Unless someone's walked across it. But where's the shadow? We listen for anything. We hear nothing. Nothing but our own breathing. I close my mouth; it tapers the sound only slightly. The breath is coming at my ears from within my head.

We do the watching round here. This is our *job*.

So we walk again – not back towards the door, as we should, but further in. Closer to the light. Now there is a shadow over it. But it's not moving, and it's not living. There's no life in this building at all, I decide, sure as I've ever been about anything – and yet being in here feels like a terrible mistake. It's warmer now than when we entered.

And then I feel something else: Starsky's panic. I'm suddenly right on the edge of being able to hear his thoughts. The man's shitting himself, and – poor bastard – he's hiding it to help me.

'Let's go up the stairs,' I say.

He nods, points his torch up at the coving all around the hall ceiling and finds where the pitch-black in the green wall is really just empty space. Down to the floor he illuminates a step, then – just as I think he won't – walks straight towards it.

Again, I know what he's thinking. He's thinking only about not chickening out in front of me. If it wasn't so silly I'd be scared of whatever's scaring him, but I just let him walk ahead, and upwards. I can't see how we're ever going to leave here again – everything seems to want us to walk in deeper.

Then the temperature goes cold again – real quick. There's no draught, no air rushing anywhere – it just changes. I'm pulling my jumper and coat down tighter around my waist, and thinking about those footsteps we heard. Thinking about them hard enough to be able to make them out, once more. Clop. Clop. Clop. Clop. Or can I?

Now I want light. I want it to be everywhere. I can't stomach the thought of not knowing intimately every dimension and surface of where I am. I want to know what's under my feet, over my head. Who put it there. Why. When.

Starsky's just waiting to be able to retreat without looking like he was out of his comfort zone. I don't know, though, if comfort zones matter a fuck of a lot in here.

'Noah,' he whispers, careful to project his voice only as far as me. 'I reckon we're done.'

And we are. We have to be. Remember not to look like you're doing anything wrong, I remember. As if we're leaving a café, the office or a chip shop, we both head out that porch, trying pathetically to give off a single-file swagger. Coving and ornamental vaulting becomes a ceiling of stars. I want to gasp, but we're gonna drown this precision darkness out with headlamps any second now. Doors and engine fill the night with noise. Noise that no one cares about.

Tarmac turns to gravel and dust again, making Starsky's dashboard start to rattle. My eyes feel as if I'm not sure they fit properly and I'm back in my own thoughts. Starsky's behind the wheel again on this one now.

Our client had to be in just then. Already so long ago, so far behind, saying there was no life in that house just can't be rational. She was there. She's always there. Why wouldn't she be? And which one of us is going to speak first and say it?

She had to be there.

'This isn't right.'

Starsky's thought.

My voice.

3

More wavelengths

Before we make our next move on the Mrs Lovell thing, Starsky suggests we eke out two days doing the maddest little job in some unknown hamlet up behind the motorway. One of those hills north of Swansea and lorries from a quarry have been speeding through some nearby road that's meant to be a speed-limit of twenty. The quarry wants to assess its own drivers, which is where we come in.

It seems pathetic: Me, Starsky and his super-sketchy mate Bob, trying to zap lorries with a speed-gun for two whole days. And it is. Worse still is that despite seeming pretty harmless, we're ultimately aiming to cost several people their jobs. Mind you, if you will draw a racing line through a South Wales village in a twelve-wheeler with an open trailer full of chippings...

All the trucks are on best behaviour though, we soon realise – all down to this ridiculous mate of Starsky's. Bob does high-end security jobs, as in he drives people to meetings or acts as a personal bodyguard to paranoid important people. He's even done a few months of it in Afghanistan, which amazes me because he's a complete div, and manages to attract attention wherever he goes. The best bit is he's also 'ex Old-Bill', as Starsky calls it, and serious ex Old-Bill, too. He's done surveillance a million times before – but he's still shit at it. Must have been Christmas for whoever he tailed back in the day.

Since it's Bob's job, we don't bother doing a recce either. Instead, we rock up at four in the morning dressed like we're going up Everest, squeeze under a frozen hedgerow and start working out how to run the speed-gun and cameras. Simple plan. Except that when it starts getting light we realise this village is slightly busier than Bob has led us to believe. By half-seven cars are pulling up right alongside us and voices are everywhere. Just before full daybreak Starsky realises why, and we're in shit:

'Boys, we're in the carpark of a fucking primary school!'

We are, too; with cameras in our hands and wearing woolly black hats. A two-foot telephoto lens peering out of a hedge, as mums drop their kids off for the day.

It's fucked, and we have to get back to Bob's van, in a lane round the corner, by pretty much making a dash for it – but not before the muppet takes a closeup of a young female teacher, just to prove he can.

From there, the three of us spend the rest of the job wedged in the back of a white Transporter, pissing in Ribena bottles that we've had to neck in order to make room for the piss. By nine the entire workforce of truckers has got us completely clocked and is on best behaviour, so it's gonna be a waste of time.

Days like this are perfect for me though. I can just think of the money, and what I'm gonna do with it. *Where* I'm gonna do it, too. Somewhere hot – with just enough of a winter not to get bored. North Africa, South America… Oz or New Zealand. What places can I realistically fuck off to and set myself up in? Lisbon? Essaouira? Cape Verde or the Azores? Got to be surrounded by the sea, to tone me down. Then Noah won't get fed up with Noah.

So we're driving back down the M4, past the jewelled lights and neon patterns of the coastal flatlands, with its steelworks that grew there some time before the ice age, and there's my mind getting caught up in these visions of a future. Me living in some simple little apartment nearer the planet's blessed middle, where it's never so cold your ankles stiffen in the morning. Some ocean-driven micro-climate where there's no wind in the mornings, so I'm always in a sea that's practically lapping my doorstep – then as it starts to get hot and the trades blow I take a light lunch and watch the cycles and seasons wander by with or without me. People say I'd get bored: Would I fuck. I'm thinking about how I wouldn't need all the pointless little things I buy to keep happy while I slave away in this country. What would I be doing with wifi or carpets? Clothes you're only gonna wear a few times? Surround sound and whatever gizmo Apple have just brought out? And as for a car... just some jalopy that gets to the end of the road will do – so it'll have to be somewhere that doesn't have a fuckin DVLA or fuel duty that squeezes you a bit harder every couple of months. Licence this, register that; yeah, I'm just saving for the day when I can last out my days without needing a pair of socks.

D'you ever get a dream where something you've always wanted is almost there and then you get woken up? Well I'm kind of on that point of no return when Starsky starts fucking talking to me, and this little terracotta roof overlooking a warm-water point-break dissolves from my imagination – just as I've almost finished moving there. Those coke-ovens of the South Wales iron works are on our right, running as certain as the spheres, and his talk is taking a turn for the serious too. Rare chance to hear his stories, but for once I'm thoroughly pissed off that he's chosen right here, right now.

'See, Noah, way it is, if you've got this ability to face up to the worst of this world without losing your nut, then you should.'

→

What's Starsky mean by the worst of this world? Well, the kind of things ordinary people shouldn't have to see or know about. He starts listing it all off, and what he's referring to is basically the many different bits of murder that the rest of us don't make a habit of thinking through.

'You know what, Noah? Nowadays a dead person can tell you more from a metal table than they'd probably manage alive.'

'How d'you figure that then?' I yawn. Got to be a sign off the motorway for the road to the Crawl coming up soon – and why's he choosing now as one of these moments to get destructive memories off his chest? Mind you, it has always intrigued me to think how murdered people are usually the only one to know for sure who did it.

Starsky's happy enough to elaborate: 'Alive, all they could do is tell you who it was. Then you have their word against your suspect. Easy money for a good, well-paid defence brief with no conscience. Dead though… dead…' He pauses wistfully, as if he misses dead people for a moment. Then he goes on: 'Well, the dead can tell you all the stuff that leads to *proof* Noah. How, and where, and for how long. In what order. When. How fast. What with. Yeah, if you're committing a bit of violent crime the worst thing you can do is finish your vic off altogether. The corpse is the most reliable witness in the entire legal business.'

Starsky realised he was one of the ones who could live with the heavier stuff when he was just a bobby on the beat. Some guy had hung himself, and his head had popped clean off but still stayed inside the skin. When he arrived on the scene the body had a mega long neck, like Stretch Armstrong – remember him? – only frozen with blue streaks and little bits of dried skin where the rope had slid before wrenching tight.

'Most interesting thing I'd ever seen,' says Starsky. 'I couldn't stop thinking about how quiet it all looked. Hard stuff to deal with, Noah, but I did deal with it. Easy as if I was cleaning up a smashed glass or spilt drink. A dead body, matey, is just that and nothing more. No longer got any sense of action, or time to it... No movement, no progression. Just still. No...'

'No *meaning*,' I interrupt.

Starsky grins, chuckles, like he's been waiting for me to say that word: 'Not exactly, Noah. That was where I came in – we'd be the ones who worked out what it all meant. Easy. You can do it now too, mate. You do it all the time. You do it really fuckin well.'

'Er, thanks.'

Is this what I'm supposed to say? Or should I point out that we only do jobs for banks and lawyers, the odd paranoid spouse and a woman with noises in her own head – and that I haven't seen anything dead bigger than a fish Scarface found on the beach once?

Either way, between two junctions of emptying, late-evening motorway, snapshots of my future little village on a warm, azure stretch of surf-drenched coast have become dead innocents, with pale faces post-*rigor mortis*, coagulating injuries and a look in the eye that still captures their last thought.

I look at Starsky as he drives and yawns. Fair enough – if you can handle that stuff then maybe you should step up to the plate. But the thought he *misses* it? That he might pine for that world again instead of hiding out in a village on just the same money, watching lorries? I'm not into that idea at all. Maybe I should read the signs here – the jobs that excite him are the ones I should run a mile from. But I don't.

Stay passive, Noah, that's what's got you by.

It's two more days before he mentions Mrs Lovell and that house again. When he does, we're headlong into it once more. No turning back.

➔

'You're going to London, matey. Today.'

This is what Starsky tells me first thing in the morning. Job as boring as the one we've just been on doesn't need any lie-in to recover, so I'm in by eight. He's already there.

'Easy little number for you to carry out, Noah. We've got the gen on this fucking husband of hers now, matey. Mr Lovell. And I've just landed you a way of having a closer look at the bastard.'

Early incoming phone call and he's taken on an instruction from some local firm of solicitors. Pretty routine and something we do a lot. Important court papers are gonna get issued by a judge in Cardiff mid-morning, and they need to be hand delivered to a desk in London the same day. It's easy; Whiteout courier these kinds of things as a line of business. For a small fortune you get Noah or Starsky, or sometimes a sub of our choice, carrying them personally the whole way. It's dull, well paid and not exactly the kind of task either of us fights the other to do. More often than not, on account of him being more important and having better things on the cards, it ends up being me. Today is no exception.

'Cardiff Crown, Noah,' he grins, waving a sheet of paper in his left hand, mobile phone still gripped in the right. 'Judge sits at ten. I'll drop you there and you can get a train after they're done. Papers won't take thirty minutes.'

This time, though, he's also suggesting I mix it with trying to watch Mr Lovell – the possible bad guy in this ongoing Vale instruction of ours – in his natural habitat. Apparently I'm going to see if I can tail him for a couple of hours. Just in case we learn anything.

Doesn't strike me as immediately likely that guys of this type will be plotting and scheming on the first random afternoon you plan to watch them – but it's an added perk to the otherwise mundane task of riding a train to the city and back. So I'm happy to agree.

'Get a photo of the fucker, Noah,' he adds, passing the instruction sheet for the court papers over. 'And of anyone he talks to.'

'Er, if it turns out to be possible,' I reply. 'I'll do my best.'

'Course you will, matey. Course you will. But worry about that Order from the judge first. That's the bit we're actually getting paid for.'

We might tout the service like it's a top-notch professional task, but there's not a lot of skill in carrying a bundle of papers in a bag from A to B. So, as is always the case, everything goes fine and by half two I'm strolling through a London Town brightly lit in winter sun.

I get rid of the papers promptly, a secretary taking all of three seconds to acknowledge their arrival.

'Thanks, do you need a receipt for them?'

I do, so one is stamped and then it's done. No more words, no mention that the bundle might have travelled across the country. Doesn't matter anyway; errand one is a useful distraction to stop me thinking too much about the ultimate aim for this trip.

Now though, with it out the way, I do just that. Here comes the time to feel the change in landscape and psyche. Time for the small-town Welshie to relish assimilation into this place that *matters*. I'm always at home here, even if I try to hate it. The anonymity, the irrelevance of who you are and where you're from. Closest the urban ever gets to being at sea.

Air rushing in and out of the Underground reminds me it's cold, despite the afternoon shine. Having taken a cab from Paddington to the solicitors, I now slip single-file into some tube station I haven't even noticed the name of. Northern Line to Moorgate. Change to Circle Line, eastbound, two stops and then I'm there, rising up some steps, backed by another of those subterranean gusts, back into that warming sunlight. Now this is London *City*. This is where decisions get made that we don't understand but which keep us all in supply of the modern world's equivalent of oxygen. Here are the lungs of Northwest Europe, or is it the heart? I look around at gherkins, shards, cheesegraters, spikes, various other oblongs shaped from silvery glass. It's all about size... ob*schlong* more like. This place can see and know all. Somewhere here there's even a file on the small startup loan used by Starsky to get Whiteout into existence.

Everything is clean, and moving – direct, smooth lines, sure of itself and its aim. Nothing cares about me, so I'm not noticed, sitting on a bench at the end of a west-facing street. There's a paved square and stone steps behind me, and I make the most of that tiny trace of sunlight to take a look at the single side of paper Starsky's handed me on the 'target'. That familiar scrawl has stuck a couple of key details down for me and, fair play to him, he's been busy finding out what he can: Mr Brian Godfrey Lovell. Forty-three. Born in Leicester. Married to Michelle Lovell of that address we already know too well. No aliases and associates. Works in the building opposite, according to a sparse professional profile Starsky found. Some sort of stock trader or investor, maybe even running hedge funds, but not for a company that we can find. Starsky's sure he isn't a director of anything. No liabilities, no secured loans, obviously no CCJs and not named in any readily available property deeds either.

This is a *thin* trail. Unusually thin for someone supposedly important. So the first thing to do is establish whether I'm actually in the right corner of the fuckin universe. I look at the address; Kinsella House. Last one of a strip of five-storey buildings, the only one of the row to lie in the shade of The Gherkin – which gives me something to smile at for a moment, just before I'm in that shade myself and it's winter again.

There's twelve companies in there, according to the door. All of them something to do with money except one which is called *Hideous CnC*, although the only reason to believe that's not a financial service is the name. Either way, it stands out immediately.

Hideous gets my vote for the buzzer, so I put my thumb over its button, press and count to two.

No answer.

Process repeated.

No answer.

Once more.

Nothing.

So I start pushing all of them. Within seconds someone responds by buzzing me in, no questions. As the door flips shut behind me I hear another voice at the intercom – but who cares, Noah's got access to Kinsella House.

The first floor's being refurbished and is taped off at chest height, but the second has a reception desk shared, it seems, by all the companies.

'Hi Sir, can I help?' A young man with black hair, neat rectangular glasses and a tea-coloured tan stands to greet me.

'Yeah, is Mr Lovell in?'

'What company?'

Fuck, I think, but press on as if I haven't heard the question.

'Brian Lovell – he said you could show me up.'

The lad pauses, eyes me hard, then picks up the phone and rings someone.

No obvious CCTV, so I let my eyes drift around the room, uninterested. Noah needs to be forgettable here. Which is something I'm good at anyway.

He gets an answer, and it looks like we're on our way somewhere:

'Yeah, it's Joel at the front desk. Is Brian expecting a visitor?'

He listens to someone the other end telling him more than a yes or no answer, then says, 'OK... hold on'. He looks up at me: 'Name?'

'Geraint.' I figure a Welsh name will rouse the subject's interest if he's got any involvements with the people of God's Land.

'Ger-ai-nt,' Joel repeats, pronunciation close enough to send him up in my estimation. 'Yeah. OK.'

Phone still live and wedged between ear and shoulder, he looks to the computer on his desk and starts typing. This guy is switched on. He's obviously been told to wait again, and sees value enough in his day to start doing something else in the meantime. After about two minutes someone's back on the other end and speaking to him. 'Yeah,' he says, nodding. 'I'd say so. Yeah, here now – he's at reception. OK, I can do. Great.'

He puts the phone down and smiles. 'Take a seat, Sir. Mr Lovell will be down in a minute.'

We walk through the unknown all the time. Happens every now and then. Starsky's oh so wise words are in my head again now. They sounded stupid at the time, but once again there's me realising that however odd something comes across at first, if it's Starsky White talking, I should probably listen.

Same with a wave, I remind myself. *You'll only know what to do when you're there, about to go over that ledge. Trust your first decision, and stick to it.*

And, as usual, that's all the time I'll have to weigh things up, because think-quick-act-fast pressures are rushing on me instead. If our client's maybe-crooked husband does walk down that stair and see my face then I'm not gonna be playing any further part in this job.

I pull a phone out of my pocket and raise it up. Pointing it in camera mode at the desk, I start focussing on Joel. He senses me quickly and looks up giving me a perfect head-and-shoulders, which is when I press shoot. It makes a big, exaggerated snapshot noise, and immediately the complaints start:

'Hey – what are you doing?'

I hit another photo as he stands up.

'Sir! You can't just take a picture in here like that. Sir?'

But I'm gone, down the stairs, ducking the line of tape and into the closed-off first floor, among a legion of painters and decorators.

From here I need two or three things to happen right – but then luck has always been essential in this line of work. First I see Joel walk past looking thoroughly pissed off, headed for the street entrance. I switch camera mode off and lift the phone to my ear. Nobody else bats an eyelid at me – I'm just someone who's stepped into these inactive office spaces to make a phone call. Staying side-on to the exit, I mumble irrelevantly at the handset. Sure enough, after presumably looking outside, the fuming receptionist comes back, and starts calling up the stairs to someone in a pretty animated manner.

This is where the chance should come.

Joel returns about a minute later, once more headed for the street door, but this time he's got someone alongside. And yes, it's *him*. Has to be. I can see this good-as-gold receptionist gesturing that the weirdo taking the photo must have gone this way – must have left the building, can't be far. Mr Lovell looks interested, and I can see straight away a mixture of calmness coupled with an intent anger. Powerful man, not sure what to make of what he's being told, not sure what to make of not knowing what to make of something, not happy about the disturbance, but unlikely to block it out either – not if he's someone who hides things from his nearest and dearest.

I walk further into the first floor, towards a whitened window pane, away from the stairs and from being seen. I have what I need now anyway – I've set eyes on him. Now I know, once they're both safely back at their desks, which of this uniformed tribe to wait for in the street below.

Darkness falls and the orange of the London skyline is washing out starlight as I gaze upwards. Freezing night, hard to keep your patience wandering about with a constant eyeball on the front of Kinsella House. It's nearly two hours after dark when he steps out – but all the waiting and self-doubt and shivering vanishes in a nanosecond. The adrenaline of a target on the move.

Younger than his allegedly beloved wife, Mr Lovell's got very short mousy hair and a long face that holds a pretty stern, shrewd-looking glare in place. He's tall too, and stands every bit as straight and erect as the sneer on his face. An open, long black coat and scarf combo hides his body shape, but stature suggests a slender, suave confidence. Hands in pockets, the steam from his breath rises gently, subdued, controlled, calm.

He starts off by looking up and down the street at least three times. Then he gets his own mobile out, dials someone, and starts talking as he walks north towards Liverpool Street.

In the waiting time I've had plenty of chance to stress out about the chances of him simply disappearing in a London cab, but he's doing nothing of the sort. We're back underground and heading for the Central Line in five minutes, and I'm eight people behind him as the escalator drops us down to the platform. There's no train so I have to keep my distance as we wait among the rest of Commuter London.

He's off his phone again by now, but seems to have abandoned looking about, and it's crowded enough down here for me to creep onto a westbound carriage only half a car-length away from him. There's enough movement, and his interest is sufficiently lacking for me to glance over a few times. He looks a bit put out by the train ride, but nothing suggesting a massive aversion. Just like every other person in here, then.

Of course any kind of contact, or speaking to him would be right outside the boundaries here, but I can't help trying to imagine my way into his thoughts. We don't even know if he's anything like the ruthless fucker his wife's described to us. But then we certainly don't know he isn't. And if there is any wrongdoing behind the Mrs Lovell job, then it's exciting to think that right here, an arm's reach away, is a soul that probably knows *every answer* to the story we want to find out.

Long journey, and I give myself a quick pat on the back for having an all-zones ticket, before he begins looking at his watch and I start suspecting the next stop is our destination.

The tube train slows into Ealing Broadway, a pretty good distance from the offices where we started, and he steps out. Quiet platform. Only the target, three others and me getting off. Tailing will get much harder from here – but you have to push it. This is how they play out. Closer you are to the reward, tougher you have to work. And it is worth my while. He's meeting someone.

Now I'm not inclined to dislike these tossers in any way. I can't. Brokers, insurance managers, bankers – they get me and Starsky plenty of our work. In fact, I tend to think something that helps me do my job well is the way I can remain completely and utterly indifferent. Benefits bludger, wife-beater, divorcee or millionaire exec, if Noah's asked to serve you, Noah serves you.

But this fucker Mr Lovell meets up with at the main exit is immediately exempt from all of the above. Exempt from being exempt. Usually in work situations there's nothing in any subject to arouse emotion, affectionate or not, in me. But here I am immediately drawn to someone's face because it is telling me in so many ways that there is one overriding sentiment I should be harbouring: *Hate*. Don't act on it, Noah, don't even listen to it. But whatever you do, be sure to acknowledge its presence from the moment you lay eyes on this pale, dark obstacle.

Mr Lovell is clearly subordinate to him – taller maybe, but unquestionably the second in command. And the relish in this guy's face shows that's the only way things will work for him. It's a smirk that can't have ever felt a discomfort of any kind, and his face backs that up. He's got super-smooth features and cheeks that kind of cuddle his mouth and marble eyes. Portly maybe, but somehow too spineless to go the whole way and just be properly fat. There's also that same monotone hair length as the guy who's led me here, but somehow softer. I can't see for sure in the darkness, but I'm guessing light blond – he's too young for it to be white. I'm going with early forties.

So what's there to hate? Well, there's his assuredness, the way he *owns* Mr Lovell from the off. Then there's the swagger in his walk, the fact this guy is like a symbol of everything that's brought our world to this epic brink. This fucker, he's got such a hoodoo on the things that move around him – as if the world seems to be warping and bending into or around his aura. Like physicists reckon space and time do for a big planet or star. But instead of dud matter, he's pulling people, *humanity* into his lure.

That's not enough in itself though, is it? Me, Noah, who never makes emotional decisions about the people I work on, going so far as to say 'hate'? But I do hate him. And it's coz there's something else telling me to. Like when you meet Mrs Lovell and catch her gaze, and it orders you to stop and bear witness, I can't disengage from the immediate impulse that there's just badness circulating all around this one.

No handshake, no real acknowledgment of each other, and they're off, slow walking pace – a stroll – towards a railing, then a park, then a long lane with no streetlights, and yes, Noah's still on them. Distant, but close enough to be able to see what they're doing.

I start thinking what Starsky would want from me now. Photos – that's one thing he said. I check the dinky camera he gave me is where it should be; jacket pocket. It's gonna have to wait though.

They stop at the end of the lane, turn to face each other and their silhouettes are cast perfectly against light in the opening beyond. I can see how Brian Lovell's hair is raised in a stiff tuft at the centre, fringe pulled down by his brow as he hears something being told to him. Side-on, this new fellow is kind of top heavy. He sways slowly towards Mr Lovell, leaning in, and Mr Lovell's head tilts slightly away. I can see the new guy's edged profile – shirt sleeves the perfect length for cuffs to protrude from his jacket top. Shoes long, with pointed toes. Firm footed. Clearly in the know, in the right, every time.

Comfort comes from the darkness around me. Halfway up this lane, I can stand in the middle of the road, feet shoulder-width apart and not be seen. I'm cast out from their range of vision but they're lit up perfectly for me. Flash and all other sound effects switched off, I raise Starsky's mini camera up and fire off a row of photos – worth a go. Can't look at the display to check the pictures in case it illuminates, but at least if I get nothing else this will be a start.

Then they're walking again, and I can feel a night breeze drawing air out of the lane and towards whatever is causing the lights they're heading for. Now my own breath is louder than anything else. It drowns out the city to our east, the wind, my footsteps. It's getting uneven as I feel the stakes rising. Freezing air, but I'm prickly with sweat.

It's a lake. At the end of this lane is a patch of water, suburban oasis, with a thin gravel path around it. A road rises adjacent the other side, elevated six feet and approaching a flyover – its white streetlights are pounding the wind-chopped surface with shimmering strobes. Nothing in the sky but it's like a full moon out here in the open again, and the two of them are about twenty yards away from me on a bench. They're both sat in a raised position – feet on the bench, bottoms on the backrest. There's no way they can't notice me now – yet neither of them turns to look where I am.

Pot-committed. Too heavily invested to pull out. Or am I? I keep walking, past them, feet away, across the lake's perimeter. I go through a little alley that leads under that road, then sit, back against the wall. My chances are less than fifty-fifty now. If they go back the other way I've lost them.

Shit, Noah. Get it right!

I wait fifteen minutes and then comes the most ridiculous noise ever. It doesn't even feel as if you're hearing it as much as *receiving* it. There's a rumble, which is sort of wet – like it's being made by steam and under some intense pressure. It starts around where Mr Lovell and the other guy must be, but then pours around the corner and sets itself up in a ring around me. The wall at my back makes no echo, no difference. This noise goes where it wants. It keeps starting up on different sides until I'm surrounded, and then starts to throb as if there like a fucking beat underneath it. Before I've even had a chance to feel anything close to fear though, or even confusion, it's kind of harmonised so that the noise is circling me and I almost like it – and then it heads off in the opposite direction. The rhythm, the stereo, it's all intact as whatever's making it gets further from me again. You know – if Starsky asked me, I'd have to say it's more about what you see than what you hear, this noise. Of course you couldn't point out how, but I can *see* it circling away, revolving off towards some outer western suburbs that nobody gives a shit about.

As soon as silence is complete again I know there won't be anyone behind me if I want to walk back. And I'm right.

I pass the lake, watch the artificial light dancing off it. There's no rhythm to this patch of water – the odd gust of foul city breeze scratches its surface and flattens out the reflections, but it's got no soul. Everything about this place is begging to be forgot.

Nobody anywhere, bench vacant, I make for the dark lane again. As I slip into its anonymous embrace I hear cars start passing on the elevated road behind, each clumsily cutting the air with familiar sound. It's the *correct* sound. Wherever I've just been is finished and the regular movements of the night are back, doing what they do.

Neither subject is anywhere in the vicinity now. Sod the photos, I think.

Noah on the train home. This has to be the pose that sums me up. Face tilting towards the dirty window pane, forehead pressed close enough to force out my own reflection and let me glimpse the outside whizzing by. Running back to where I belong.

This is when I remember the hate again. It's the thing I can recall easiest – although back in that clearing by the lake it was long gone.

Through the window, my mind processes the successive squares of yellow light that flick by, punctuated by the whites, reds and oranges of roads and highways. Sometimes the patterns are in clusters, and then they spread out as the city drops further away into memory. In the dark, the offbeat clacking of the rails diffuses my anger, keeps time with the hum of carriage on metal underneath. The journey rushes by, and I complete the escape by thinking of the beach tomorrow morning.

Crisp, convex lines of swell bending into the bays around the Crawl. If I want to go, I'll go. That will arm me against anything back there. The city can only come for me if I choose to believe its values.

Which I won't. Whatever we find, however this pans out, I'll always be able to freeze-frame to that other moment in my life when there's no deficit of understanding, no need to find out more. Noah on the train home… Nah, bollocks to that: Noah in the ocean, Noah on a surfboard, dropping into a bomb set, back foot pushing down into the water.

My body twitches as my mind goes there. Weight then unweight, and I swoop off the bottom and back up that wave face. Knees in tight, economy of motion, I push ahead, down the line, water cutting neatly in my wake. Torque, poise, precision – the wave tells you what to do. I lay an edge in the face, and head for the beach with a swish – take a little look back at the fan of spray in my wake. That's how to win this game. What doesn't matter will fizzle – like it always does when I decide to call time. Remember why you do it, Noah.

'Any swell?'

'Dunno, man. Wind's pushing over. It looks hanging.'

Something to love about the sea – coz believe me there is fuck all else you can do about this – is the way it just never turns up to order. When you're planning wind, tide or current to do something for you then that's rarely the ocean state you'll end up getting.

Next morning's a classic example. There's me on that train home gliding my way across waves in my sleep, big ideas about how a great surf's gonna wash away the bullshit of the night before, that fucked up little labyrinth in Ealing. I creep through the door to my place in the early hours, not even using the lights and dive straight to sleep with visions of swell lines stacking the horizon when I wake. Then dawn breaks – well, *fades in* really – to the sea looking like a frozen vat of puss.

Bad sign; ocean's not hearing my pleas. That surf session is off.

So let me take a good look at your perfect line, so I know just exactly how I don't want mine, chants my stereo as I drive up the beachfront, hoping the lyrics can help me say something defiant back at the salty deep. I think the song actually says 'life' – perfect *life* – but I change it. Coz after all, the line you choose is far more important anyway, isn't it?

Little mini-details will stick in my mind from now for evermore. I phone the office to say I'm coming in after all. Starsky's on the odd bit of his cycle already coz he wants no sugar in the coffee I'm fetching him from the Trawlermans' Café, our favourite. He does this once a month – tries to cut down on the fags and other unnecessaries, and it always ends in spectacular failure. So in my mind, for good now, is my dashboard clock saying 8:17am as I lock my car and walk through the sliding doors, then the steam gurgle of the milk machine, old men tilting hats and saying 'Heya Noah, boy. How's things?'

And of course the sea – vile as can be. It's got no order to it, and the lumps that are rising out of the foamy mess are getting hacked to pieces by a blustery gale that's whipping around the headland like it's lost its way. Beyond the white caps, the whole channel is moving like a procession towards Cardiff, Newport, Bristol, Avonmouth. It's filthy and brown too, ahead of a horizon that's shifting flat layers of grey onward in the same direction. Weather so foul even the ocean is rejecting it.

The reason I'm gonna remember it all is what happens next. Like that day we first meet Mrs Lovell, the minutiae seem relevant for their significance. Turns out today is when the new girl, the one with the ideas – Alys – comes into the equation. Mind you, it's the last bit I end up remembering clear and crisp before the blur.

When I reach my desk those coffees are perfect temperature for drinking and Starsky cuts straight to it. He's read messages I wrote him on the train back – although they didn't contain the half of it. Don't know if they ever will either.

'Right, before we take this any further, Noah, I wanna know what you thought...'

I try telling him I *can't* think, that there's this *thing* in the way of thought when it comes to Mrs Lovell and her weird fucking husband, but Starsky's already there. He's felt it too.

'So what would you do?' he asks me. It's like we've shared something dirty we shouldn't have. I almost wonder if my little walk in the dark last night was just something my own mind whipped up to while away the time. And I'm also questioning if we were actually in that house, acting like such tools. Maybe it was all just some farce I imagined while bored the other day. Were we really justified getting all panicked out like that, as if we were a bunch of teenagers doing a Ouija board? And why the fuck didn't I sing to the rooftops yesterday about all that wasn't right with the London darkness? Where were my yells of terror? What happened to the come-and-take-me-away moment I should have probably had surrounded by noise near that flyover?

I think before answering – and then fudge it completely anyway.

'Me? I'd... I'd probably...' Hesitation is best broken by what I think he'll want to hear. I know he hasn't banked Mrs Lovell's money yet: 'Well, we're not really gonna find out if anyone saw us in the house the other night are we? Also, we know now that Mr is easy to find. And she's made a payment. We've got a written instruction from her, so I'd... er... agree to the job for sure now? Probably.'

'*Uh... er... uh...*' he mocks. 'Well, Noah, I think your head's telling you the right thing there, matey, but my head – my head ain't thinking that at all.'

'It ain't?' I try to mock back.

'No, it ain't, Noah. And you know why?'

'Why? Coz you don't believe Mrs Lovell?'

'Oh, I believe her alright. That's not the reason, no...'

He's pushing the window open and craning his neck out into the corridor to check no one in the other non-smoking offices can see him sparking up a cheeky fag, which he blows into the street outside. Howling ocean winds, still strong in these inland side-roads, blow the ash off and sharpen the lit end. He leaves his hand hanging out the window – the room's freezing already, and the slatted blinds rattle a second time as warm and cold air continue to change places. He loves this shit; slow delivery, me hanging on his next word:

'Problem I have with it all, Noah. Well, truth be told, I have two problems. One; the kind of story she's on about reminds me of jobs I done back in the day, and let me tell you, there were bad fuckin people at the end of the rainbow on that one. *Bad* people, matey.'

OK. A little surge of something close to adrenaline, probably mixed with a bit of bravado makes me shrug and go, 'Right... And?'

'But that ain't quite it. Bad people we can deal with. I'm getting alarm bells about it for something else, matey. And when I get them, it's *always* for a reason.'

'OK, so what is that reason then? I mean, this time? What's up?'

'Dunno.'

'That's it?'

'Yeah. Dunno. That's the problem. It just *feels* bad, you know. Like a sort of feel-it-in-my-water type thing.'

And one step leads simply to the next. Cash job with a high margin. Questionable client, 'alarm bells' as Starsky's calling it over reasons unsure. Not sure how to play it, but wanting the pay cheque, so here comes the idea of bringing in someone else. Logic dictates it, so we follow.

But *this kind* of someone else?

He closes the window, checks the cigarette butt is cold and bins it. 'Noah, you ain't seen me do this before – what I fancy we do next – but I can tell you mate, it works.'

'What works?'

He purses his lips, puffs out air through his nose and says, 'Misc advice, mate.' He actually pronounces it like that – 'misc' – Starsky loves his abbreviations; 'disqual' for a driving ban, or 'enq' for enquiry. This one's perfect, because it's telling me nothing.

'I've done it before,' he says. 'This is exactly the kind of job where they can help.'

'Misc advice?' I repeat, as if to check he's said it more than fishing for what he means.

'Yeah. Either that or I can tell Mrs Lovell to get a big dog. But that won't help us make any moola, and neither of us wants the job to go away, eh?'

One thing he's sussed correctly.

'So what d'you reckon then? Got a problem with it, Noah?'

Before I can say anything he's harping on about all the jobs he's done in the past where various weirdos with no qualifications beyond reliable hunches have helped him get out of impossible scrapes. I hear how he was stymied watching ninety hours of CCTV waiting for some terrorist to walk across the screen, only to call in this wizard or druid or something similar who tells him what hour to go to on the tapes. He wasn't gonna buy it himself that first time, he tells me, but then there's the arsehole suspect, walking straight past with a can of paint, like they need him to be.

'Loads of coppers use this shit,' he stresses, as if trying to convince himself. 'It's even led me to bodies, Noah.'

Great, we're back on bodies.

Maybe just to end the conversation, I tell him fine, let's do it. And like that he's on to the practicalities. One of his old colleagues knows someone who knows some girl from over Cardiff-Newport way. She's meant to be worth ringing. He's thought about doing it before for other jobs, 'But you ain't meant to disturb that kind of stuff when it's just over money.'

And this isn't?

'Nah. Something else going on here, isn't it. Right thing to do, Noah, I'm tellin ya. Misc advice it is. Trust me; these kinds of people, mate, you get em in when you have these one-in-ten-thousand jobs that make the hackles of your back stand up. When things aren't right.'

I'm trying to work out if it's shit scary or actually a bit reassuring to hear Starsky offering these admissions about the Lovells, when he hits me with a few more of his probably-not-tall-in-the-slightest stories about killers and rapists and hired torturers all wandering the same world as me, you, little Josie – shit that you don't want to think about, but that he's lived with for nearly two thirds of his life. Then, once he's got my fucking skin crawling all over again, he tells me how his mate reckons the girl we're gonna call can be trusted with big, nasty secrets, with life-and-death stuff. Everything I'm hoping our Vale gig isn't.

And whether I like it or not – no matter if I'm in or out – that's where his line is turning next.

He's got hold of this Alys within the hour and fixed up a meeting. And here it is upon us: the point from which my world gets complicated like it's never been before. Me, Noah, no one else. In theory.

She comes to the office first – just before I'm planning to go wandering in pursuit of another coffee and a steak bake – talks only to Starsky, looks straight over me, sounds far too serious for someone who does a job I don't even think exists – and isn't the least bit interested in any sort of smile, unless it's to make us feel small. She's chewing a piece of gum like she means to do it some harm, which doesn't really mix with being dressed like a trainee barrister – and we have got to know and detest a few of those I can tell you. In fact, it even crosses my mind she could well have come from some canny law firm, or even be Mrs Lovell's wicked hubby's younger mistress. The gum and the slightly inelegant walk are the only giveaway – she's not from that sort of stock. And it's confirmed when she speaks.

'There's things I have to know before I get involved with a case that's not criminal,' she tells us, 'and I have to know them straight away.'

Her accent is tough, straight out of Cardiff past, and between her and Starsky I feel like I'm in a fucking pantomime. They talk business – or at least it sounds like that – and I'm frozen to the spot listening: Noah, ineffective, sitting, wondering why he's not just walking out for lunch hour, as per the plan.

'Fine,' says Starsky. 'Ask and I'll tell.'

'Your company,' she says. 'You gave it your own name. Why?'

'*What*? Why did I call my company by my name?' This is a question he's had no inkling was about to come up, and his reaction is classic. 'Why's that matter? What's it got to do with… Oh I don't know. How am I meant to be able to tell you something like that?'

'It's your company,' she says. 'And it matters a lot. So tell me the answer.'

'Er, well, sounded good for an ad I suppose,' he says.

'No other reason? Not that you like hearing your own surname as a trademark?'

'Definitely not,' he says, almost pleading. 'I'm low key. I guarantee you.'

'And why did you carry on doing this kind of work when you left the police? Why not just retire?'

'Skint,' he says.

'Why *this* then?'

'Only thing I can do.'

'Fine,' she says. 'So, this instruction. You said on the phone you want to know about a client's health,' she says, 'as in mental health, right?'

'Yeah.'

'And nothing else?'

'Don't think so.'

'So a case of speak to someone, suss them out, then tell you if they're...'

'*Speak* to them?' Starsky chokes. 'Hang on.'

'What else did you have in mind then?' she says, throwing back a glare that he looks like he thinks he deserves. 'You're assuming I can sit here and just tell you the answers to questions simply because you're someone who needs to know them? Come on...'

'OK, fine, I can arrange a meeting,' he says. 'But it's more than her, you know, head that we want, er...' he coughs, '*read*.'

'Read?' Alys looks like she's going to get up and leave. 'OK. I see. Well then...'

'No – I don't mean... You know... I... well, what's the word?'

'Get me a drink of water,' she says. 'Please.'

Starsky isn't moving quickly enough to his leased drink

dispenser, and when he finally presents her with a tiny plastic cup she looks like she's forgotten what we were talking about.

'So what were you going to say?' he asks, and, immediately, she's back alert.

'Well, it would be better if you said it,' she laughs, 'but since you...'

'We need advice,' says, 'on whether she's...'

'Good or bad, Mr White,' she tells him. 'Good or bad. That's what you need to know. You need to know if you're signing for the right side here.'

And then, don't know why, but it just twigs in me. This girl's only a few years older than me – maybe just thirty – and she's already wiser than Starsky. I hadn't thought it could be done, but clearly there are some people out there who have such a skill.

'Trust me,' she says. 'I'm *here*. You can already assume where your client is, relative to "good or bad" because of that. My interest in your case, if you want it, is not going to be the issue. The issue, Mr White, is going to be whether you let me get involved *enough*. Either I get to find out a lot more, or you can take the advice I just gave you – call it a simple favour if you like – and we'll all move on.'

'A lot more?'

'Yes,' she nods, switching the gum to the other side of her mouth. 'A lot more. We meet: us, your client; how and when I need us to meet. You won't have a problem getting her to agree. And that's how this will have to happen.'

'So no different to how you guys do this stuff for Old Bill jobs then?' he says.

'Tighter,' she says. 'I'll need the boundaries even tighter. No more questions.' And then she winks at me – yes, me – with perfect timing, eyelid and cheek in sync with jaw, the whole thing a flash unnoticed by Starsky. A clear, deliberate wink, right as that worn out lump of gum gets bitten with intent.

Yeah, she's got him completely laid out. Which, now you think of it, means she's probably got me down too.

This is what suddenly makes me absolutely fuckin *fascinated* by Alys – quarter of an hour in. It creeps up on me but then seizes my ways of seeing without a prayer of recourse. She's clocking everything about me without even trying – maybe without even wanting – and I'm seriously excited by it. After all, what should I be afraid of? At face value I might come across as a bit of a knob sometimes, but if someone gets beyond that... I mean, I'm not bad. I don't prefer to harm, I don't destroy. There you go – the right side of good. Getting that across is the hard bit though. But I don't have to do anything to show myself to this Alys. She can see. She knows – knows *me*. Or today's me at least. I start winding myself up, thinking she must be able to appreciate Noah and all the layers. She must see the Noah everyone else misses.

And then she leaves.

So soon and I'm left with only memory of her, slipping away, thinning treacle through my mind. A receding tide. I'm trying to grip it, but there's nothing that can hold something this fleeting, this scattered. I'm trying to pull up the image of her slightly awkward stance in the doorway. It was just showing at the end – the look of someone who can't bear wearing these corporate trousers and jacket a moment longer than she has to. I'm fighting against the static to see that weird silver necklace, a twisted twig of metal hanging way beneath her long neck. Dark eyes, the colour of deep water; fizzing points of intriguing life in a face that's just... Smooth... It's leaving me again.

'Whaddaya reckon then?' Starsky's asking me, and the drag back from the there-and-then is done. On goes the slip-slip-slipping of this oh-so-important figure, back through the time that's passing since she left – deep into parts of my psyche I can't ever access. Already it's like she never came here.

'...Uh, whatever.' I'm ready to change track now.

Which is what he arranges, pronto. Statutory demand for some plumber in Ebbw Vale who didn't pay for boiler parts on time. A maxed out credit card too – £95 if I can get it by midday tomorrow, only a mile away from the serve. And can I do a drive-by of some vintners near Caerphilly on the way back through; need to get Starsky a photo, even if it's dark, to prove they're trading. But none of it means much – beyond a dark night alone in the car with my rambling thoughts – all of which I reckon Alys already knew, before I ever did.

In need of solid ground, I find refuge in the familiar. Maybe someone does know more than me about the shit that matters, but I still know that poor fucker in Ebbw Vale's story before he does:

'Someone else owes me money, man. Did a whole boiler and system on a buy-to-let and the company went bust.'

'How can a *letting agent* go bust?'

'I dunno. They owe me three grand though.'

I think of all the tosser solicitors who don't pay me and Starsky for half a year at a time easily, and can see my mum going on about the safety of her repping work in the pharmaceutical trade with its monthly payslips and handy bonuses. People are always gonna want cures aren't they? Gonna be willing to pay to feel better? Limited use though, all that extra as disposable. As long as you're above the breadline, I reckon. Some things exist whatever your take-home, and some others wouldn't fall into place if you had all the made-up account balances in this pale blue world.

That card comes in, too, and I cut it with clunky metal scissors, right through the chip'n'pin. What a gesture, eh? Feel the awesome retribution of the bank manager. A faceless, ceaseless, motion. The laws of finance. Only need the vintners to look in rude health and Noah's centrifuge will be running after itself.

Money? You know, if we all just stopped *believing* in its value then, then – well, who knows? But we don't, because we like spangly thingies and land and tasty food with rich drink and digital TV channels that beam football matches played on felt-green pitches and – don't forget this one – we like power too. So people play along, and get into trouble, and that makes work for me, so *I* can play along. So I can buy my own glittering lures.

Oh well, at least I know it.

We go hard again for a couple of days. No mercy, and no scruples. A student's dropped out of Cheltenham Uni and didn't pay the rest of his hall fees. This is the most pitiful of them all – just a couple of days to realise he'd done the wrong thing, and then he's back in Wales with a massive debt and no plan. I remember that happening to half my mates; they were all laughing about being on the run from the loans, the halls, the tuition fees – and it never mattered a fuck. They didn't have Whiteout Legal Investigation Services after them, though, did they?

I keep a Hollister sweater in the back of the car and some poncey stonewashed jeans – just for use in these instances. Into costume, into character, and time for some basic pretexting.

His old girl comes to the door.

'Hiya?' I say warmly. 'Craig in?'

'No, sorry love. Moved out he has.'

'Oh, gutted. Coz I heard he'd come back from uni? I've got my car with me, mind – d'you reckon you could tell me how to get to his new place?'

So Craig is added to our list of victims, and on we go. Fake bad backs, loan defaults, car repo, bankruptcy petition, injunction with power of arrest, moped repo, house repo. People weep, they swear, threaten, admit it all, beg, shout, hide. It's a crawling, sprouting mass of financial rot. Insolvency in bloom, with me making money from it all.

And then, at last, a few more days after Craig's date with destiny, my provider, the hand that feeds me everything I need of late, Starsky White, says we're gonna be carrying out the next part of the Mrs Lovell instruction.

Alys is meeting us both, near that massive mansion, the void in the Vale, and we're gonna get on famously.

It's on. And I'm still in. This is all going to take *shape*.

4

Still plenty of light

It's easy to forget how sketchy Michelle Lovell is about people coming to the house. It's the same rigmarole again, with us sweeping past in Starsky's car to collect our fragile, living payload. Then we whiz into the network of lanes and around in all sorts of circles until it's 'safe to talk'.

We may be due the spring mists any time soon, but, when it wants, winter's still got a wrist-cracking hold on South Wales. Undeterred by that, Mrs Lovell's out, immune and ready for us. The front seat has been left for her, so I'm shoe-horned into the back. I can see how her skin has tightened from the frigid air. Red-cheeked and fresh-faced, she's obviously stood there a little while waiting for us. She pushes her hair behind her ears, and settles into the seat as Starsky lets the engine down. Then we're in a gravel trap at the side of one of the B roads again, and I hear the ground crunching under the front tyres of Alys's Corsa pulling up just behind.

One more interview, Starsky's told our client, with a freelancer we want in on the job. And sure enough, it was fine. No problem, as long as we keep it on the move like before.

The second engine dies – a door, then footsteps. I keep looking ahead, feigning indifference, my breath and heart-rate steady as is within my power. Alys wanted to pass the house on her own, to get a feel for it, but now she's going to sit in the back with me, and get her own first shot at trying to read Mrs Lovell.

The intensity is lost on Starsky, who makes pithy introductions, and tries to keep all personality out of it. To me he's suddenly become the third most interesting person in this enclosed space. I wonder if he knows it?

This is dangerous, my head tells me. Starsky's the wisest man in the universe, and he's pulled this together because he got freaked out by the Mrs Lovell job, so I need to sharpen. Can't miss anything.

But I am missing things, everywhere. All I can focus on is the exchange between our maybe-mad client and Alys:

From the off, it just doesn't look as if these two are actually taking part in the same conversation. Mrs Lovell is talking straight through both Starsky and Alys. She's probably closer to addressing *me* if anything – and that's not what's happening in anyone's world. Then you've got Alys. What can you do with someone like this? If Mrs Lovell's wavelength is shot, then I'm fucked if anyone's gonna keep up with Alys. She's the conductor here – pace, rhythm, Alys is running it. She can make this dialogue sound any way she wants.

Starsky finishes up the introductions, like he's expecting everyone to shake hands formally when we're having a meeting in the cockpit of a car that smells of damp and decaying nicotine. A meeting arranged so a girl neither of us knows anything about can hopefully tell Starsky what story we should go out and look for.

Alys doesn't even bother to ignore his gesture, says to thin air, 'Probably nothing to worry about,' and smiles, effortless, affable, direct.

Usually the man with a plan, he's thrown by this straight away. Mrs Lovell doesn't notice anything out of kilter though, and as of that moment me and Starsky are just onlookers.

Mrs Lovell goes: 'That house. It's everything.'

Alys: 'What makes you think that?'

'The pines at the top end, around the back. Did you see the tips coming over the roof? Those are trees of such importance. My great-grandfather planted four – the year my father was born.'

Alys doesn't pause for thought and keeps firing questions, but they never quite match the answers before or after.

'So what sort of times are we talking about?'

'The copper beech is in the family too. The laburnum. And the monkey puzzles. The land has been with us for two hundred years.'

I wonder which of these trees was the one Mrs Lovell turned into a stump fifteen years ago, while Alys comes up with another question that seems not to match.

'How often?'

'Fourth generation. But my husband wanted changes. I could see his point – it was old. Same as when my grandparents had it. You could tell someone was growing too sentimental. My sister never had the same attachment as me...'

'How sure are you?'

'Oh, I couldn't begin to tell you. Extremely important. I'd say this is so important. It's the most important... thing I'll ever face.'

On this goes, Starsky waiting to intervene and try to pull this whole exchange back from la-la-land, because he needs facts and stuff to note down. But I'm drawn totally to whatever's going on behind the ephemeral bubbles of language these two women are releasing without real worry for meaning. They both look so involved, so engaged.

When Alys starts being more specific, Mrs Lovell drifts even further, but I can feel some sort of complex circling game going on. They're striding around each other, light-footed, looking for the moment to connect.

Alys, the first to draw straighter lines: 'Why the sounds?'

But then this: 'The best man at our wedding... he was my husband's art tutor – not how to *make* art – how to *buy* it. He wanted something you could *touch*. That man – they fell out since – they get tutorials in taste, trends. This is his *retirement*!'

My mind seizes that last word, the way it's said. You sounded vengeful then, Mrs Lovell, and it doesn't suit you – that's what I want to say if I had power of speech. Alys half wants to say that too – I get that one. Hang on... Her thought! I'm picking it up, I'm sure of it.

But Alys hides it well. 'The sounds,' she repeats. 'They're not chosen at random?'

And Mrs Lovell shuts down.

'I can't go through telling this again,' she announces, cold and confident. 'Do what you must.'

'We're trying to help,' says Alys. 'I need your perspective.'

'I don't have one,' says Mrs Lovell.

'Why?'

'Someone else's perspective is what's important here.'

'Who.'

'You know who.'

'When you were being watched before,' says Alys, smashing taboo right out the way, 'was it *him?*'

'I hope not,' says Mrs Lovell.

'But you think it was?'

'You know what I think too, don't you,' says our client, dead of tone, no question, just a statement of fact.

Starsky sees his way in: 'Did you manage to write down some information about your husband? Nothing more than some handwritten stuff will be fine. His name, and if you can, office address?'

Of course, we know most of that stuff already. I've eyeballed the fucker and Starsky's been back on all the land reg, credit databases, electoral rolls, Companies House, insolvency

70

registers – anything that might give the slightest sniff. And guess what – that 'Hideous CnC' label I saw *is* his City incarnation too! So really we know as much as her already, but here it comes anyway, lined paper, page of a notebook penned in midnight blue ink by the hand of this stately woman. I want to know why she's trusting us with this. Why she's willing to have more people come in on the plan yet-to-be-made. And what she's really thinking of Alys's intense, magnetic eye-contact?

Mr Brian Godfrey Lovell. Forty-three. Born in Leicester. Always with a so-called business partner when in London, she says, not to be confused with the best-man art-dealer we just heard of. The business partner is Haydn something – she doesn't know the surname, even though he's stayed in their house plenty of times. She doesn't know where the partner's from either. Or who they bank with. No mention of Hideous CnC or hideous anything else, obviously. How can you know so little about your spouse? Especially when you reckon he's got it in for you. There's also an, albeit insultingly basic, description of his appearance, and of the partner, Haydn, who I know right away is the prick I saw at Ealing Broadway that night when it was probably my own intrusive behaviour that flushed them into such a sketchy looking tête-à-tête.

I'm not looking forward to it, but already know we're likely gonna see both these morons up close before that second twelve and a half grand of Mrs Lovell's sits in the Whiteout trademark's account. This is all being done with no hold, no grip, on anything.

'Thanks for all this, Mrs Lovell,' Starsky mumbles. 'Descriptions are handy,' he adds as a bare-faced lie, before tentatively pushing for more. 'Would be helpful if you've got a picture too, just for precautions. I'm not thinking it'll come to it, but you never know. Could be a big help if he should ever walk up on one of us.'

'He won't,' she says. I feel the need to gulp air. She really doesn't have a fucking clue.

'Still,' Starsky says, placating, 'wouldn't hurt. Better to have and not to need an' all that. I can copy it on my phone. Not planning to make contact or look into him at first anyway. Not without your say-so.'

It occurs to me, if we know this is bollocks does it mean Alys probably does too? You're on your own again, Mrs Lovell. You come in alone, and you're going home alone. To lots of noise.

'Plenty of time,' I find myself adding, and it's immediately obvious I've spoken out of turn.

Mrs Lovell looks at me again – straight on – and I can't handle it for a millisecond so my eyes twist away towards the window. 'Plenty of time if you don't have to go back to *that*,' she fires, quick and monotonous – the words trying to escape before emotion catches up with them. These fractions of time in which she baulks, where the composure shakes, they're getting more prominent to me, I realise.

And that's not because they're happening more often – they're not. If I had to guess why I'm starting to see more, it would be this: Alys is looking out for it too. These things I'm seeing, they're coming to me through someone else's perspective. I want to shout. It's happening again. This is going both ways. Alys: I can feel what she's looking at.

I start trying to turn around and catch Alys's glance instead, but it's not going to happen. Don't know if it's Mrs Lovell pulling my stare or Alys pushing it away. Noah's not at the controls though. Thoughts chase me, take me, tell me.

So what we both end up waiting on from there, too keen to know, is what version of that meeting transpired in the world according to Alys. To start with, for someone so eager to get this big payday moving to the next stage, Starsky goes a week doing nothing to arrange that precious bit of info – the Alys verdict. That's too fuckin long, when something so meaningful has *almost* happened. But that's his way. 'Hurry up and wait, Noah.'

His contact warned that mentioning cash, prices, instructions or contracts would put Alys off finding anything. We pay what we think it's worth, is how it goes. Is the wait worth it? This gig of hers is all about the flow, the energy, says the bloke who told the bloke who told Starsky about her. You know, any day of any year I would be fobbing this crap off, saying I'm over it. But we believe what we feel, right?

So what happens when your grasp of what you felt is starting to get a bit shaky?

Eight full days and nights pass, and when this new 'misc' consultant of ours does pop back onto the scene, Starsky can't do anything about it. He's got to go to Aylesbury for another job, to interview some tool under caution – investigation of an insurance claim, everyone's favourite. So I'm left in the sublime situation of being the stand-in.

She's coming to the Whiteout office, first thing in the morning. 'Pay what it's worth,' Starsky says.

'How the fuck do I do that?'

'Just fill out a cheque – here – and stick the digits on it. Everyone knows how to write a cheque.' He tears one away from the book he keeps above his desk. Such a dry bastard, no idea of my plight.

'Yeah, of course I can fill out a fucking cheque – but how much?'

'I told ya: What it's worth. Your decision, Noah. Think about what we're getting paid, what we'll have to do to see the job out, and then weigh up how useful she is in helping us meet those ends... Oh, and she won't ask for it, so you'll have to bring it up – at the right time, mate.'

'Great. Yeah, leave it with me.' Already, a basic 'professional' meeting with this girl is gonna carry the awkwardness of a fuckin date, as I have to walk that cheesewire tightrope of etiquette. How to pay, when to pay. How *much*. And then there's the fact you can't hide from her – not even inside your own head.

Sleep harder to come by than it has been in ages, I'm in the office early for that day of reckoning – before any of the others who rent space in this block. I have to tap in the code, turn off alarms, hit the heating and open the blinds. In an hour or two a communal receptionist will be sitting at the front desk reading a *Daily Mail* or something similarly offensive. We all chip in for her wage, but she has orders not to know Whiteout has an office here – so people have to ask for us by our names instead. Generally Chris White's status is 'not around', like today; out at a meeting – Noah as a reserve. But Alys will know the way through, she'll know which door to tap.

With no one around I start psyching up as if I'm about to paddle into big waves or jump off the cliffs of Acapulco. Breath drawn regular, tweak my neck from side to side. I go put a filter coffee into Starsky's old percolator, and leave it to gurgle and sigh. The appointment's been set for early, and hopefully she'll arrive to a freshly brewed pot of Nicaraguan just as it's the perfect temperature. Cups are clean – Starsky wouldn't have it any other way – and the milk is fresh and full. It's times like this I should be a proper smoker. You can see why people like him and Bob got onto the cancer sticks when they were younger – all those hours of surveillance or getting ready for a show-down interview with someone who's made a real-life video nasty but won't admit to it. I get to thinking how this morning's work wouldn't be the slightest cause for worry in their worlds, but still that sense of high-stakes doesn't go away. It's as if there's an outcome to strive for in the next couple of hours, an outcome that will have wider and more serious effects than I can possibly realise. Only I don't know what that outcome is, how it can have any effect at all – or what's required of me to bring it about.

At the end of a corridor that we share with a chiropractor and a couple of other small businesses I don't take much interest in, there's a flat window set into the wall at chest height, which lets you look out the side of the building and over a little patch of marsh and grassland. I've turned a company phone on and kept it with me, as I walk to that window and watch a dawn murmuration of starlings swirling about, getting ready to split up for the day ahead. They're late leaving this year – or late arriving. I forget which – just heard it on the radio a few days ago. Either way what are they waiting for? We humans have to pay a grand to fly to another continent.

I lean my elbows on the cold plaster of this windowsill and let my thoughts follow this swarm as it twists and shifts across the wetlands that separate the Crawl from rows of hills behind. Atlantic one side of the town, heights the other. Just as the novelty starts to wear off, she calls. Running late.

It's just gone eight, and she's not going to make it this side of midday. Given that she lives within an hour of here – so Starsky reckoned – this must mean something pretty significant's come up. Traffic doesn't delay you half a day. If this was a debtor or a subject making excuses you'd swear it was just avoidance. I don't want to ask her why she won't be here, so just offer to reschedule instead.

She sounds reluctant. 'It's going to happen,' she says. 'It's just a push for me to get to *you*.'

'OK,' I tut, cool as I can. 'Well, is this stuff something we absolutely need to talk about face to face, anyway?' And as soon as it's out it feels like this is just the wrong thing to say. Don't people like her take their shit really seriously? I mean, Starsky takes it all serious enough – so what am I thinking?

She's fine though, and seems to animate a bit – or at least the voice coming over the receiver does: 'Not really – nothing ever is. We've done the hard bit. Of course if you've got paper and a bit of time we can cover *some* of this stuff on the phone. But we won't make as much progress as you want though. It's not ideal.'

'Er, OK. No problem,' I say. 'So just set me a time and place. Whatever suits…'

'Your office is…' she begins, then tails off.

'You want to meet at the office still? That's fine. Right, so same plan then. You just need to say when?'

'No. That's not what I'm saying. Your office is… it isn't ideal either, see. There's a lot to go through, Noah, so why don't we try and catch each other in a more neutral space? I could get somewhere neutral quite quickly.'

Hearing my name makes something jar in my temple, a quick flush where my blood twitches in temperature. My first name? Starsky was 'Mr White'. I'm sure of it. But if I think that makes me special in some way, I'm probably not onto much – at this stage, anyway.

'Your "client",' she almost coughs the word like it needs anonymising, 'Michelle…' OK, so there's another one who gets first name-referenced too – and Noah isn't too keen to be chucked in the same basket as her. 'Michelle,' Alys continues, 'I think, is someone we should all take very seriously.'

The shrewd part of me says I'm not liking the 'we' in that. Like she's deciding this is partly her gig now too. Digits scroll in my head, bottom line getting thinner. But it's said with such conviction, as if the only driving force here is that of necessity.

Pay what it's worth. Starsky White's words are echoing to me.

'OK – you say where, and when,' I offer again. 'Are we talking about today still?'

'Of course.'

'Fine with me. Like I said, just give me a time and place.'

And then – direct, calculating, elusive – that place and time are both set, and Alys's voice is gone, losing gravity and substance as it falls away from memory swifter than it arrived. The venue for our meeting is as neutral as you can get.

A services on the motorway; lunchtime.

Burger King wafts its flame-grilled tentacles my way as I settle for a plastic-wrapped, four-quid tray of sushi rolls and frothy coffee from the newsagents instead. She's late again, and I'm thinking I could have got away with a Whopper Meal. Doesn't matter who it is though; you can't shake hands with someone professional when they might have been watching you stuff fries into your mouth with those same fingers seconds before.

Professional... now there's a thought. I'm supposed to do business with this girl over something I don't even understand.

Handshake doesn't go ahead either. Dunno why. It just doesn't.

I half stand as she strolls over, and then ask her if she wants a coffee or anything. Scones with jam over there, I note.

'No thanks.'

'I'll probably have one myself in five.'

'I'm OK. Don't let me stop you, though.'

I do let her stop me – but that probably has a fair bit to do with the way she plunges us both straight into the cold, hard facts of the 'case'. And she's really busting out the terminology too.

'Right,' she says, 'you wouldn't want to set up an OP near that place under any circumstances – can I get that message over to you clear and early? The voyeur gets *squashed* if this goes where I think it does.' Then she says something else, low, to herself which I think I can just hear. 'Torn apart. Yes, no OP. Whatever we do.'

OP – that's 'observations post', by the way. She's talking fuckin surveillance. OK, so she seems to think there are reasons not to act sketchy around that house... As if we'd get into shit like that right off the bat. It's only been a matter of days since she got involved and already I'm wishing we hadn't done any of that extra-curricular crap, as, I'm sure, is Starsky – wherever he is right now. What chance she doesn't know something of it, anyhow?

Now, completely coherent, Alys is again in total control. A mentor; someone who knows the answers already to this puzzle but who still has the humility – or the sardonic sense of humour – to let us do some figuring out for ourselves. I'm realising the cryptic shit she threw at Mrs Lovell isn't her run-of-the-mill way of doing it. Not by a long stretch.

'Noah,' direct, piercing eye contact, 'I need you to tell me how Michelle first came to you.'

'Er... Not sure. I think she rung Chris – you know...'

'Chris White?' Starsky's full and proper name always sounds odd to me. But so does mine, come to think of it.

'Yeah. Well, he just said to me that he had this interesting case, and didn't think it should be first enquired alone.'

'He had that right.'

I want to interrupt the course of this now and ask her what she thinks. Coz she clearly does have something to say – but she invites this confessional out of me further, so I go on:

'She got us out of the phone book – we keep an ad in there. For debt recovery. It says private surveillance and process serving too. But small-time. I mean, to me it seemed as if – well, you know, she seems to think this is all a big deal, and that everyone involved is big and rich and powerful – so I, er, just thought she wanted to pick a little firm like us coz they might take it on a bit more serious, you know?'

She's nodding, and has glanced more than once at a little notepad. Nothing's been jotted down though. The nodding has a sensibility to it – makes you feel you can go on. So I do. 'When we spoke to her it all seemed quite, sort of, well, far-fetched?'

Alys nods. 'It would,' she says.

This is the time to go *And is it?* But I don't. Instead conversation takes a short hiatus during which time I'm twitchy to say the least. Without a voice right in front of me to tune into, the background chatter of the room swells back into my ears. I'm feeling the shit sleep I had stressing about this meeting, the breakfast I never ate. The back of my neck is tight from too much coffee and thought. I'm wondering why I do it to myself.

Now Alys does pull out her notebook, and I watch the precision with which she unclips a pen, twists it and scrawls a heading or date into the top left margin. She scribbles the underline hard until the paper must be razzed with it, and her pen makes a gentle whooshing sound as she does. It supersedes the rest of the building's noise and yanks my attention back.

I get asked in quick succession, but with calmest patience, all about the house – the route we took to it, and what I think of its appearance. Then Alys tells me she hasn't seen it. Didn't go there the other day before meeting us roadside. She doesn't want to see it either – which makes me baulk with guilt again about what I'm concealing.

She knows it anyway.

Fuck. There's that low-frequency alarm, pinging in my soul again. It lights up the core of me. This person *doesn't really need to be told anything*. She's not fishing for info – she's just observing what I will and won't admit to. Alys is only quizzing me to calibrate what she's already decided.

The writing is still going on. She's moving slow, relaxed. Tiny marks on the page – could even be shorthand if it wasn't for the fact time looks like it's never managed to panic this girl into anything. I try to guess what she's penning into this notebook and my mind hits a wall. She moves to say something, and I fill with adrenaline. The moment passes.

In thought, she presses nib against page, holding on to whatever mark was being made. And it invites me to talk again.

'We went there; the house.'

She stops. Then looks at me, and her face shows warmth. I see wide eyes lose their intensity. She tilts her head to one side, a few degrees, gradual, precise and I watch gravity adjust her two-piece earrings to point at the floor again.

'Did you,' The words come out forgiving, no question intoned, and she smiles. 'Your idea or Chris's…'

'His.' She looks impressed.

'And what did *you* want to do? Were you keen to go along with it?'

I think, for a moment – about how I don't know what to say – and then realise that's bullshit. I shouldn't be trying to create any kind of impression here. Just tell her what you know, Noah, and how it happened. See what that leads to.

You pay what it's worth? How do I do that? This isn't worth anything… yet. But it could be. How do you measure this up against cash?

I'm dragged back towards that confessional again.

Nothing is held back as I recount in full and frank detail – the walls, their height, the peculiar way they didn't seem to add up to where the ceiling should be, the air we felt in there, the stairway, drive, gravel surfaces and surrounding lanes, the floor inside that porch and the way it just drooped open, as if the house wanted us to take a peek. I tell her how Starsky bet me it'd be unlocked, how he seemed so sure of the plan and then so lost when we came to talk about it back at our desks. Now

Alys writes nothing; hears everything. Sees even more. I'm sure of it. And when I am done, she has ideas beyond, or thinks she will soon.

'Could you hear running water anywhere in there?' she asks. No.

'Are you sure?'

Yes.

It's going to take more time – but time is something we have. For now. She's not worried about this. As it stands, we're ahead. We're where we'll need to be.

I'm buying every word. There's nothing out of place in the way she tells it.

'Noah, we should talk about this again soon.' She wants to be 'kept in the loop'. Nothing can pass without her knowing. We're going to meet within a few days, whether there's more info or not. And then this:

'Where do you go to think, Noah?'

My answer, without need to deliberate on it at all: 'Beach or a hill.'

'OK,' she nods. 'Let's go day after tomorrow. I'll have more then.'

'Eh?'

'Or even tomorrow might do. Depends. You decide. Beach or hill. We'll do it your way from the start. We have to.'

Fine.

'It's found me, you see,' she says, 'this job. You're the guys the client called, not me. So you need to be listened to as well. Let's go where you're most comfortable. Where you're at your best.'

In my plastic seat I stall – almost beyond re-starting again. I just about get a response out before she notices:

'OK,' I say. That's all. And it is OK.

'I'll use your landline,' she says. 'We'll make a plan once I know.'

'My landline?' I'm half a thought behind again.

'Yeah.' Then she tells me my own phone number. Starsky must have given it out.

And Alys goes. A departure that's followed by that draining of short-term memory again. I clutch at the image she presents, the sound of her voice but again it's futile.

All that I'm left with is an insane hunger. I want to eat immediately, something full of wheat and flour and sugar, wash it down with half a litre of soft drink or strong coffee. I need to get outdoors too – but not before she's well out of range.

Is she ever well out of range? I never mentioned a word about London. And that's not all I've neglected.

Shit, Noah! You didn't pay.

It's an easy run back down the motorway, the Corridor to the Crawl. Rush hour beaten and still plenty of light. Short days seem much more accommodating when your imagination kicks you out of bed before sunrise. I spin up along the coastal road and take the long way back to the town centre. There's still no swell anywhere in the North Atlantic, and if there had been I wouldn't be up to a surf anyway. But that doesn't stop me taking a look. Light southerly winds are sending micro sets wobbling across the shoreline. They'd be perfect A-frames if you were three inches tall. The brown muck that's normally chopped up from the mudflats on the seabed has settled, and the water's a greyish blue. As close to clear ocean as the Crawl sees.

High-stakes days are coming around too often. Hoping they're behind me, but knowing the only chance of that is if I turn my back on the whole thread, I leave my car outside the stairwell behind the Whiteout office, and wander. Couple of other tenants still there – but our unit can stay locked for the rest of today. I need solid ground, blue skies. Soles feel out the earth below, a brief diversion across sand – massive high tide pushing everything it can against the shore – then up onto the promenade again and back into the streets I grew up in. Mum's house passes by, empty by day – Josie still in school, if she hasn't gone on the road, accompanying her mother to a string of sales meetings again. That girl can already do a stock take and fill out mileage logs. She likes being close to Mum, being useful for something, but teachers are on their case. Apparently the kid misses so much that by the time she's twelve it'll amount to a whole academic year. Can something be that black and white? I mean, the girl asks *questions*. Doesn't that count?

Scarface should probably be on these walks with me too – probably in that house having a kip, and like I said, he's technically my dog after all. I swear to pick up the pair of them, sis and mutt, and go somewhere special sometime soon. That's what I'm about. But not now. Not today.

There's almost nothing left in my tank now. I'm beaten, bludgeoned, bereft. No energy anywhere in my frame, so I head straight indoors and flip the latch. Noah not available.

Ah, my shitty space. Bland – showroom style. For now it's all I am. But this is just a waiting room, if I get my way. The lounge has got a masked edge of sunbeam cutting across it, adding another pointless abstract line to the Ikea rug I kick my shoes over. No energy for TV, radio, a surf mag or book, listening to some music. I sidle upstairs to the spare room – west facing. Sun dropping towards its daily exit; now is the only time of the only kind of day when it's worth sitting in there.

I lie against the far wall, propped up by a beanbag, and stare out the window. Those southerlies coming off the Bristol Channel are causing tree tops to sway. The street behind backs onto the marsh fields out back from the Whiteout office, but if you lie at just the right angle all you can see is sky and a handful of branches from a massive oak in a garden from the street behind. Reading the season wrong, like the starlings this morning, the oak is just starting to push out a few tiny buds, while magpies sit at its opposite reaches, calling to each other.

Way, way above, mackerel-skin layers of cloud are starting to fall apart – each patch of emerging sky empty all the way to the edge of the atmosphere – apart from one pinline plane trail. Lower, about halfway between the treetop and upper vapours, several thicker, cotton blobs drift, quicker, through my range of vision. Nothing that could carry rain, just innocuous patterns in the sky. Then I notice one isn't moving at all. It's whiter than anything else in the frame, and three birds, also magpies, are perched right on the cloud. I blink to be sure. No doubting it. One bird flaps briefly, then settles again, shaking its tail to sink a little deeper into the soft surface. I know straight away this isn't right, isn't logical, but nothing changes in my mind. For some reason, at this moment, it's nothing beyond the usual. The sight settles in; my eyes accept. I watch for ten minutes, then twenty, or longer. Rows of other clouds come and go around it, but this one keeps floating there.

A fourth magpie eventually arrives, sits on the very edge of this unchanging, brilliant puff of white. Another steps slowly across a rise in the cloud to meet it. Side by side, tails tilting into the air, the two look over to the tree branches below.

Then all four birds up and fly away, as if they've noticed something.

I sit there for an indefinite, irrelevant amount of time, eyes still fixed on the same spot, limp. No muscles in my body doing anything beyond keeping me conscious. Eventually, with the cloud still not moving or changing shape in any way, I drift off.

When I wake up the cloud's still there, and another bird has returned to sit right in the middle. Going downstairs for a tea I take a look out the kitchen window but no change. Still there, although getting redder as daylight recedes.

It's been only a couple of hours, yet Alys phones just as I'm ready to declare it dark. She's ready to meet. And tomorrow will do.

5

Elevation to reliable witness

So here's something that fucks it all right up: Mrs Lovell's dead the next day. And don't think for a second that's dead as in ran out of breath or heartbeats. No, the woman has been absolutely cut to ribbons in her garden by some fuckin sadist.

We find out only a few hours before the press. Another one of Starsky's mates from his time in the police tells him the story in some café where they all network over greasy breakfasts – you know, wades into sharing confidential info with just the sort of person you shouldn't. It's too interesting to keep it to themselves, the tale of this rich bird who's been hacked up in the Vale, so they pass it on merely out of morbid interest – as if sharing views on a film, or narrating a good goal or try scored on the telly last night. It means that we know all the bits they leave out of the report that appears on *Wales Today*. Without realising he's talking about Starsky's client, this plod spills all the most gruesome details of the case. Just fishing for advice from an ex-member of the force – as if Starsky will do no more than chew it over...

She's been found by nine in the morning, because the whole thing happened right in the middle of the garden. And since her house is on an incline it means neighbours gazing out the windows as their coffees boil are able to see this semi-naked lady lying there on the grass, drained of blood and organs.

Three people from those new-builds at the bottom of her cul-de-sac have made the discovery simultaneously. Doesn't sound as if the killing was done quickly either, or as if there was much of a fight. She's been hit over the head – it'll be a few days before we know if it was hard enough to lose consciousness – and then stabbed in the sides of the ribs too many times to count. Her face has been cut up too, and her throat slit to make sure. Bits are missing – and not the usual bits. We're talking little bits of flesh from the most obscure places; the side of the cheek, a knee-cap and then there's a big hole in the side of her back, as if the killer's tried to reach in. There's bite marks too – all over. It's fuckin foul, and they're borrowing detectives from everywhere for ideas.

Despite bite marks, there's no obvious sexual motive, which is something else they don't like. Means they can't compartmentalise the case. Mind you, the attack has happened by night and she's in a thin nightgown that's now in bits. Nothing's been taken from the house either, that they can see, and the aggression of the whole thing is suggesting someone who's done it before. This fucker's got style, and it's a style none of them purport to have seen in decades of combined corpse analysis.

You know what, Noah... Nowadays a dead person can tell you more from a metal table than they'd probably manage alive.

So anyway, by lunchtime I'm able to warn Alys of the rapid changes too, ahead of supposedly seeing her at the Crawl's western beach in a few hours' time. What the fuck do I do? Cancel? And shouldn't we sort of declare our part in this nightmare to someone?

These are the calls Starsky gets to take responsibility for in return for the far bigger slices of the pay cheques he takes home. And they're calls he's looking for advice on, too. He hasn't been here before, on this side of the fence anyway. If he were still 'Old Bill' he'd want to know all he could, of course. But what happens now that it's partly his problem?

'Big shit sandwich this, Noah. And we're all gonna have to take a bite.'

I've always been stoked on the details of my life, and how it works. I mean, I'd wanna be me. We get to see the edges in this game. There he is... Noah with the stories, Noah who can't be ordinary. Noah who stands out. Noah who has a plan. Noah who can't be phased coz Noah's *experienced*. Noah's shifty. Noah's hard. Noah plays under pressure. Noah's going somewhere more important than you. It's total bollocks. Noah's as weak as anyone.

And now Noah's involved. Can it be more fuckin clear? Death. Someone's been killed, and been killed mucky. It's someone we know had issues. It's someone who called *us* in to help with those issues. So whoever's seen this poor lady off wouldn't be too happy if they got wind of me and Starsky either. Dying's something that actually happens, you know. She's just proved it. If someone sticks enough steel through you in the right places that's *it*. You're gone. State the obvious, I know – but how often do we actually *think* it?

I drive out of town from the east and the sky is all high drama. Some kind of front sifts thin slices of daylight over the sea in barred rays. The rocky point at the far end of the Crawl is out in the thick of it. Black boulders dropping into green ocean. Frontlines under frontlines. It's all about confrontation. The sea's million-year standoff. Turn your back on it. Go on. Behind all that somewhere sits the sun. Servant to the master. It moves. We grow. Winter, move over. I mean it. Move out the way.

SPRING

6

Sessions

'You're involved, Noah.'

This is the first thing Alys says when, still a few hours before it becomes public knowledge, I tell her what's happened to our client. Well, sort of the first thing – if you don't count the 'I know.' Of course she knows. I don't ask how, because that way I can still assume she's heard it from somebody else. Yeah, one of the coppers maybe – or even Starsky.

'Did you hear me?' she says as I send silence back down the phone at her. 'You're involved in this.'

She's not reading the same signs as the fuckin police though, because they've decided it's *Starsky* who's most likely to be 'involved'.

He gets pulled in about a week after and it's a pretty relentless attempt to pin shit on him from then on. To start with he's full of bravado and even reckons he smacked one of the coppers in the interrogations room – the big-mouthed one who told him about the case in the first place. 'Dent police pride and they always get funny,' he tells me. 'The twat's just embarrassed that he run his gob off to me without thinking.'

But in Starsky's case it's clearly more than that.

OK, I can see how it looks. I mean, we are among the few fools who had their connections to the deceased open for all to see. Whiteout Legal Investigations is definitely in and around her affairs during the last months of her life, but Christopher

91

Starsky White has alibis – and a clean DNA trail – and no motive – and doesn't fit the profile – and has a million other strong defences too.

Yet they want it to be him so badly they'll do nearly anything. Watch your back Starsky. Filthy coppers in South Wales can pull strings. They hold him overnight.

So, given all this *you're involved* nonsense, I'm on the phone to Alys about ten times wondering if all of us shouldn't just go to the station to try and reason with Starsky's captors. Because let's get this super clear right now; that guy is not a murderer in any way. Ever, ever, ever.

'You can't,' says Alys over and over again. 'You of all people have to stay away from the police right now. *You* need to keep quiet. Because I've told you, you're *involved*.'

There she goes again. I keep pushing for more on what she means. The reply is she wants to meet. Not now, but soon. 'Lay low. I'll come to you when I can,' she's telling me. 'There's still more for you to do.'

Meanwhile April comes in, then moves us closer to May and early spring's thick palls of wet greyness give way. Rain-soaked ground starts to throb out deep, plush greens that echo the blues of the sky overhead. Sun's the same height as it will be in August now, and the only thing keeping the brakes on this whole warming-up thing is the sea – which will step out of its freeze any time.

Surfing's easy again, and as usual it's what saves me from life. Solid, long-period waves – these springtime swells are organised where winter swells were angry. The power comes with a crisp edge; ruler-straight lines through the ocean's surface. You get to bask in afternoon heat as you suit-up and wander to shore.

Once in the water, sunlight reflects off the surface to your face, under your chin. And afterwards comes that feeling of drying salt water starting to strain hair.

There are people about too – other surfers emerging from hibernation. Community thrives again at the beachside carparks of the Crawl, and for the next few months we won't need to wish on living somewhere else.

I'm working on a tan-mark too – an important one, from a wetsuit, right on the throat. Just above where I'd knot a tie, if I ever wore one. Coz these days work drifts down my priorities like silt making its way down the channel to the lighter, bluer waters beyond.

And what of the Vale? Leafy, rolling, breezy, fresh – well it'll see its changes too. Starsky gets pulled in another three times, he's even in the local papers as a suspect, but the truth of it is that trails left by Mrs Lovell's real killer – or killers? – are every bit as dead as her.

According to *me*, *Noah*, at least. According to the version *I'm* trying to push.

But whenever Alys does get in touch she's banging that same drum again and pretty soon I'm gonna find out more about this 'you're involved' shit. I don't want it to be the case, but it's obvious from the off that she has a better idea than anyone of what happened in the Void in the Vale during those few night-cloaked hours of blood-letting.

And sooner or later I'm gonna hear more. It's inevitable. Sure as the force sticking me to the earth.

She keeps phoning, about once a week, asks nothing much beyond 'have you heard anything?' then seems to go all vague on me before hanging up. She never appears to want to talk to Starsky and I've taken it as read not to tell him this is happening. The calls keep coming, promises to meet, warnings to lie low. And then, just as the plan is made and Alys is agreeing to another impersonal dinner conference at the motorway services, they come for me too with the words we all dread and relish – *You do not have to say anything but it may harm your defence if you do not mention etcetera-etcetera* – and instead I'm being taken for a ride to Barry HQ, where the Vale's murder detectives keep their sparse and dusty offices.

They knock early, pre-dawn – usually my own trick when I'm out card-collecting, so I'm well aware who's at the door – and tell me to change into some half tidy clothes before I get to join them for a chat under caution. There's two male coppers about Starsky's age, one of whom stands outside the shower as I get ready. It's forty-nine days after the night she was killed. I know coz I've been counting to fifty as if it was gonna represent some important quantity.

First thing they do is set me up with a Swallow viewing, run by some pint-sized PCSO; a computer slide show with mugshots of about twenty women Mrs Lovell's age, none of whom I've ever seen in my life. Then the two coppers come back, hostile from the off, calling me by my surname, and finding great intrigue in the smallest things.

'According to this then... Noah *Lloyd*, you're in a four-surname family eh? How's that happen then. Mother, step sister...'

'Deed poll,' I tell them before this can go anywhere else. 'Nothing exciting.'

'So... Lloyd – where's 'at come from then?'

'Phone book.'

'Phone book?'

'Yeah. Random choice. Flicked through. First name the pin landed on.'

'Bollocks.'

'That's how it happened,' I tell them. 'Anything wrong with doing that? Where's *your* surname from?'

This rubbish is obviously not big on their agenda, and these questions put an end to the pre-shit shit that they're giving me. They introduce themselves promptly – the one doing the driving so far is a Mr Whitfield, the other Starsky's embarrassed 'mate' Sgt Davies – and then get straight on with it. After another caution, of course. Conversation is something pretty close to this:

Whitfield: 'So you're here to help us, and you definitely need to. We've got a simple situation – someone dead, with you and the people you work for having an instruction for discreet enquiries on your books.' (Looking at notes quickly – for theatrical purposes only. He'd have to be thicker than he looks to need clarification here.) 'Instruction made *by* the deceased.'

Noah: 'Fair enough. What d'you need to know?'

Whitfield: 'Well, that's really simple,' (addresses me by surname again). 'What was the instruction for?'

Noah: 'No problem telling you that, boys. Although can't you tell me why I'm looking at mugshots of middle-aged ladies first?'

Whitfield: 'In case you recognise one of them.'

Noah: 'Yeah, but don't I need to know *who* I'm meant to recognise? As in where I'm supposed to have met the person?'

Whitfield: 'If you've ever met the person we're thinking of, you'd only remember them by face. They wouldn't have made themselves known.'

Noah: 'Bit fuckin pointless, then…' (except I don't actually say this last bit, as being an out-and-out prick to the police doesn't work in real life quite like it does in films. Unless you're Starsky, of course, who's forever gonna be seen as one of their own.)

Whitfield (repeating, slightly tense): 'So what was the instruction you had off Michelle Lovell?'

'Straightforward stuff. She wanted her husband followed and observed – coz she didn't trust him, I'm assuming.'

'Her husband?' Whitfield, unsurprised, unimpressed.

'Yep.'

Then the other one – Davies, the one Starsky walloped – speaks up, using my first name this time, and the conversation takes a turn I don't like:

'*Husband*'s missing, see, Noah.'

So there's your fuckin man then, I'm about to say, but then they spell out the rest of it.

'Not what you're thinking, son. We know he wasn't there when she died. But he has gone AWOL since. If anything… well… it's a case of going on the run.'

'On the run? From you?'

Davies, smirking: 'No. From whoever slaughtered his missus like a farm animal. Can't blame him really, eh? Surprised you haven't split as well. They probably know all about you, let's face it.'

As you can imagine, that gets my attention.

The coppers go on like this for a while, not so much trying to pin any kind of blame on me – it's blindingly fuckin obvious I'm not some devil-worshipping woman-slasher – but instead seeing if they can shit me up with the idea the same people might have me within their sights too. Pretty ropey really, if you ask me, but it's a game they like to play. Authorities of all kinds don't like things going wrong on their watch, and if you can't help them clean house you'll often become a scapegoat for the fuckwittedness. It's an honour, really, isn't it? Sit back and watch them go. One of the many times when the policeman's manual must allow for a no-strings-attached bit of bully-boy power-tripping. As long as you see it for what it is, this is the easiest thing in the world not to get pissed off with.

Besides not being any sort of psychopath, I'm not stupid either, and singing away about things I've seen in London – about going into her house, when DNA would have told them that by now if we'd left any – it would all probably get us into more trouble anyway. And not just with the police, either. If her killers are the same people supposedly filling her property with funky noises then… well, I'm not even going there.

I give a few moments' thought to what these two 'detectives' must be thinking right now – probably something along the lines of how little reason there is to talk to me much longer – and this reminds me that what I really need to know is what Alys must be thinking. I'm meant to be meeting her right now, after all. Yeah, I'm projecting the right attitude now. They can't hold me, can't threaten me, can't even ask me anything I don't want to answer. Hold on Noah, I tell myself. Keep waiting, blank-faced for the moment when they give up and let me out into the Barry sunshine.

And it works. I'm walking into daylight soon enough. But the whole thing has done what it's meant to do. The injustice of being bothered in the first place. The threats made by them *about* the real killers. They've done what they wanted. They've made me need answers myself.

Only it turns out the answers need me just as much. Or so she says.

Once these two muppets are done, Alys calls me straight to attention, and I realise once and for all this thing is never going away.

She carries the scent of the whole sordid gig with her from the off – only, once more, I don't see it until it's too late to do anything about.

➔

I'm less than an hour out of the nick when she calls, and she's suddenly gone all soft-voiced and friendly. Getting my head around the original Alys seemed a task in itself, let alone dealing with this new approach:

'We were meeting up, weren't we, Noah *Lloyd*?' she goes, down the office phone, five minutes after my bus ride back is over and I'm at my desk. No checking it's me on the receiver, no 'Alys here' to let me know who's rung. Although in fairness I had an inkling who it would be. Anyway, the softness bowls me over and everything I say next starts with 'Uh' or 'Er'.

'Uh, er, well we were, like, but uh, things kind of...'

'Yeah, I saw,' she says.

'Saw what?' as if I think she might have been there or something. My voice sounds like Starsky's or those knobhead plods Whitfield and Davies – accusing, aggressive. I don't mean to, but I'm so on the back foot already.

'I saw... your problem,' she answers. 'The detectives.'

'Uh, right? Er, well, er... And?'

'There's still somewhere to go, Noah.'

'Er, somewhere to what?'

'Will you be in the Crawl this afternoon?'

'Uh, er, it er, depends. Wouldn't Mr White need to come along too, now? He's a better person to er...' First time I've mentioned his name in ages and she dismisses it right out.

'He's fine,' she says, 'but you're more use and you know it.'

'Uh, er, you what?'

'I'm happy to keep dealing with you.'

'Yeah, but shouldn't I...'

'Don't worry about coming to me,' she says, over any queries I might be about to raise. 'You choose where. I know you'll get it right.'

The plan *had* been, before the police complicated it, that I'd nail this daytime meeting with Alys and be on to an overdue hang-out with little sis by early evening. But with our mid-morning slot long gone and office hours ebbing away, anything we do now is gonna run roughshod over that idea. Interrupting time to think, Alys is there, again, saying 'I'll come to you. Just say where – like you were going to do before...'

Then her voice saying my name sends a sting through me.

'...Noah.'

Scarface and Josie both look equally gutted when I say something's come up – but work's work, eh? Even if this is the first time I've done business on the shoreline.

Yeah, my choice – Alys did tell me to say where so I've opted for my stronghold. It's three hours later, and even then talk of Mrs Lovell seems to be both out of bounds and essential at the same time.

It's when we get to the low-tide mark that she stops, stares straight at me and carries on with her direct way of saying everything and nothing at all:

'I'm glad there's an excuse to get near the sea,' she tells me as we step off the last yards of dry sand towards where it's permanently wet. 'So many of my meetings are over coffee or in rooms with no windows.' I remind myself that Starsky first heard of her because she freelances for the police a lot. Yeah, so a beach probably is a pretty cool place to conference.

'Er, d'you live near the water?' I try.

'Overlooking it. Further that way though,' – she points east – 'where it's a bit more ordered.'

'Yeah, bigger tides towards Cardiff and the Vale,' I add, as if it matters.

'Maybe. But this is the place,' she says. 'You've got it right. What time's low water, exactly?'

'Got to be nearly now,' I tell her.

'So high tide would have been mid morning?'

'Yeah – about right, yeah. Twice a day. Moving on by about three quarters of an hour each two tides. You've taken an interest in this stuff before?'

'I think I might well have,' she says. 'But it's only now that I know it.'

We step further forward until we're at the ocean's edge, feet slowly sinking into soft sand that will be reclaimed by the sea in a few hours' time. And she stops again and looks square at me so hard I want to yell for help.

'Noah,' she says. 'I have to keep in touch with you for a while now. You're involved.'

No words in reply. There's nothing. Not even the thought patterns needed to create them.

'You're safe, but you'll have to do the right things. Even if you don't know what they are, or don't want to. It can get lower than this still, can't it?' She points at the sea. 'The tide. Its range goes further out, still?'

Yeah, past the shipwrecks, I think of telling her.

'Good,' she says. 'I'm working on something. Something this could all be part of. You'll have to trust me. We need to wait for the next part, though. When I know more, you'll know more, as long as you're ready for it.'

Tiny waves trickle along the shore. Behind her a clearing sky brings Swansea and the western horizon into view. Minutes pass, easily. I'm held by something so strong it doesn't matter what else this short passage of time is capable of. Then she adds:

'Keep an eye on those tides, Noah. When it does happen, you'll be the one who hears.'

Obviously, once Alys is gone the first thing I do is phone Starsky and tell him. Tell him about getting pulled in by the police, about my walk on the beach, how he wasn't in the office when I got back or otherwise I'd have let him know back then. I tell him anything else he needs and his first reaction is absolutely tamping.

Not with me, though – no – I can do no wrong.

All his ire is for the coppers. In fact, what he wants is to drive straight to the Vale HQ and plant one on Davies, again.

'He's the fuckin arsehole who's been on my case, Noah. That other one, Whitfield, he's just a plod who can't think for himself. But it's that Davies you have to watch. I've known that prick fifteen years, matey and he's bad news all the way. Did he mention me?'

'Not much,' I say, moving the receiver closer to my mouth and hushing my voice, as if even talking about this stuff in my own place is sketchy. I explain how their main aim seemed to be convincing me that Whiteout employees might pop up on the killer or killers' radar at some point.

'Yeah, sounds about right mate. They want you shitting yourself so you'll cry into their laps about how scared you are of being next. Then you'll get this line about how the only way to stay safe is to tell them exactly what you've gotten yourself into, you know, trading everything you have on Mrs Lovell – and probably me, not that it's anything of use – in return for the protection of a force so stupid they couldn't catch a dog shitting.'

'Yeah, I gathered that,' I tell him. 'But we haven't really got a lot for them anyway, have we? Apart from the fact she thought her husband was into some bad stuff.'

'They know that anyway.'

'He's missing,' I say.

'No shit.'

'Did you know that?'

'No, but it's not really surprising is it.'

'Isn't it?'

'Nah – probably the one theory they have got about right.

Think about it, when you've got DNA and other modern forensics arriving on the scene before her blood's barely cold you're not gonna get away with that sort of domestic violence. If it had been him carving her up like that they'd have known it straight away. Oh yeah, I can assure you there'd have been a *lot* more fuss about his whereabouts. A *lot* more.'

I change the phone to my other hand. 'So he's split to avoid someone then?'

'Most likely really, when you think about it, matey. OK, it's possible that he's just shagging in the Bahamas somewhere. But most likely thing is he's worried about being next.'

'I've been talking to Alys,' I say.

'Good.'

This catches me out. I've been worrying about telling him this last bit. But *good*? What kind of a reaction is that?

'She got any ideas then?' Starsky asks me, as matter-of-fact as he was when going on about Mr's disappearance.

'I can't really tell.'

'Nah, they're often like that, mate. Don't worry too much. Those fuckin psychics – they have their ways and you just have to go along with it. Just keep her sweet. If she's talking to ya then that's great. That girl will have as much chance of finding out what happened as anyone.'

'Why should we care though?' I ask. 'I mean, our involvement with the Lovells – with anything to do with them at all – it has to be finished, right? We can't go on caring about that business now that this shit is going on?'

'Maybe. You never know though. Keep her sweet, matey. There shouldn't ever be major shit we don't know in this profession. If you've got a chance to find out anything about a client – past, present, dead or alive – that might help you make decisions in future then you should always take it. You've no way of imagining how knowledge on that case might help you out in a squeeze some time.'

'Really?'

'Oh, for sure. Always take a chance to know the answers, Noah. And anyway, aren't you interested? I'd fucking love to know who was tormenting that old bat. Fucking *love to*.' His television comes on the other end, loud. You can hear ads booming down the line.

I thank him, and ask if it bothers him – all this shit his company, Whiteout, has come under. He says not in the slightest, and I believe him. Coolest geezer in all of Wales – although being a Cockney blow-in has to make that superiority a bit easier to project.

'Oh one more thing Noah,' he says before I hang up.

'What.'

'Don't, under *any* circs at all, tell the coppers we've been dealing with that Alys, right? It could cause all kinds of shit, for you, for me, for her. Just take that one to the grave with you, alright. We've paid her in cash, it's off the books, and for all intents she's a ghost, OK. Don't fuck with that rule. Absolute pillar for dealing with her type. You happy with that?'

'Yep. Fine by me.'

'Good. Now fuck off to the pub or over your mum's if you wanna talk to anyone else tonight. There's football on in ten and I've got a car to repo at dawn.'

So there's gonna be something to hear then, is there? And I'm the 'one' who'll get it? *Wait for the next part* and *keep an eye on those tides*? Maybe it was the background noise of the waves licking the shore in front of us, the steady, swinging tug and push of fixed ocean. That has to be why the words have worked their way into my head with that rhythm, why they pop up so predictably on the same intervals as some long range swell that knows its place in the ecliptic.

I don't know, though. Can it be that simple? Is it just the rhythm of the waves that have embedded what she says in my mind like that? I'm listening to the other things she's told me now, too. On the phone, one stage at a time, sometimes almost too quickly for me to be sure it happened.

It did though. She's had a lot more to tell me – it's just my willingness to register it that's held us up. But now, I'm starting to run it over. *There's this object, or law of motion, starting to appear ahead of you now, Noah. No need to question, or worry. It's just there, as if always…*

'Ahead' is the key word too. That's the bit of perspective I don't want.

To start with I think I can ignore it. Bury head in the sand, and all that.

She says it won't work, though. *Not even for a moment Noah.*

But this is me.

Isn't it?

For now. But you will be more.

I want to groan, to shout, to fight. And it's not happening.

Yes, now I can be clear about this. Definitely true. It's once she arrives that the forward view starts filling my horizon. *Everything else gets shoved out*, I'm told. *Whether you like it or not.*

End of the same week, last day before dogs get banned from the beaches for summer, we walk again, this time with Scarface, and early morning coz the tides are six hours later.

And again, it's there at low water – as if she thinks the

encroaching sea can wash away the facts of our meetings afterwards. The dog runs straight into the waves but we stop just before that point where the ocean's murmur takes over.

'I see why you come to the beach,' she says.

'It gets me away,' I reply, turning back to face the land behind. 'Look how quiet it is. We're as far from it all here as if we were looking down from a mountain or something.'

We both gaze back at the silent frame of the Crawl, miniature motion of vehicles and walkers the only sign it's really there at all. The sound of water peeling off the shoreline is all we can hear.

'I prefer this to the top of a mountain,' she says. 'You mentioned that, didn't you? We could have met there too.'

'Oh yeah, don't get me wrong,' I say. 'I love hills, like. It's my thing, you know, apart from the surf. I walk up them when I can – or even run. Always will.'

'Suppose. But haven't you ever wanted somewhere else again?'

All the time, I think. *You're not using any special powers to tell that though, eh?* I stop short of telling her about my terracotta roof and warm water pointbreak, and how I'm gonna ditch this life for it when the time is right.

'How come the dog's yours then?' she asks.

'Ah – two mates of mine picked him up as a stray four years ago in North Africa.'

'Picked him up?'

'Yeah, well – they were spending the winter there, living in a van, like. People from here do that a lot. Get away from the dark and the cold. Anyway, the dog kept jumping in and hanging around with them all the time, and had some cruel owner who kept coming looking for him to wash him with detergent. My mates would hide Scarface away, and then when it was time to come back home to Wales they just went sod it and brought him too.'

'Right,' she says, slow and sceptical. 'So why isn't he with them now?'

'Yeah, they, er, went back,' I explain. 'For good. So I took him on.'

'His name?'

'Random choice,' I say. 'Ran through a list of film villains and that's the one that came up.'

'And then you didn't keep him at your place?'

'Sort of. He was like best mates with Josie from the off, and then I was always busy and then my mother used to walk him with some boyfriend and now he just lives, well, with those two really.'

'The friends who moved…' she says. 'Surfers?'

'Of course.'

She looks at the horizon, a flat line of grey-on-blue lit bright by high-angle sun. Then her eyes drift east to where you can see the shadows of land across the water.

'So can you surf over the channel?' she asks, nodding out to sea. It's such a clear day you can just make out the hundred-yard cliffs of North Devon.

'Yeah… Lynmouth,' I tell her, pointing over at the tiny clusters of village nestled in those cliffs. 'There's several spots all along that stretch. Huge winter storms only. Takes so much swell to round those headlands. Most people go there in summer, though… when it's flat, and all you want is an ice-cream or a stick of rock.'

She laughs. 'My father was from over there.'

I pick up on the *was*.

'Never met him,' she says.

'Really?' She can sense my curiosity.

'Dead before I was born.'

'Oh… That's shit,' I tell her.

She doesn't comment back directly on whether it is or not, but adds, 'D'you know how long life expectancy is, now?'

'Er, eighty?'

'Depends what you do,' she says.

'I suppose. What did he do?'

'Deep sea fisherman.'

'Shorter than eighty then?'

'Doesn't really matter. I do think about it though. Of all the moments in your life to die, the odds on it being the few months when you're expecting your first child?'

I think about how many days a year we can see this far across. Haze is in the way of that landscape most of the time. Alys's eyes are still fixed on those outlines.

'My grandmother's eighty-six now,' she says. 'Never forgave him.'

'For what?'

'Dying.'

'How can she hold that against him?'

'For what it did to my mother... His death... Made her into a useless woman.'

'Tough times, though, probably,' I suggest.

'Yeah,' she agrees, taking her gaze off the horizon and looking down at the sand around our feet and the distraction it provides. The ground is wet from the lapping tide, and we're both sunk in to the ankles as she dwells on this murky past a little longer. 'But it'll always end tough, for all of us,' she says. 'Whatever you do, your last moments won't be comfortable. There's no sweet resolution really.'

I smile at her conclusion, and almost nod.

'My grandmother used to read me stories coz my mum couldn't,' she says. 'I always wanted to say, even when I was about four, that the endings had one line missing.'

'How d'you mean?'

'Well. You know: the bit that goes *They lived happily ever after*. It leaves out, "*until one of them died*".'

'Yep. About right.' I'm doing a shoddy job of being sensitive, but then that's not really what she wants, I reckon, because now she shifts it to me.

'What about your dad? There's something similar with you isn't there?'

'You reckon? Shit, that's a pretty big leap to make isn't it?'

'Sorry. It's just…'

'That you think you can tell?'

She doesn't say anything.

'Nah, it's OK,' I say. 'At least I could still meet mine if I wanted.'

She almost smiles. I'm about to apologise, although I'm not sure what for, when she adds, 'Your surname. Is it his?'

'Nope,' I say.

'It's not your mother's or your sister's though.'

'No. You'll laugh.'

'Will I?'

'Yeah. Coz it's from the phone book. Random choice. Ran through a list and that's the one that came up.'

She does laugh. At least it means she believes me.

'No connection at all then?'

'Well, not exactly.' I hate telling people this next bit. 'He ran some big company my mother worked for, see. Pharmaceuticals. Medicines and medical equipment. I think she's had a lifetime of promotions for not holding him to account over my existence.'

'OK, but why the surname change?'

'Well, she pinned his name on me for some stupid reason, anyway. Just like she did for Josie – that girl's got her old man's, too, despite the fact she's met him like five times at the most. Dunno why my mother does it really, the surnames. As if maybe that's gonna make these guys feel they owe her something and return one day to complete a happy family. Don't matter – my sister can do what she wants – right now she probably doesn't care too much. But once *I* was old enough to have a choice I sorted that shit right out.'

'By becoming a "Lloyd"? But isn't that...'

'Yeah, a chain of pharmacies. I know. Great isn't it? Some escape.'

'Why not just roll the dice again?' she asks.

'Against the rules of random,' I say. 'You know the guys who brought the dog here? Well, they helped me. Like umpires I suppose. We all agreed. You aren't meant to choose your surname, so if I was going to pick a new one then it made sense that I had to have no choice what that would be either. Same went for him.' I point at Scarface, who's also taken to peering out to sea.

'So you've never met your father?' she asks.

'What? No. And I'm pretty sure that's worked out fine for both of us.'

'But you could.'

'But I could,' I say. 'If I really wanted.'

'I don't get that – why you wouldn't want to. It's the reason I do it,' she says.

'Do what?'

'You know...'

'What – your...'

'Yeah.'

'Work?' This has never been mentioned before. Not using that word, 'work', at least. But now here it is, because I've raised it. Alys being asked to talk profession. Seconds after Alys talking life and family. It's clearer now. I was right to think you don't actually embark on a trodden career path of being whatever it is she calls herself – *Misc advice*, I remember Starsky saying.

'Yeah, my... work,' she mumbles, as if thinking about something else. 'I wanted to know about my dad. They hardly told me anything, my mum and gran – except the really big bit, coz I'd find out sooner or later anyway. He was killed by someone, Noah.'

'What, like an accident?'

She sneers at the word. 'No. It was about as deliberate as you get. Murdered – that's the industry term, for it, isn't it? And whoever did it put an end to me finding out more than the most basic stuff about him. It's like my mum and grandmother were ashamed, raising me after that had happened. So all I ever had to work on as a kid was a photo of him. It's the enquiry I can't complete. There's no source for anything when it comes to that. It eats me. The one question that sent me on my way in this field would have to be the one I can't answer.'

You pay what it's worth. More logic in that now than there's ever been.

There's so many places I want to take it from here. What does she want to know about her dad? Why? All well and good to want to do her line of work, but how did she find out she *could* in the first instance? Trouble is, if I push for any of that, she'll just ask me the similar things in return – and then she's gonna see connections. Or she's gonna think she's seeing them – ones that aren't there, too. And all this heavy air is already enough for now.

Then comes another sudden change of tack to something more like what we're meant to be on about. But there's no easy route now. She was right about happy endings. Whatever she raises, Noah seems destined to feel anything but comfortable.

'This client of yours,' she says, stopping and twisting the balls of both feet in the sand to face me, 'I can't warn you enough. She's why I'm here. Let's not forget. There's gonna be more to this, Noah. And you might well not like it.' The tone brisk, is as if I'm meant to understand. 'I'm getting something about this Noah. For all we know this might tie *everything* together.'

There's a lone longboarder fooling about on a tiny, wind-blown peak that will probably be head-high when the tide rushes in. He's doing well though, cruising a true line across the shallow sand-bar so that he makes a good distance on every wave he gets. He seems to know the pockets of power, where to turn, when to weight himself in order to hit the speed line. I distract myself by watching him – his rides are my rides.

'I want to do that,' Alys adds, after another moment I can't measure.

'*You* might not like it,' I say.

Halfway back up the beach, Alys finishes the train of thought.

'But then I might,' she says, again looking back at the longboarder. 'I want to try at least.'

Starsky rips the piss – but then again so would I if the tables were reversed. I take a second to imagine how it looks. Noah's gonna take the girl from the Lovells job *surfing*. Yeah, even Starsky, someone who hasn't ever set foot in the sea – 'I think what you lot do is wrong,' he always says, 'that place is for fish and sharks only' – knows this is normally a dead no-no. And it is – well, as far as dates go. But this isn't what's going on here – and who cares about that anyway? It's not Noah's way to do what the crowd orders, and I'm getting the feeling it might not be hers either.

Another mate of mine, who also doesn't give a toss for the code, has got a girly wetsuit in his flat that he uses precisely *for* dating. It's like the third or fourth outing in his get-to-know-you routine, and he's all over it when I tell him I want to borrow it to push a girl into a few waves.

'Get her hooked, and you're laughing,' he tells me.

I don't want to be laughing though, do I? I want to be getting somewhere towards the bottom of something, even though I don't really have much of a feel for what that something might even be.

Starsky, again a fount of wisdom, puts it in finer terms – once he's done giving me the obligatory five minutes of shit:

'Remember matey, that she's there for the same reasons. You're *using* each other here. Feel free to think that at any point. Here ya go, as your boss I'll give you official instructions. I'm askin ya to get info off this bird. She's got a read on what was going on with our client. She's apparently more forthcoming when she deals with you, and we need to know what she's got on the Lovells for the security and prospects of the company. Happy with that?'

'As I'll ever be.'

I'm round my mum's for a Chinese with little sis straight after leaving the office, and the whole thing drifts into the background. The food's my shout because Mum isn't back from some conference yet. Josie's let herself in and placed an order for both our favourites before I've even turned up with the cash.

Scarface on the end of the couch, we watch the silliest film ever – the one with the talking penguins who ride waves. We've both seen it a million times too. I put her on to it hoping it might give her the bug, but it's too cold round here for kids to like surfing outside of summer until they're a bit older.

After the film finishes I'm in the garden waiting for the dog to piss when our mum gets back and thanks me for whatever I'm meant to have done to help out tonight. Josie heads up to bed and I walk straight back, slowing through the dark, anonymous patches between orange pools of streetlamp, before finally melting into the darkness of the side street behind my place.

'Got to head back early,' I told Mum on the way out. 'Big day at work tomorrow.'

'Are you chasing anyone?' – Josie, eavesdropping.

No, is the answer I'm glad I never gave. *They're chasing me.*

Shit. It's happened. I never get this. Super nasty night's sleep. Second time in a year – last one was just after me and Starsky first ever went into the Vale to meet the cause of it all. People in my line of work are meant to get it all the time – that's why they booze, fight or whatever else. It's the restlessness.

Bollocks to that.

There's truth under something Alys spouts at me. That's what's holding me up. I *want* there to be. Thinking about it makes me roll to face the wall, wedging pillow below neck in ever more awkward ways.

In the half-light of my flat, I give up, get a bowl of cereal and sit on the sofa and drift. Mixtures of sleep and other nonsense wash over, all in the image of Alys's face. Like the first time I saw her – the edges and definition of her cheekbones, the straight, strong lines of her neck, the expressive, slightly creased forehead – it's all draining away behind the dominating lights and darks of those open, round eyes that seem to be seeing more than they want.

Then I'm there: REM. The fifth stage of sleep. From nowhere.

I don't know it yet, so the horrors that set on me are too real. If I've had a gnarlier dream than this then it couldn't have been later than about three or four years old, when it's still just about OK to piss the bed and scream for your parents. It's one of those swirling fuckin nightmares that you take a few minutes reminding yourself didn't happen when you lurch awake again. In it I'm me, and walking some street just before a sunrise which isn't coming coz nothing moves but me. The pink-toned pavements sink into mossy cracks and there's stagnant rainpools everywhere. Then I'm fighting – for my fuckin life. Some bloke whose face I don't see is raining blows to my temples that make them ping like a telly on mute. My ears are getting heavy and bleeding, and then I'm giving it all back, slamming this guy's head and neck and foaming at the corners of my own bleeding mouth. I'm baring teeth, and I keep pounding so that there's gonna be nothing left to come after me again.

But, under a luminous cloud with a bird on top, it does come after me, and next I'm being dragged out the doors of a building and down some steps to the pavement by someone else in a shirt. I'm yelling at him to let me stay inside. In the road, the arsehole I battered is waiting to start working on me all over again. Still no face, but he's got an iron bar, and hard shoes, and my legs are giving in so there's nothing I can do and still sunrise is hovering somewhere below that gory horizon.

Stir, Noah. Shake. Just go on as before.

I'm up. Dispassionately pushing tasteless cereal into my mouth again as a kettle boils too noisily for me to yet be completely back in the land of the living. The sleep's got its hoodoo on me yet. It's the kind of thing that'll stay with you for the day – maybe even screw with me when I'm trying to nod off the next night too. Anger... fuck man, it's been a long time. I hate that shit.

It's howling a gale outside, so I sit and watch rain make my front window look like I'm inside a carwash. Then I realise it's only been light half an hour so I set up bed on my sofa again, close my eyes and wait for round two – which never comes coz I'm out cold a minute later and into a dreamless, uninterrupted coma.

It's Alys who wakes me, banging on the door and ready to go. Weather is no deterrent. We're out there.

And she's into it.

This is really up my street now. Out the boot of my car, she flings off the smart-casual type clothes she's been wearing down here, like a seasoned pro, wrapping herself up and catching the towel under her arms perfect. I watch the black neoprene tighten neatly onto her thighs and hips, before she wriggles the top half on over her bikini and turns round for me to do up the back-zip. The wind even slacks off for her – and the skies clear, too. She is meant to do this.

We're inside the lee of the harbour where the waves are cleaner and lined up. For about ten tries she can just about cling, laying prone, to this huge starter board. But then I tell her to have a go at paddling after one on her own and she catches a bomb first time. She hobbles to her feet and then goes over straight away, but it's only a few more before she's picking them off herself and actually riding them.

Lesson one – if you can call it that – out the way, we go again the next day.

And again.

Until soon enough she's angling across the cleaner lines that roll through. In between sets, during the ocean's lulls, we sit behind the breaking water and talk about anything that doesn't mean too much.

And, like some sort of psychological antibody, my alter-ego starts trying to think of ways to fuck this up. Soon enough, it finds one, of course. I'm thinking of Starsky, and the washed-away idea this whole thing is meant to be some kind of work-related networking attempt, as I push on towards messing this little arrangement up good and proper. Well, it's what's meant to happen next anyway, isn't it?

We're back at my apartment, tea-time after a decent session on the dropping tide. The wind's blown in and it's gonna be a few days before the sea is worth checking again. So Noah, the moron that he is, leans over as if to kiss. Disaster. Of course, I've read it all completely wrong, and all I get in response is a smile and an awkward moment. I don't know whether to say sorry, to blame something else – it's the ocean that's let me down in a way, right? I've shared it with someone else. Big mistake. *Irreversible* mistake.

And then, to make it even more complicated, Alys is actually pretty cool about it – well, not *completely* cool, coz then it would have been a two-way thing – but cool enough to tell me she's happy this just happened.

Why? Well, it is part of the plan for us to get close, apparently.

Eh?

Yeah, it is. But then there's varying 'ways of getting close'. I won't know the difference, goes the explanation, but she will.

Maybe. Clutching to any hope that I haven't totally fudged the entire thing, I listen as she tells me again, slower, eyes levelled at mine, that I am important to her, in ways I don't get.

Ways I don't get?

But apparently I will. And here it comes again. It's expected – I'm meant to love. And then I'll hate.

Then I'll run off…

I don't know why I listen, but I do. I can't find solid ground, she says, without perspective – although where I'm meant to get that from is anyone's guess.

Then she heads off, with plans to return once the ocean's finished throwing the mini-tantrum the Met Office has predicted over the next forty-eight hours. A great, anti-cyclonic Atlantic hissy fit that is immediately matched by one in my head. Because it's the last night of the wailing winds when, for a second time, I'm stuck in this vile dream of darkness and blood where this figure just beyond my sight is working me over with mashed knuckles and a toothy grin that is the only object

I see with definition. Like before, blows rain on me and as I push to get to my feet I hear noises further in the background. They're noises I won't reach because when I jolt awake it's past dawn and my place is beyond silent.

I make straight for the window, wanting to open it and exchange the stillness in the room with anything outdoors, and that's when I see that the cloud is back – *outside* of the dream.

You can tell the sun has risen coz of how light it is, but fog on the eastern horizon has kept it from showing. Lower in the sky than makes sense, over the trees to the north of my landing window, is that front-lit puff of hovering white, with two dark birds nestled perfectly in its flank. They sit there, twitching and preening, and all I can do is watch, checking what I can see for what it might mean.

Then the phone rings downstairs and by the time I'm done taking details from Starsky of an injunction that needs serving in a rush there's no longer anything to be seen outside, and the yellowing sun has made its way out above the haze.

With a morning's work to do it's a relief not to have the option of trying to sleep again. *There's your perspective*, I say aloud, as I fish for a towel and turn on the shower.

First afternoon after the storm, to test if she really does mean to be this mellow about it all, I still pack boards and take Alys to a beach out of town – mile and a half walk through dunes and tall, sharp marram grass. Everything I say needs to stay trivial unless *she* changes the rules. I want to tell her about my dream, or even about what I've been seeing out the window, but I know I mustn't. If it matters, she'll ask anyway.

We hit the water straight away and with the sun right overhead it's see-through and clean. She's up and cruising, her back to a wave, right foot forward, accelerating towards the foamy inside section on her best ride yet.

It's exactly what we need – all about finding nothingness, an act, a ritual, we're absolved. Lifted entirely from the path we were on. Through the pushing tide, as the swell builds, we drift, and ride. Cool sea droplets running out of my hair drag away the need to be anything to anyone. And this, there's no doubt, is for both of us. This *is* shared. Right here she's being someone she shouldn't. She knows it too, and still she entertains it, over and over again. That deadly-serious fire in the eyes is almost out. You know there's not gonna be some cryptic statement about things I don't want to know about.

Change is all over her, and on the way back she suggests a detour up into the valleys. Big detour, we drive an hour out of the Crawl, ascend to where the sky starts lifting the land far beyond the sea's pull, and I know that of course she's got a motive here – she always has done – but I can't do this any other way.

We park up and walk higher. There's a mist stagnating across the mountain's midriff, but from above it we can peer back on the fog blanket, small holes in the vapour below letting us see strings of road, thickets of forest or woodland. We've gone from below sea-level, now, to as high as Noah gets. She's seeing the full range – and I'm signed up for whatever it'll all go on to mean.

Ages since last I heard any of it, on our descent, I'm the one who starts silently running off the various incantations of Alys predictions that crept up on me in those early meetings. *I'll be the one who hears. I will not like it. But then I kind of might. I'll love. I'll find solid ground.* I let them roll around, pushing at the fabric in the deeper bits of my mind that seem easier to find away from sea level. And then I realise that's why she's got us here.

'We had to get away from the ocean then,' she says.

'I know.'

'You're coming to terms with it, aren't you?'

'Yes,' I tell her.

'You know you've got a big part to play.'

'Fine,' I say. 'I'm fine with it. Bring it on.'

If you told me now that I'd see weakness in this girl one day soon, I wouldn't believe you for a second. But like everything else about Alys, when that moment comes, it all falls into place again – and I know once more that we're all just doing what we always would. It's just that she can see across the whole storyboard. Most of the time, at least.

The missing bits are what I'm for. Whether I like it or not.

We drive, through patches of summer flies in the evening air. I flick headlights on as we enter the main roads again and skip back down the motorway to the Crawl. When we get there it's night, but sun magnified through my windows in the afternoon has stored warmth indoors.

I chuck keys in a draw and my coat over the bannister, and have to try again. This time I don't lean in, but leave the decision to Alys. We both know what's going to happen anyway.

As we embrace the lights still haven't come on – no need to confuse senses any more than they are already. My hands rise from her hips and drag her jumper and t-shirt up over her head. She does the same to me, and we press close. I'm walking backwards, but she leads. We're over my living room couch as buttons pop open, and socks drop off. Sometimes it's too much to be face to face through this, so we look beyond. Her breath on my shoulder reminds me it's happening.

No repetition – every movement matters – nor crescendo. Just a rite of trust taken on together. Nor is there a spoken word when we're finished, but some time later – could be minutes, could be hours – we head upstairs in almost pitch black. Ascending, I make out her silhouette on the stairs below me, now with her t-shirt back on but stuck perfectly to the outline of her breasts, and then we're asleep, apart but under the same cover – touching only at the feet.

Then I realise again how close all that violence from the other night is, eyelids closing then gulping for air as whatever's chasing me lurks just beyond the moment I switch off. But when I do go under, there's no time to get disturbed before I'm up again. I go to writhe against the visions of my own soul, but can't move, and when my eyes open and the world comes back, it's because I'm tied to the bed.

Curtains are open and a streetlamp outside cuts through the space in my room. This is real. Alys is sitting up watching me, and she's bound me to the bed. Both my hands are together – I think it's with tights or a long sock – which has been lashed around one of the wooden legs. I can't turn fully round to face her, but can't roll away either because she's used a sheet to press my feet flat to the bottom end.

She's still got the t-shirt on, and its hemline is just below her belly-button, but I can't see the details of her waist because she's sitting sideways, hips slanted, leaning on one arm with her lap hidden by shadow. Her look is neutral, and safe.

I don't fight it. Why should I? And I don't speak either. But she does.

'Keep still,' she whispers. 'We can't let them down.'

Then she laughs, too quietly for me to be sure it's what I heard.

'We're OK here,' she adds, almost inaudible. 'As long as we stay just as we are.' It's clear the words are meant for no one but us. Then she adds, 'It isn't you. That's perfect. You're outside of the main thread now. This is exactly right.'

And it sounds like sense, just because of how it comes out, so

I do what she says, and when sleep comes back it's clean, and full.

At dawn, or rather a few hours after it, I don't even want to ask her what was true and what wasn't, but I try.

When we drive up to the beach to see if the swell might have lasted one more day of building high-pressure, she talks again.

'Would there have been waves over the channel in the storm just passed?' she asks first of all, but it's obvious where that's going to lead.

'You mean did the surf spot at your dad's village break? Lynmouth?'

'Yes. That's it.'

I think about it – weigh up the size in the Crawl and the power of the winds now receded.

'Probably,' I say. 'It's rare this time of year though. You're interested in going there?'

'Of course. I don't think I've seen all its moods yet.'

I laugh. Coastal towns this far up the Atlantic are like that. They take years of live-in knowledge before you feel you know them. I tell her this and she seems intrigued – but lets me change tack, like I knew she would.

'It's working,' she says. 'Riding waves taps you in, doesn't it?'

'To what?'

'To that *everything* I mentioned.'

'Is it alright that we're getting close, then?' I ask. 'You know, for whatever is to come. Are we OK like this?' I try to use some of her words from that mad moment in the middle of the night, when she sat up and stared at me, tied down, like she was waiting for a ritual to start: 'Are we "OK here"?'

'Yeah, it'll help,' she says.

'You know in the middle of the night, was I...'

'What do you think?'

121

'What was that about?'

'Making sure your role is clear.'

'Eh?'

'Just putting you the right side of the story. Making sure you don't get caught playing the wrong part.'

She looks at me. I remember how this same look was almost impossible to bear during the first days of knowing her, how it would core me and make everything shut down. At least that's something of the past.

'Don't ever watch me like I did to you though, right?'

'Why not?'

'Just promise you won't. We've got to keep you outside of the main plot.'

'That's what you said in the night,' I say. 'What d'you mean?'

'It's not really that essential to you, is it?' she says. 'The trust is there anyway.'

'Well, maybe, but some of these things you say…'

'Don't worry about it, Noah. You'll know when you need to. For now you're doing fine.'

'So it was all OK, then?' I ask. 'You know… Us, you know…'

'Not too often, right?'

Because of what's ahead.

She doesn't need to say it. I can tell.

We've made it, done whatever had to be done, just in time for the moment when it all comes back into motion.

And I don't mean the sea. No. I'm talking about the Lovells. It was always there, really, wasn't it? The questions, the noises. The dead. And the Void in the Vale.

Well, the ignorance was fun while it lasted.

It first happens after one of those inexplicable days on the prowl when everything you do is just wrong from the off.

Noah's still Noah, don't forget. Even with Alys on the scene, and the beach days and heavy talk that have come with her, I'm not forgetting to go out working people over. No way, not me. Got to keep accruing, haven't I? My future no-winter plans won't just pay for themselves.

Back in the darker months those early nights played to my advantage. But now most of the estates where I hunt, the fields of play for me and Starsky, are places where sunshine brings everyone out to the doorsteps. Once the real summer heat-waves start to come, the collective resolve of the poor, destitute and lazy to stand up to you is strong enough that it takes a moment of guts to walk up to those flaking front doors and demand payment. In just one day lurking on the streets outside a Newport council house – trying to tail some bellend who's on the sick for no reason – I get asked by three different passers-by if I'm a copper, a paedo and if I'm 'Dave who sells cheap phones'.

In the afternoons when there's no waves back in the Crawl to wash the guilt of what we do out of my hair, I cruise between instructions wanting something to happen. And a bankruptcy petition on my way out of the same estate isn't enough. Order of only a few grand, and this bloke comes to the bottom window of a ground floor flat screaming and yelling 'Clear off!' and how I've got my wires crossed. Ten minutes of banging on the glass, during which I disturb every neighbour in the block, and he blazes out the buzz-locked door, unwittingly completing another day's work. Face to face, I can hand him the papers now. *You're served, mate.* Too easy.

It's not fair, I know. Probably a useful sole-trader a year ago, fitting roofs, taking care of his own, hurting no one and cutting out the middleman – before everyone on earth seemingly went bust.

Yes, Noah's still Noah. Out I go, plying the trade that's been given to me. Someone else will do it otherwise, anyway. I know one day there will have to be an end – to this version of me, at least – but for now this is my means.

Hot as fuck, no wind, days getting longer. Spring swells are fading, and that summer-oppressed ocean is starting to go to sleep on us. There's a two-foot wave forecast for tomorrow – and I can probably push Alys and Josie into a few while sneaking out to weave a couple myself. But in the meantime it's car windows down and waiting, sweaty in the traffic of a city bypass. Hot Tarmac and drying, yellowing grass holds the sun's energy. Restrained by a box junction and red light, I can see sizzling air trembling and rising off the ramp up to the motorway, masking the passage back to the south west coast.

A police car is flashing at us all to part and let him through, and I end up getting squeezed out of the queue and stuck between the box junction and the three-lane roundabout without the traffic lights' permission. Safest place to go is to filter myself back into the lane the blazing siren is taking, and then without thinking I ignore my exit, miss the motorway and realise I'm following the car to its scene.

Side road to a trading estate and a group of chain hotels; Travelodge, Comfort Suites, all those sorts. The panda car is going up to the one privately-run B&B in the lot, the 'Manila' with a mossy car park under the shady lee of weeping willows and taller pine trees. I'm yards behind the flashing lights – gonna take this all the way.

There's no need to think of what to say when we all draw to a halt, because I'm so fuckin close and behaving so gormlessly that there's a bollocking coming my way for sure – but at least that's breaking the humdrum of it all. I need it.

One copper runs into the building – the driver, a woman PC about forty – while the one in the passenger seat, a younger guy, also PC, who looks a total knob from the moment he squares up, makes towards me, angry and ready for mistakes.

'What the fuck d'you think you're doing, Blue?' he yells at me as I lean out the window and lift my shades up to look at him. 'Can't you tell we're on our way to a fuckin scene?'

'Sorry buddy,' I say, clicking a pen and flipping open my notebook. 'We're all here to make a living.' I play being something else, someone even lower in their food chain than what I am in real life.

He's purpling up on the cheeks. Gonna be a hard life in the force if he's getting this angry this young. 'Fuckin hell, man,' he trembles. 'You fuckin scum'll do anything won't you. There's no fuckin story here, mate. I'll fuckin plant one on you before you get anything out of me.'

I laugh. 'Give us your number then, officer.' I look to his shoulder, and make as if to write down his ID.

'Fuck off. You'll have a number in a minute, and a fucking night in the cells.'

'Stress less, *2487*,' I say, soft and smiling. 'We've probably got a lot in common.'

This sends him over the edge, and he raises a fist, maybe to see if I'll flinch. 'If you follow me in, I'll fuckin nick you,' he screams. 'Now *fuck off!*' A trace of spittle catches my cheek, as he makes for the reception door into which the woman copper went.

I'm buzzing. That's all I needed to change the day's direction. Pleased with myself and resolving to do this kind of thing more often, I search radio stations as my car rolls back towards the big roundabout. Then up I go, through the heat-shimmer towards the motorway. Something loud with plenty of drums comes on. I wind the windows up and look for the air-con.

But when I get home Alys is outside my apartment in her car.

She meets me at the door and I can see something's wrong. I can't find the key quickly enough, and she's already got a tear going down her right cheek as we follow the draught into the cool, dim indoors.

'What's up,' I say, instinctively holding her.

'Noah.' Her voice is weak, sounding like there's been anger very recently. 'I'm fucking scared.'

It takes a bit to get it out of her, and I should know she wouldn't be rattled like this over nothing. She's been tailed herself, the same afternoon, in Swansea town centre – got so sure of it she confronted the guy – and her call was spot on. He had all the gear you could want in his passenger seat. A short telephoto lens, miniature camcorder, clipboard with logs scribbled in pencil and Post-it notes so he could forge any bits that didn't read right. Thin guy with whitening hair and designer glasses, who didn't say a word back to her but pulled away fast, nearly taking her foot off. A red VW Golf. Drove away at speed too.

I'm fuckin speechless in Alys's presence again, only this time there's nothing natural about it. Once more I've got no feel at all for what to do.

'What made you notice him?' I ask, after five minutes in which the pair of us stare somewhere between my back window and the ceiling.

'I could *feel* him,' she says, 'for ages.'

'How long? What d'you mean ages?'

She starts sobbing again. 'Oh, Noah. I'm getting careless, Noah. I knew it, but then I didn't.'

'What d'you mean? How long?'

'Ages.'

'Ages?'

'Weeks!' she chokes, then drops her head away from me into the edge of the sofa. 'I don't know how it happened. It's been weeks.'

'What's been weeks?'

She looks at me, not sure if I really am this slow catching on. '*They've* been weeks,' she says. 'They've been *watching* for weeks.'

We're in all evening, and then when it hints at getting dark she says she's staying. Don't blame her – she's properly rattled by something. But it means I'm stuck awake all night, partly since this woman is on the end of my bed and I'm into her – but mainly because I want morning to come so I can head straight down to the Whiteout offices, get Starsky on the case and find out who the fuck has been tailing Alys.

When something which I wouldn't exactly call sleep does take me down for a few moments, it's to a waiting train of thought that says I've somehow caused this. Funny how the most irrational things seem to be crystal clear truths in the restless hours of the night, when the dance is happening to a different rhythm.

Then the sun gets back around, and the shadows shrink. Dawn brings less space to hide.

I leave Alys asleep and, as the streets first warm to the new day, get through the office doors before anyone else is in the building.

When Starsky arrives he's as thrown by it as me. Bad form, people in our business turning lenses on each other, he reckons. He's on about an action plan, last bit of which is ringing around to see which agencies have a red Golf in their fleet. Subtle.

'Sold one myself once, Noah. Ideal car for mixing in with the boy-racers. Although you say this one had an older fella in it, eh?'

'That's what she says.'

'Yeah. Odd one. Sounds like he knew his game – although he couldn't be that good coz he got caught.'

'Doesn't mean shit and you know it,' I tell him. 'What about your mate Bob? He's a total kook and you reckon he still did a decade in surveillance squads?'

'You'd be surprised about him,' Starsky says. 'He's lost his edge now, but that geezer could do anything before he *cared*. That's always the way it goes Noah. It's other people who will do for you. The ones you're attached to. Just look at you now. You're gonna run all over the place on the trail of some fuckin PI who could be absolutely anyone, and it's all coz you're caring about a bird.'

'No it's not. The prick might have been looking at *us* too.'

'Not me matey. Last time someone tailed me was four years ago. And I broke his hand. Told ya before, I know what's in all my mirrors, all the time. Don't buy milk without knowing who came in and out of the roads behind.'

'And?'

'Take it from me. Piss enough people off and you'll have to live like that as well. That's when it's easier not to have anyone needing you.'

'Who says I have?'

'I've warned ya, mate, and I'll do it again. Remember why you were dealing with that girl. And watch who you're tight with. If you ain't comfortable for them to be in shit with you, then don't let em in.'

'Yeah, but Alys works in dodgier stuff than me!'

'Tell yourself that if you want matey. At least she probably knows where her casework is leading.'

'But that's exactly it! She doesn't.'

'Well I'd be fuckin worried then,' he tells me, clear and frank.

'Thanks,' I tell him. 'Nice to know. So what now?'

'Well, you *do* need to find out about it, Noah.' And here

comes the bit where he fills me in on how to play this out, nicely and normally. Only this time he's not offering the usual guarantees:

'You could be getting yourself further in the shit like this Noah, but you're right. There isn't much else you can do. Usually my advice is leave sleeping dogs lie. But what's happened is what's happened. So you had better take a bit of responsibility. Need to look out for the both of you here, now. Double trouble. Don't say I didn't fuckin warn you.'

Ideal. Starsky's gonna start briefing me on his how-to of inter-agency snooping, complete with its non-guarantee of safety.

But there's no need, because by tomorrow we know who's behind the red Golf. Or rather *I* know.

Me, Noah Lloyd, and Alys, both summoned to a meeting, in the Vale, on a seafront closer than I yet know to where she lives.

The person who makes this demand? My next client – and I say *my* because it's clear from the off that Starsky's not coming in on this instruction. I should have seen it on the horizon. We knew all along there would be more of them, didn't we? Michelle Lovell told us herself that she didn't come into this world alone – even if she went out that way.

Her sister's voice is distinctive, it has the same hollow, wide-eyed weariness of the world that I struggle so hard to recall in Mrs Lovell, even though I know it was there. And when we come face to face the resemblance is eerie. I'm seeing, lurid and superimposed, the blood and gore of our last client's wounds, on this healthy woman, still breathing and sentient in the same world as the rest of us. The same woman who ushers both me and Alys into the veranda seats of a café on a warm afternoon, overlooking a slowly drifting expanse of sea.

On the horizon you can see the cliffs of North Devon again, but my eyes are fixed to the next stage; Mrs Lovell's return, in the form of *Miss* Clare, her sister, again age unknown, unguessable.

At first I'm relieved it's her behind this and not, well, you know, *killers* – but pretty soon it's all getting heavier than I'd really like again, and coz everyone else around me is going through the motions I end up hooked into it as well.

Maybe she's heard Alys's gripe about meetings with coffee, because this time we're served sweet white wine, cold and in clean glasses, by a waiter who leaves us well alone at the far promontory of this place that's just out of the Vale and on the outskirts of coastal Cardiff. Our newest prospective client seems well at home here – clearly a regular.

The same sort of intro is offered. I'm re-treading ground here, I know it, but the helplessness is all over me, and for the millionth time this year Noah is hanging on the every word of women who know more than he ever will.

'I'm grateful, she says, for your time, Mr Lloyd,' and I wince as she says it. But Alys stays still, focussed, more echoes of places I've been and can't seem to stay away from.

'That's fine,' I nod.

'I was quick on the telephone, I know,' she adds.

'Also fine.'

'But these are things that should always be done on a face-to-face basis, I'm sure you'll both appreciate. I hope it wasn't far to come.'

'No – it's no problem. This is a nice spot around here, Miss Clare,' I say, getting used to the name.

'I can assure you this is not a waste of your time.' She looks over a pair of darkened glasses at us both. 'I can buy your assistance, starting from *now* if you like.'

Well, you paid to have this girl snooped on, I remind myself, so it's gotta be worth our while eventually.

But what I actually say is, 'Let's see what you need to discuss, first.' Then I look at Alys for approval, which *is* a waste of time. The finances of it seem to be something Alys has never considered for a second – which reminds me once more that we probably won't share similar goals in the end. Can I imagine Alys whiling away the pointlessness in a dusty surf town until kingdom come? Can I bollocks. Anyway, no time for that now. Get the crap out of the way, Noah. Concentrate.

→

Good to see, meeting this sister, that there was one person on Mrs Lovell's case who wasn't after her money and land. I mean, even me and Starsky were in a way – and I sort of am now, too. Not that Alys looks close to mentioning anything of the sort.

You pay what it's worth. Ah, how fondly I recall Starsky's sage advice. Going to a meeting of this kind without him is probably really fuckin stupid in the long run – but I shut that notion down before it has any chance to get moving. Listen, nod in the right places, and this could be worth yet another chunk of my perfect wave fund.

Then, just as I'm in danger of thinking us masters of the whole situation, there is this hint of bitterness in the sister's voice that puts me right back on the alert. It's when she talks about Mrs Lovell living in the family house – and the time she cut down a tree, how they *knew* she shouldn't have had care of the place. Maybe I have got it wrong? Are even her blood relatives thinking of land before love? Maybe this dead madwoman really did have no one.

'I was happy moving to the Marina here,' Miss Clare tells us, dismissing the idea just as quick. 'It got me out the way. We were worried for her, though, because there was always something about that house that attracted greed and trouble.'

So she's thinking *Mr* is our slasher incognito then?

'Look, Noah.' She's using first-names now, at my request – although she hasn't given me the go ahead to return the informality. 'We've both had to talk to the police over this too much already. It wasn't a secret in our family, or what's left of it, that Michelle was having issues, and we'd all considered them to be...' – pause to pick exactly the right phrase next – '...*her* issues.'

I start writing things down – right as it occurs to me this is probably the middle-aged woman I was meant to spot in that swallow viewing for those two coppers. My notebook is like a comfort blanket as I try to figure things out. Why they were interested in her, why she's interested in us. The nearly forgotten shorthand scratches itself on the page before me as she talks, slow and careful:

'We'd tried a few times to ask Michelle to see someone about this, this... *invention* she kept sharing with us. Brian did as well. He'd been very patient. A busy man too, always getting closer to bigger and better work...' and she falters, just like her sister used to.

A deep breath, disguised gulp, and then back on track. Family traits are amazing eh?

'I'm passing on a lot of confidence here,' she nods at both of us, wresting back that sense of authority. 'I'd really be happier about it if you were taking instructions from me. It can go through a solicitor if you'd rather things in writing. Fees are no problem.'

So I ask, what would 'instructions' mean doing?

'Firstly,' she says exhaling, readying, 'it would mean sharing your professional opinions, and what you were doing with my sister in the first place. I'm advised there are rules about sharing information, but I'm sure you'll know ways around it. I certainly can find one for you.'

'OK… It depends what information, Miss Clare. You're right about one thing, we don't *sell* findings from another instruction. Data Protection is black and white on that.'

'But I do need to know what my sister told you and what she wanted from Mr White and yourselves.' She looks at Alys too. How does she know Alys also met with her sister, Mrs Lovell, when even the police had no idea about that bit? Oh yeah, that cock in the red Golf might have somehow managed to figure it out. Mind you, that would involve *super* up-close-and-personal tracking of us both. Like she says though, there are always 'ways'…

'Right,' I mumble, hoping she'll just get on with it.

'Whatever my sister has asked you to do is key. I need to be able to move on, so does the rest of my family, and this is something I must know about.'

'Don't you already have an accurate idea, Miss Clare?' says Alys – although it hardly sounds like a question. I wonder how cool I'd look if I could wait my turn in a conversation so clinically, so efficiently.

'Yes. I do.' Those eyes, similarly intense to the dead sister, sear towards Alys's. 'Of course I do. But I can show you both something which I want your opinion on. Your *informed* opinion. An opinion that could build on any conclusions you'd reached about my sister before her death.'

That last word drops between us, commanding its own moment of reverence.

'Find out what was going on at the house,' she says. 'That's what I want. To know if what she told us was true. Was it the same as what she told you? Find out if she was being watched. And who by, if you can, but that's not the most important bit. I just need to know what was on her mind in the end. Find out if she was right.'

'Not by selling you any info we gathered,' I say, ever

conscious that there probably isn't much beyond what Miss Clare has already guessed.

'It's none of my business how you find the answers.'

'I can see what you're saying,' I tell her. 'And I understand what it means to you all. But I can't just ignore the boundaries this probably crosses.'

'Once you return to your superiors and stand by the choice you've already made not to register this meeting in your company's logbook, you'll cross a boundary, Mr Lloyd.' she tells me.

'And what makes you think I plan to do that?'

'You will if my price is right.'

I look at Alys. This is the one part of the gig that won't sway her anywhere – even if it does me. Cash will be my route out one day. Suddenly I can feel myself pulling off the end of a long ride at this mysto right-hand point-break, the self-same one I'm gonna fuck off too once I save up enough of the bankers', lawyers' and – maybe – landed gentry's moola.

'You can have two minutes to think,' Miss Clare says. 'But bear in mind the parameters might change as soon as I share *my* info. I'll settle this table's account.'

Account? Settle? This woman stinks of Legalese.

Once she's out of earshot Alys tells me more of this wonky shit about how I might be the one – the only person – etcetera.

'Yeah, I know,' I say. 'But you know this woman is asking me not to tell Chris Whi...'

'Noah,' she's saying. 'We're so close. You'll find out *imminently*. It's bigger than all of us. I can see where this is going.' She piles it on, all the freaky stuff normally reserved for low-tide or the flank of a hill until I ask her straight:

'Alys, are *you* saying it too then? That we take this job on, away from the Whiteout books, you and I? We don't even know what it's going to involve yet. And that I don't tell anyone else we're doing this? It's not just that woman there asking me to do this. You are too?'

'Yes,' she says, clear and certain. And before I can reply, she's ironing out the details, or lack thereof: 'Don't set a fee, Noah. Don't ask for one. If you take this on you take it for the *meaning*.'

So that's how Alys does business then? Now I'm hearing it direct from her – another part of her 'professional' view. Pay what it's worth.

Miss Clare returns. It's either a yes or no first off, please, no inbetweens. Either way, she has to know now. Sign up and we'll thrash out the small print. No we won't, you can pay what it's worth, Miss. Expenses then? Fine. I'll be in touch, there'll be an allowance. Alys needn't use it. Nor me.

But I will.

Somehow.

Should I be thinking about money before doing whatever I'm about to do? Faustian pacts are readying here, my blood the ink. Nah, bollocks, just take it all. Sort *yourself* out, Noah. That's what you've been taught. Everyone else will, won't they?

There's a letter. It arrived the day after her death. From Mrs Lovell. A farewell note. Only it's nowhere near that simple. We shake hands, let sister go her separate way, then me and Alys drive out to the headland at Lavernock, planes falling into Cardiff Airport behind us and I get ready to take notes. But none get made.

Nowhere to go, we lean in and read Mrs Lovell's perturbed, shaky handwriting. A tortured soul with days, maybe hours to go, borne out on a cream-coloured page.

I will not like it, but then I kind of might.

Clares:

Firstly, this note is for only the most ~~most~~ ~~of~~ of you. My husband **MUST NOT** be made privy to this if you ever see him again.

I am well aware you have all held dubious opinions about my sanity. If you're reading this it's unlikely you will still be concerned with that sort of thing. You're only going to get this note if I fear the worst. Peculiarly, I'm feeling no pain writing. I've thought about this moment, as something dreadful beyond what we are engineered for. Now it's here I haven't got a worry in the world.

Where do I begin to best give you the picture of what has happened to me in the last three years? I'll cover Brian first. He is as powerless as me, probably more. You know I met him in closed circumstances, but you always agreed he seemed to know the world better. Certain parts of us though, I've learnt, are in equal balance in all of us. Brian's ways, like the rest of us, are just as bound up in something carnal. This is the only way we better ourselves isn't it?

The claims I've made against my husband are well known. However, in the last few days that game has taken place across other senses. I've <u>seen</u> something ~~too~~ too now. In person you wouldn't give this a moment's time, but that is of little importance. This is the last of my voice. All I want you to feel is acceptance. I am neither happy nor sad. I am neither angry nor calm. Everything that passes understanding, but that keeps us human, has cancelled out inside me. I have been neutralised. I am pleased it's happened this way. I'm ready, which is why I'm so afraid for Brian and anyone else who isn't.

As long as you know the physical facts, then I can say I've done right by you. So here they are:

Four nights ago the disturbances in our _family home_, reached a height and I felt something more than just sound waves moving through the corridor. ꓯꓶꓵꓹꓲꓯ꓾ꓫꓷꓜꓭꓚꓛꓯꓵ꓾ꓭꓯꓼꓽꓵꓡꓴꓯꓫꓭꓷꓼ I've abandoned bed as a place to sleep for the past two months, because that's where these things seemed at their most (sorry to call it this) **sensual**. Instead I've sat up all night and used thought for company. Then, a week ago I was drawn to walk towards the windows. This spell of frost and clear skies was at its most striking. I had to go outside.

I didn't for almost an hour though, because the warmth indoors was holding me, but when I finally stepped out the beauty of those unexplained hours revealed itself to me. The first time I did this there was a pain accompanying the knowledge and it was exquisite. I stood longer than it's probably possible under a cloudless winter sky ~~the sky the light the~~ for a dangerous length of time.

Can you remember how clear the stars overhead could print themselves on your vision here, when you looked long enough? The great hunter was swinging overhead, facing up to the bull. His pack of dogs was following loyally into the confrontation, as they always did every night over our heads as children. The cluster of seven sisters was flashing to the right. I lost my breath, and woke on the ground having missed even more time. I was warm though and, immediately relieved from all the worries the inside of this house inflicts on me. I had been freed from my angers and fears. I wanted to dance with happiness. This was when I saw a cut on my arm.

I knew then I was being offered a trade. Physical pain for relief from my ~~corrupted twisted tortured sick~~ imagination. It's something you would accept too in this situation.

The following night I knew what to do. I went out again and the same events took me as before. The second wound wasn't of any concern either. On the fifth night though, <u>last night</u>, the noises followed me outside. If I wasn't certain there was an ending around the corner then, I am this morning. What I saw last night has ultimately a ~~[struck out]~~ ~~[struck out]~~

There's a part of us that pleasures in violence, and will seek to harm and destroy the beautiful. When I look into the sky that's all I see now. Violence, destruction and force. The more fragile the more admirable the beauty, the greater the prize and satisfaction taken in its annihilation. I wasn't aware of this, as you aren't yet. At first I couldn't understand the why or how of such laws. I did though, last night, when a figure presented itself to me.

Later than the previous nights, under a sky even

clearer, I picked up the trail. The warmth in our house was transferring with the frozen weight of outside. Every noise I've ever come upon in the house was alive in all rooms. The male voice, grunting its urges at me in the dark would come and go, drowned out by motors, whistles, swaying branches, running water and pounding rain. There was smashing glass and thin metal sheets shaking. I could hear fire, falling rocks and then the cries of animals you'd never have imagined existed. The rises and falls were unified and organised. It all had a beat. The noises were getting in behind me and lifting my steps. I was walking on air to open the doors I had already shut. There was no light in here, except from the stars pouring through the house from each door and window. I felt excited and when I set foot on the ground outside there was a shift under my feet. It was as if the earth had turned to go back on itself.

The noises were there too, and where first they'd been behind me they were now surrounding and moving everything else. I saw fire overhead and a shadow at the edge of our property. It was a figure. There were legs, long and powerful. I felt safe and so I walked towards it. Now my own body weight was back. I had come too close though, when I realised what I was looking at.

Oh, this is hard. I don't want to write it. Maybe it can still be held back as nothing if I don't share it. Maybe I am just a fool with no awareness any more. The figure was barely human. No, it was _inhuman_. The legs and body were in our image, or rather in the image of a man. I couldn't

139

see clothes. The torso though, it was too long. I was so happy and secure in its presence that I took it all as normal until I looked up. This creature was taller than a man by two feet at least, and as I lifted my head to search for its eyes the noise rose with me. It was going to be too loud, unbearably so, to get to the eye line and hold a stare but I caught the shape.

The head was not human. I don't know what it was but I can see the silhouette now if I blink. There was a long jawbone like a horse or zebra, something bovine or equine. The neck and shoulders went straight into it. I couldn't see hair or skin but there were, oh I don't know the right word, but <u>antlers</u> is close, rising from the forehead on both sides.

There. I've done it. It's for you to interpret now. I saw a man's legs and torso, but the head of a, oh I'm simply writing as I think now. There's so little left to say. The head of a ~~horse bull thing~~ There is no doubt in my mind of this shape, half-human at best. It controlled everything though, I knew immediately. The noises were in and out of this figure's <u>soul</u>, and it was moving me where it wanted. I can't say where that might be but it wanted something from me, something which it didn't take. I felt nothing. No fear, no pain or excitement, not even perspective until dawn, which has now moved in and I can't tolerate it.

You're going to read this in days. I'm going to walk now and decide whether this really does need to happen as I think it does. I'll post this to you if I must. This winter sun is so weak today, and there are even a few clouds. I don't care if it's cold. Even now at the softest this sun will get in the sky, day is horrid to me. I'm going to face light one more time, but if night gives me the same feeling this evening then I'll know. I've cleaned out. There's no love in me now, no aggression, no desire, no concern. I am neutral. I am cancelled out.

I may never act on these thoughts, but in hours I'll have decided. If you're in receipt of this then I have done, and here's my explanation as best you may be able to understand.

I'm not even sure if goodbye is appropriate.

You can say it though, if you have to.

M

7

'Misc advice'

On the horizon, lights off the overnight fishing boats are starting to ping on in the late dusk as we each raise our eyes up from the paper before us. There's a blood smudge on the reverse of the sheets, concentrated around where they were folded into an envelope, stamped and posted first class apparently, but which we don't have because Miss Clare has been keeping this letter in a plastic zip folder.

The shifting waters around Lavernock Point bring their chill into the air. Orange haze from the industries of Avonmouth, Portishead and Weston-super-Mare over the water are just coming into sight as I go to speak and then don't.

She's had this note – journal – diary entry – confession – whatever it is, for months, Miss Clare. Months, just sitting on it, waiting until the question of how to take it forward – *if at all* – was somehow answered.

And now it's our problem too.

Straightforward really, then? Mrs Lovell seems to have believed in some freak that had been threatening to carve her up, so she knocked out a letter to her sis, then went in for the whole twisted game. Yeah, that's it, she's signed up for some hideous S&M thingy that's gone too far. Maybe she really was a mental case, into some nasty weird shit, and her husband is just the normal one who knew.

But then all the things that *I* know about this come to mind, each contradicting the next. She wrote a note that seemed to imply her impending fate. She went to meet this... thing. The husband is missing, evidently not obsessed with her money after all because he's done a runner rather than stick around to take care of all the hanging funeral- and estate-related nonsense her death must have left – probably stuff Miss Clare got lumped with in the end. Nice work if you can get it, eh?

What about my own experiences in London tailing that fucker, too? My senses don't deceive me. I know that for sure. Same goes too for the things I've seen and felt around that house, and the deceased woman who was in it. Me and Starsky were there – the place *was* creepy as fuck. I *didn't* just imagine it.

Then there's Alys. That's the bit that really gives me the chills. All this weird premonition-type jargon she's been spouting. The conversation she had with Mrs Lovell in front of us, and now how ice cool she is about what we've just read.

I set off dismissing it, and then she overrides me.

'This is really interesting,' she mumbles. 'Amazing. Now it makes sense...'

'What?'

She's looking back at earlier pages. 'I need to spend a bit of time looking at this, Noah. We should go somewhere else.'

'Hang on, what d'you mean "interesting"?'

'Probably a bit simple to say straight away,' she says, totally detached in face and spirit. 'I've been this close before, and it was nothing. So we don't need to rush around assuming. But... well, you read it too? It's all suggesting we've... been on the right track.' She drifts again, then adds sternly, 'More than we could have ever imagined. Come on, start the engine.'

I try again. 'Hang on now, Alys. Are you suggesting that...' I struggle for how to put it. 'That... that... like, d'you mean you might sort of... you know... think there's *something in it*?'

'Why not?'

'Hold on… You serious? You're looking right at why not.'

She smiles, calmer again. 'Well, it's obviously not that simple…'

'The, you know, supernatural, like,' I cough, then immediately feel like a tit for saying the simplest of all simple terms right as she's telling me it ain't simple. Moron, Noah. What are you playing at?

No, what is *she* playing at?

Her living. Her trade. That's what.

'Er, ok. Whatever you say. Alys, I'm cool with whatever you wanna think, like, but so long as you're cool with me, you know, probably not believing it.'

She's still smiling. 'It's fine, Noah. And I just want to go somewhere else and think.'

'OK.'

'I live near here, come on, I'll show you the way.'

And we're driving – well, I'm driving, she's co-piloting. Alys arrived on foot to meet Miss Clare earlier. I'd been assuming she got off a train or something similar, but then she did tell me she overlooked the ocean up east, *where it's a bit more ordered.*

We're no more than three miles from where she lives, and fifteen minutes later I'm in her own apartment for the first time, fourth floor studio, clean and swanky. The coffee machine is on, and I'm all gooey and ready to believe in funky shit I shouldn't.

And there's plenty of it – I can assure you.

She's got books on it all, there are theories, there are rumours, there are sightings. All things weird and wonderful, Alys knows them all. Now I'm being let in. She's known everything about me and where I'm at regardless of what I've actually told her. And now I'm getting more of it back from her.

She shifts closer, *way* into my personal space, and starts

running me through illustrations and verses about creatures and rituals that she wouldn't seem to mind existing. People eating each other's hearts and surviving, reincarnations and all sorts of wobbly ideas that make me think the cops maybe are wasting their time and money calling on people like this to lead them to bodies or serial killers' lairs.

'It's following the codes of something bigger,' she's saying.

'Bigger?'

But Noah still listens. Quite why, fucked if I know – but then, truth be told, I'm not sure I'm caring either. Her knee is touching mine. There's a page on both our laps with diagrams and lines and incantations and people turning into things and other ideas that go over my head but which she cares about so clearly and so passionately. This is Alys as tangible as she could ever get, I reckon – now could be a time to lean over, to push closer. Really? Come on. In these circumstances us two fucking again is the last thing that's gonna happen.

But why am I sort of getting off on listening to all this crap which I hardly take in? There's so much advice, said and thought before, telling me to be wary now, but it's all worth nothing when the time is on you.

'The patterns, Noah. The codes and symbols. They're fitting right into the story. Keep a close record of this. That's what we need to do. You too. Match it to the right threads. If we listen carefully, we might even be able to tell what happens next.'

Beyond her, on top of a shelf filled with reference books to all these signals and threads and intertwined messages of the occult, there's a picture. Not black and white but it's got those crayon colour contrasts of something taken in the early eighties. A couple, on a beach.

Family portrait, she tells me straight away. 'I'm in it,' she adds, standing quickly and pointing right at her mother's waistline. 'By there. And somewhere in their eyes too. They knew I existed when that was taken. It's the only picture of the three of us.'

I can't look long. Now's not the time. She sits straight down and once more all she can think about are the contents of her books below, and the decade she's spent studying and thinking about stuff that the rest of us wouldn't credit with a place in this world. This is when she animates. She's talking about the sounds described to us the first time we met Mrs Lovell.

'Remember, Noah. How many of the noises can you remember specifically?'

'Well, there's... hang on, why does that matter?'

'It does. She heard sexual sounds in the mornings? First thing in the day? What about running water – was there running water? Did she list the connections she thought existed between the various noises?'

'Yeah, but it was all over the place...'

'Think about it, Noah. Just for now. Remember her voice, then work from there.'

And this is precisely one of the things I can't do. Mrs Lovell's voice. It's never been there. Her face, of course, her mood, the way her presence made you feel. Her house! But not the voice. Sound seems to be beyond the void.

'What d'you mean you can't hear her voice?' The admission has Alys up again and pacing the room. 'Try. You have to try. Don't tell me that, Noah, unless you're really, really sure. Why can't you hear it? D'you think you were ever meant to?'

I dunno. Maybe not. It is like it was never there, I'm telling her. And here come the questions in return. *What else do you think?* and I can't say anything because I don't think anything. I *can't* think anything.

My wrists tied to a bed-leg, and Alys's gaze and tilted shoulders and shaded hips are flashing in and out of my vision. Along with other dark figures at that park in Ealing – and that house, the lanes through the Vale, all the things that don't agree these last few months – even the moving tides out on Lavernock Point just now. Wonder how the clouds behave outside Alys's windows on a breezy afternoon? Maybe I'll know one day.

'And what about you? Did you ever hear running water in the house? Think, Noah. It's so important.'

Leftover heat from the afternoon is dissolving. A VELUX window in the sloping south-facing roof of her flat is open, catching a night breeze. South east; the warmest summer wind, but after dark it's a current of dry, cooler air. The tension in me has nowhere to go.

We are professionals after all. This symbiotic relationship is just about business – apart from the times she doesn't want it to be.

'Things are coming into motion here, Noah,' she says. 'I think I can see where, too.'

'Good. I can't'

'You will.'

'Yeah, you've said that.'

'You won't need too many more directions once we get there,' she says. 'Stay here tonight. Tomorrow I'll tell you how this works – as far as I see it.'

Starsky would be pulling out action plans and next steps and what-will-we-tell-the-client and who's-gonna-carry-out-what-inquiry-and-next. And why. Like he probably is right now for the question of the red Golf driver – which he doesn't know has been answered yet.

There's someone reliable for you, someone who keeps control. Starsky doesn't let others too near, but Starsky will always do right by Starsky. And by me, if I honour his ways.

Alys's bed sits in the middle of this wide, open-plan room. Skylights put it under a spotlight. A single sheet, all we need in

147

the warmth made by the sun through the day. She shifts the window-pane down an inch to let some more of the outside air in, and I can hear cars and the noises of a town outside. As the air cools her skin hardens, heightens the sensation of my touch. I'm going to lie here for hours, as close as I can handle.

'Just sleep,' she says, then presses against me.

OK.

Just sleep. Yes, of course, I always knew it. Silly Noah for doubting, for hoping. We're just conferencing what to do next – but without talking, with hands on each other's hips, moving across each other's thighs.

And what will we do next?

Take the job.

Trail the left over guy, I hear myself suggesting, somewhere in tomorrow morning's future. The one from the Ealing Broadway freakout. That Haydn Whateverhisnameis.

She goes back to the beach. Ride waves, watch the tides. That's keeping her in touch. But for me, no such luck – but then we don't need luck, anyway, do we?

Easy. I'm the go-between. I'll be the one who hears. Her ribcage opens and closes in my hands as we move.

And I'll be the one who lays the idea on Miss Clare too, says the Noah of tomorrow morning, the Noah with a plan. And Miss Clare will let us do it. We'll get the official instruction. The client will sign us up and we'll go to work. Nothing wrong with any of that. It's what we do. Both of us.

As sure as I can be of anything, I get an idea why Alys has got me in her bed like this, but then I lose it. Does something need an explanation to make sense?

I chase pay cheques. That's all people are to me. It has to stay that way.

But once she's asleep I can doubt in private. Is my path really going back to London again? Through the tube-train, after those figures, to that darkness and vibrating, swirl of noise I don't want to be too sure I really heard?

And though I only feel it right now, it's no time before I end up knowing that it is the next move. I am going back. *This* is what makes Alys need Noah again – when it stops being just business.

She sleeps so still I don't want to move anything. It's too light in here, and a long time till tomorrow.

My naivety is my biggest virtue. If only that were true.

SUMMER

8

The alley

The walls and windows and cornered structures of the City are flicking light around this mid-August morning. A cobalt sky has only the blazing sun sitting in its middle, and everything is lifted in brightness. Clean, synthetic concretes and mirrored glass bounce photons around, filling this grid with the unstoppable energy of life fighting life. Even greed and pretence can't stop the world feeling awake. We're all here, whoever we are and why ever, sharing the same blissful, fleeting experiences of sentience.

Leaves filter reflected sunrays as they tremble in a light breeze. But the way everyone else is seeing this beauty ain't anything like the way Noah sees it.

Most places you'd go on a dry day in high summer, someone, somewhere will engage you – notice you're there, like. Even just asking you the way, without knowing you're not local, or a comment on the weather as you wait in a queue. Instead, my only interaction with this canvas is an imagined *how are you* with the immigrant teller who scans and takes payment for my scotch egg in a One Stop near Aldgate.

Not gonna get more than that here. Conversation is a waste. Everyone knows where they're going, and if they don't it would be revealing weakness to let that show. It's on their faces. Purpose. Possession of their own affairs.

Kinsella House, and *Hideous CnC*'s door, is fifty yards away. Subject is in the building. Noah outside and ready.

153

So, packet of shitty junk food in one hand – need good nosh for jobs like this, not least so you can fit the fuckin image – twinky camera in my pocket, pair of shades for imagined anonymity and the info is etched in my memory of who and what I'm on the case of.

And I'm set.

Now to wait.

→

Miss Clare bought into it from the get-go, and I mean *bought*. Don't you just love the way the proper wealthy can't ever take things to the real Law? How they end up trying to deal with stuff in house? Even with murder, the ones who can afford it will always want to find out for themselves, to be the most in-the-picture, to have the experts on *their* payroll. It's always been how Whiteout gets its biggest and best bits of work.

Mind you, that's the one bit I am still stressing over. Starsky hasn't got the blindest idea I'm on the tail of the Lovells, Clares or this 'Hideous' company again. The red Golf driver never showed up, and didn't really seem to worry us again. His conclusion: these things happen. A hazard of the job. The pretty obvious continued involvement of Alys in my life since hasn't tipped him off to it, either. He just thinks Noah's knocking around with some bird met via work – that Alys would be a decent enough catch to any person not employed by Whiteout to keep things impersonal – and that if it does come back to bite me the consequences should be manageable at the time. If only.

Alys can't ever live up to a promise as narrow as that. I've come to terms with it by now. But even though she's behind most of my thoughts and pulling the strings – of that there is no doubt – she's still pretty content to leave me to the turgid musings of my mind without too much fuss. In this case it means allowing me to handle the nasty business of the... well... *business* bit of the Miss Clare job, as I see fit. And handle it is what I did, calling in a wedge of cash off her, while still unleashing the best of Alys on a customer who was keen to lap up the whole story for whatever we say it is.

'I'd like to allocate some time to researching cases that match some of the contents of this letter,' Alys had announced during our next meeting, turning up as the unofficial chair all of a sudden. 'Meanwhile Noah will make some discreet inquiries into Mr Lovell's associates – since finding your sister's husband is likely to help us all.'

Miss Clare thought about that one for a moment, before asking about the first comment.

'D'you mean to say there are incidents, *murders*, that match what happened to my sister?'

'No,' I cut in. We couldn't have left that idea going round her head.

'Not, as such,' Alys backed me up. 'It's your sister's story I'm more thinking about.'

This is something else I've been told umpteen times now, too – how there's something *central* about that whole chain of events that Alys is really, really drawn to. She's pushing and jabbing at it, turning it over and cross-referencing it all over the place – to cases, to stories, to customs and rituals. 'It's still around us, still to play for,' she keeps telling me, despite my attempts not to take it in too much. So yes, Miss Clare, your sister's story is of interest to us.

Anyway, that left our client chewing on something, before we got a clean and lucrative go-ahead to build a trail on the business partner. Alys's idea. My task. Our mutual interest – I think.

And whether it would turn out to be in Miss Clare's interest, well, it would be my job to make that happen.

As well as ensuring Starsky stayed out of it. A far tougher task. Maybe I shouldn't wonder how that fucker came to believe in people like Alys after all. Coz like I said before, his senses border on the psychic most of the time too.

First of all I try to lie. We're off somewhere for the week. Me and Alys.

Where?

There's a swell coming. Lynmouth, north Devon. Over the channel. Got a few bits she wants to do over there with her work, too. I try something at least founded on a sort of truth – she does want to go there, one day.

'Can't fuckin lie to me, Noah.'

He's right. I can't. OK, OK, I'm going somewhere else.

I try to be honest, about being dishonest. I'm going somewhere that I can't tell you, mate.

Merciful bastard doesn't give me the dilemma of a direct 'is it to do with…' question, which may suggest he's so far off the idea it hasn't even occurred to him. But that's about as likely as him giving up the fags for good. So really he's avoiding giving me enough rope. Which is either kind, or, well, I dunno, dangerous really?

'There's stuff I need to resolve,' I tell him. 'Personal. Relationship shit. Family things. You'll know when you need to know. Please understand, please trust.'

Do what you must Noah. Go ahead.

But there's gonna be serious rebuilding of our working arrangement once this is done. Make no mistake about that. I know it from the tone, the disengagement, the detachment. Right out on a limb now. Things are mattering too much. I'm caring about the outcome – engaging my *self* in a job. My strength becoming my weakness. Can't be good.

The trail of this Haydn fucker was easy to pick up at first – even bearing in mind I couldn't have Starsky knowing what was up. Greggs, his surname is. Like the bakery. Haydn *Greggs*. Now I know. First I photocopied the whole Whiteout file on the Lovells late one night in the office, which included the various company director, Land Reg and Experian checks we'd done on him – all through his connections to Mr Lovell, and all using *Kinsella House* or other office premises, including one in Jersey of all places – as contact address. Other online hits turned up a few more mentions, but only in lists of associates or officers of various companies that were all probably tax-dodges or efforts to wash fake VAT around – the stuff good accountants will do for those types and that the rest of us only find out about after the next dodgy holding company is up and running and the assets shifted to someone else.

Then, though, it all went kind of blurry. Only other hits on him were a handful of networking pages – a Linkedin with no profile pic – probably set up by someone else with nothing more than what we already know. So up to London I've come, a four-day mission to just hang around the various addresses we have for him until I spy the fucker.

From there this is a wing and a prayer. Best plan is follow him until he sleeps the night somewhere – preferably his as-yet-unknown home address, and then it's probably back to the computers to see what stuff that new address flings up, before a bit more surveillance and hopefully something that hints at how he's managing to keep all the affairs afloat that were so dependent on his vanished sidekick Mr Lovell.

Easy in theory, but Noah's still the poor fucker who's got to do it all. I wonder if detectives Whitfield and Davies tried this stuff out too, or if they just walked into his office and introduced themselves. Odds are they spoke to him – and when they did it was probably a hell of a lot nicer than when they had me and Starsky in.

Two days roll by, crashing in a shit Travelodge off King's Cross before I spy my target sliding out of Kinsella House, which is when thirty-six hours of boredom dissolve in an instant. He's only coming out for a fag – although I'm sure there are places inside or on the roof he can use, so even that tells me this guy is looking around.

I'm feeling all sketched out straight away, but when he emerges again later and starts heading somewhere my fuckin stomach turns round. Something about him gives me the willies all over again – the way he slides out of this doorway without a cursory glance in any direction, not even to check for traffic as he wades over the road. Purpose in his every jolt. He's got a sort of swagger to him, but it should be dampened by this portly sluggishness that makes me imagine him every night swigging the first glass of an expensive bottle of bubbly, leaving the rest to go warm while being a cock to some long-suffering waiter. He looks greedy – he's got soft features, but eyes that shoot bullets – all the time scanning, weighing, imagining opportunities to take, to use, to command and chew up. He's had life his own way, and he's still getting it. This is as worthy a target as Noah will ever work.

We're in motion through a crowd of pushy Londoners, all walking the opposite direction, all with the energy of summertime in their step.

It's really hard to tail people on foot. In a car their ability to get away from you is controlled by the speed they can go through traffic, and only the keenest of crook – or Starsky – would gaze at the rear-view mirror enough to spy that the same car had been close up behind for too many junctions. On foot though, without wheels and a metal box dulling your subject's instincts, you often need that extra bit of luck to avoid being sniffed out.

Last time it helped that there were two of them, clearly absorbed in some important discussion. Now it's just Haydn

Greggs – and Noah, forty yards in tow, wading through a crowd of automatons in suits.

He's got a light grey jacket on, even though there's this moist type of heat in the air. London heat, you know? Stale air. It's not anything we get on the coast. His darker trousers are cut tight to his legs and there's a pace on him as well, each step twisting his feet firmly against the ground so his hips and shoulders tilt to where he's headed. We bear west, towards the city's iconic structures and spaces, before he stops and I have to shimmy a little so as not to stride straight past. He's stopped to swap chit-chat with two coppers at the side of the river, and it looks like they know each other. I imagine him chewing the fat with Davies and Whitfield somewhere comfy, giving them all they want but nothing they need. Sleeves rolled up but wearing black flak-jackets, the officers doing the best they can to look casual for a brightening summer stroll, but coppers are still coppers. MET coppers too. Sharper, faster, harder, better than the shitty little Welsh ones I deal with.

I picture Starsky as one of these – but then remind myself he left that world. He won't like them anymore than me these days. Haydn's smiling now, but it ain't the kind of smile that shares goodwill.

As he starts to move again he knocks one of them sideways, playfully, like – with a knuckle. You know, a light, pat-on-the-shoulder sort of gesture. But there's an 'I've got you where I want' air to it. Fucking creeps me out. There's nothing in this guy that someone like Noah can warm to. Ever.

I don't have to, though. All I need to do is find out *something* more about him, so we can carry on with this game of cat and mouse – a game in which Alys says the roles still haven't been set.

Anyway, he keeps going for about twenty minutes, along the edge of the Thames, and smokes again as he's going. He gets to where I think I can see the Westminster stuff coming around the corner at us – and that eye thing is getting taller and taller over our heads, and then he turns back. He's stubbing a ciggie out between fingers as we cross paths and I have to avoid eye contact and pull my own about-turn without getting noticed.

Then it's straight back to Kinsella House, same route as before, except for one weird little detour in which he goes down a tiny alley I swear is a dead end. It's the back of a big furniture showroom – but only the fire exit – they must take deliveries from the street. I have to keep walking, but see out the corner of my eye that he's down there and looking up.

This is fucked, I think, so I step into the showroom, politely refuse the offer of help from a smiling salesman, and look around with an eye out for Haydn again through the window. If he doubles back on himself now and heads west, I'll lose him – but he doesn't. Instead he passes a minute later rubbing his hands on his coat. Back in the street, I can see him touching his top trouser button and that's when it occurs to me the most likely thing he was doing down there was having a piss. Pretty primitive for someone in his layer of society – but it is my best explanation.

Then he disappears indoors again at the first place I picked him up and, as is good protocol in this situation, I decide to call off for the day. I know he can be found here again, and it wouldn't be clever to stick around and push luck any further.

Argy-bargy with a copper, a smoke and walk on the bank of the Thames and probably urinating in an alleyway mid-afternoon.

Interesting maybe, but nothing so far that's gonna break open this instruction. It is enough, though, when I get back to my Travelodge, to phone and get permission from Miss Clare to do several more days of observation – times chosen by me, probably at random, to see if anything else shows up.

Two more spells on his tail unearth pretty much the same kinds of stuff – nothing at all to do with any business he may conduct and, obviously, not a whiff of Mr Lovell – or even a hint of a whiff. There are several more smoking walks and an exchange with a passer-by he seems to know. There's a time when he's whispering shit at an unimpressed security guard three doors down from their offices. I also see him greet three more coppers, buy a paper, go into a bank, a Caffè Nero, talk to a cabbie, sit at the river to drink a bottle of water – all 500ml of it in one go – as well as going into a newsagent to pick up a cereal bar. Oh, and a pomegranate, too.

It's getting to the point where I'm having fun. This guy's just another tool who wanders the earth chasing his own impulses.

But then, fourth time I follow him – fuck, it could have been never, and I wish it was, but it does happen – I'm led to horror. Horror, yes, that's what I said.

Armed with a camera, which I'm dull enough to fuckin use too, I see the sight that ends my desire to do anything in this fucked up, wrong, wicked, useless endgame of a job – ever again. And I realise that everyone else is right and I'm wrong, right the way across this perfect line.

It's a street somewhere off Brick Lane – towards Bethnal Green says my phone's navigator – although you never know where one place ends and the next starts. He goes the whole way there on foot, and slowly, so it's like almost an hour's walk. No trains, no buses. No taxi – which remains the one thing he could do to lose me immediately at any point. I pick him up outside the *Hideous CnC* offices again, and once more, with Noah his little parasite fish attached, Haydn Greggs keeps his usual pace through the city streets. We cross one of the busy arterial roads

– which would lead to one of those famous bridges over the Thames and then a southbound highway – only we turn north instead, away from the river. He slows, looking in shop windows several times along the way – always dusty newsagents or pawnbroker- and bookmaker-type places. Dressed in pricey clothes, he seems somehow drawn to the city's bric-a-brac, and its food too. He reads menus of kebab shops and second-rate pizzerias, and then pauses to peer through the whitewashed glass of a place that's 'to let'.

When we're far enough from the money bit of the City to have completely lost any sense of its gravitational pull, he quickens pace even more – like he's losing inhibitions. He's a cooling outer planet now, but I'm still sucked into his orbit, a captured comet, losing mass by the second.

But then we're somewhere else again – and another pull resumes. The ramshackle sole-trader shops and dingy, uncared for buildings end, replaced by sparkling office spaces and fake marble porticos. We slow before he heads into a small backstreet that heads behind a row of properly posh restaurants.

And this is where it's going to happen.

Noah on red alert – and I mean it. I lose my blood for a moment – as if the stuff switches to oil and back again in a nanosecond. I'm hot and cold at once and my finger tips prickle. The sun, high as it ever climbs in a British sky, is still getting into this street, but it's cold anyway. Like I've strolled into a walk-in freezer.

Someone's waiting for him, out the back of a restaurant, wearing a chef's apron and with the sort of slightly wet, greasy hair of a person who's been in a sweaty kitchen with a hat on. There are smells of good food wafting down towards me, but I feel sick instead of hungry.

I'm close to him now – I could throw something heavy and it

would reach Greggs from here, and I have to slip in behind a green wheelie bin to avoid being seen. I can't hear what they're saying but the conversation is serious. They're looking at their watches, and are clearly uncomfortable. This isn't a friendship. This is two men forced together by something else.

I fire off a round of photos, wide-angle and closeup so that there's clear ID of the pair of them, and enough surroundings included to get a definite location on them after the fact. I try scrawling times and places in my notebook, but I can't pin this down to a named street. Maybe it isn't one.

After a few minutes I hear a beeping and have to crawl even further back, towards a litter-flavoured wall drenched in the sweet smell of spilled alcohol from the wheelie bins. It's a lorry in reverse, coming towards them, down the alley.

Shit. I'm penned in. I can see the driver's eyes in the side-view mirror, which means he can see me too, if he looks.

It's a mid-sized vehicle – just too big to be a van – with a boxed rear, and it has to tick-tack a bit to get around the bend so it can have a clean run of reversing up to the two fuckers I've been watching. It could just crush me if it wanted, and I'm breathing in its carbon monoxide for a moment. When it passes by I'm hunched down low, and on the passenger side, starting to think I may well have avoided being spotted.

But I have to get a better view for myself. I've been waiting for Haydn Greggs to do something, anything other than just wander around looking important, and if this is gonna be it then Noah needs the money shot.

Priority is knowing what's in the lorry, so I step up to its slipstream, facing downwards in case there's CCTV around here. Palm on one of its headlights, I walk carefully forwards, using the lorry to cover me as I get three more wheelie bins along, and then there's no option but to jump right under the last one and scramble forward, belly-down in the anonymous stains on the concrete below me. There's just enough room to wriggle to where I have a view of what's going on. I'm less than two car lengths away.

I still can't hear voices, what with the engine and the intermittent beeps of the reverse warning. An industrial fan over my head doesn't help either. But I'm gonna be able to get a picture of anything and everything.

The truck stops, engine still running and I hear doors. The driver's feet hit the floor, and I see him walking around to the rear.

Side-on, I can just see the horizontal metal slats covering the lorry's back, and there's a jarring, clacking noise as they start to mechanically rise. A sort of heavy steam pours gently out, rising too slow to be water vapour, and then I realise it's coz this is a giant ice-box on wheels. I edge forward to get a fuller view. As the shutters rise further I glimpse, through the frozen mist inside, a row of dark pink objects swaying lightly. It's a meat delivery, and there are about a dozen carcasses of big animals hung from the roof of the hold.

Haydn Greggs and the man in kitchen overalls are peering keenly in. They both flick fag butts to the floor – still burning, drawn right to the filters. Perfect smoker's timing, both of them. The driver climbs in, and they both move right up to be in touching distance. The intermittent bleeps have stopped, but now there's another perpetual electronic whine coming from the vehicle – like a waiting security alarm or something. There are pneumatic noises too, and I see the stop-go rhythms of hydraulic movement inside. One of the carcasses is lowering gradually, until the bottom of it brushes the floor and the driver has to give it a push so that it drapes off the back of the lorry and over the road.

The man in the apron takes the lead, and gets right under so as to lift the carcass up, and then Greggs joins in too. I'm wondering what fuckin use the super-important Haydn has with helping move meat into a restaurant when, firstly through the camera lens's grainy way of enhancing vision, I realise this lump of meat poking out the van has toes, and is in fact human.

I'll be the one who hears. I will not like it. But then I kind of might.

Now *all* noises become irrelevant, as I grow fixated on the dark red, blotchy tones of a frozen corpse, most of its skin missing. There's no blood anywhere, though. This is meat, ready to be used for meat's main purpose.

They're in no urgent rush, maybe because they know they're in a private place, or maybe coz they reckon too much haste could lead to a mistake, like dropping this horrid carcass on the filthy Tarmac underfoot. Then again, it could even be that they don't think they're doing anything wrong. He's visibly uptight, but Haydn Greggs still has that look of complete authority over what he's doing.

They've dragged it out as far as the torso now, and still there's hardly any skin – it's been neatly peeled off across the whole body, with just some yellowing patches of gristle that look like the bits of glue on a can or bottle when you tear off the label. The ribcage has been sawn short, an arc cut neatly around the bottom edges and all the insides removed.

My only way of dealing with this is to focus on taking pictures. Disengaged, viewing through a screen, like the way most of us like to see the world these days. Gradually, as this thing is moved out, I start to hear faintly, over my own breath and the idling engine, the three men calmly communicating to each other, as if they're about to move a sofa into a house.

The driver jumps down, gets ready to lift the top half free of the truck, and I'm hoping, just for my own sanity, that it's gonna be headless. That's when I notice just how fucking *big* this corpse is.

This was someone – a man I'm presuming, although genitals have been taken out too by that big butcher's gouge – of enormous height. Probably almost seven feet tall. No wonder the three of them are so put out.

It's cold all around, and yet the meat is still leaving little pink marks on Haydn Greggs's shirt as he grips the middle section, wrapping his elbow around a thigh. Then comes my first sight of the head, and I wretch.

Not out of disgust – let me make that clear. I wretch from *realisation*.

Ahead of me, and burning itself into the digital memory of Noah's dinky camera, is the outline I refuse to believe. Tall, enormous, strong, a man's legs, skinned but thick, the wide-shouldered torso of a giant human but with the head of a... I'm just as lost to identify it as she must have been – as anyone would be looking real-time at something that cannot exist if the world you know and rely on is built the way you think it is.

The horns have been sawn off, but I can see a long, equine nose and jawbone. The neck doesn't really cut in from the shoulders – which themselves aren't pointed outwards like a human. There are big lumps of messier flesh hanging from where the skin was pulled away further up towards the head, but still the muscles attaching the skull are intact, so that it won't flop limp when they finally manage to clear the whole carcass off the back of the truck. Taking pictures stops feeling worthwhile – what the fuck use are they gonna be to anyone? How will *ever* sharing what I'm seeing here give me anything but trouble in the life ahead?

I think how maybe the *Daily Mail* or *Mirror* might be the best place to send these shots, but can't imagine them taking this seriously. Then I entertain it being a wind-up, before my senses override, and remind me of the blood-burning shudder that hit me when I arrived here. Now I realise I'd known all along something was gonna happen here. And anyway, the smells, the cold air, the texture, the way it's gradually staining the clothes of the men lumbering it indoors and out of sight – it's all too real. I'm part of this event. I'm in it, therefore it is.

The three of them – plus deceased guest – disappear into the rear of this building and I start questioning anything I can. Where is this? Am I somewhere that can be pinned down to a simple London postcode or a location on Google Maps? Can I be sure that's a kitchen in there? Is this really a lorry? Was that definitely my man Greggs?

I stay still, lying in the same place, too cautious to move anywhere else. This is life and death, Noah, I tell myself. Or even more than death.

Silence starts to settle around me, despite the engine and its echoes. The back of the truck is still open, and I can see inside better than ever now. It's cleared of mist, and the other carcasses look nothing out of the ordinary – pigs without heads or trotters, four halves of two cows, I can make out various cuts and strips of rib and bone. It's just a bog standard butcher's wagon. I log the number plate of the lorry, and look to see if there are logos or contact details anywhere on it – there aren't – so I start trawling through the best ideas of what to do next.

Top of the list remains nothing. Keep motionless and silent, Noah.

It's like an age, during which the lorry's grumbling motor starts to allow some of the further off noises of the city to penetrate the bubble around me. I can hear buses pulling away, something further off that's either a drill or a saw, roadworks maybe. There's the odd car horn.

I've no sense of time anymore – not even when I'm actually looking at my watch – and then two of them come out again. The driver, and Haydn Greggs. I don't study them closely this time, because avoiding detection is my only care now. I hear the cockpit door slam closed, then the truck drives off in only a fraction of the time it took to get here. Greggs is left on his own. He lights up another cigarette, and I can see front-on how his shirt is smeared with patchy stains from carrying whatever it was inside. Then he sets off, briskly and confidently, striding forward with those sure-footed paces so familiar to me.

I don't follow him, but stay here for as long as it takes to get dark. I drift; my mind thinks of everything and then nothing. The sense of what I've seen doesn't come to me at all – but it doesn't need to. I've documented most of it, I think.

Hoping there's not gonna be any other sordid shit to see in this backroad that I wish didn't exist, I let my mind into that state of semi-concentration you get in a long stakeout. My eyes never leave the closed door into which that thing went – right now that rectangle in the wall ahead is the primary hazard. Observations locked where they need to be, Noah wanders around his own head, distraction enough to make this work bearable.

And then it is dark.

And then I run like fuck.

And then begins the process of dealing with where I am and where I was.

Variations of things Alys says are never far from entering my train of thought, but still I don't let them – like a tune you avoid getting stuck in your head.

Running slows to a quick march. A flight of stairs downwards and then the Underground envelops me. I count off the tube stops back to the hub, King's Cross, and check out of my room, quickly. Then it's back to the station, onwards to Paddington; a rapid retreat to God's Land. Wales needs Noah and Noah needs Wales.

I don't look at any of what I'm carrying – in case it somehow changes. I'm only about the business of getting me, and my immediate possessions, back to *my* space, where the ocean smell is in the air and the importance of *that* place behind might just dilute enough for me to see what it all means. *Might*.

➜

Fears concentrate to a single point.

I get home to the reminder that Alys, of all the things she could have been doing, was *surfing*. Yeah, I know that was the plan in the first place, but it shows just how far off my thoughts managed to roam – you know, that it was a surprise to get reminded of it. I quiz her on yesterday's conditions, look at the tide tables and realise she was cruising into a few out beyond the dunes west of the Crawl at the exact same time I was seeing the gates of hell squeak open.

Oh, yes, fuckin love how far apart our worlds can get, eh? There's me, following the devil down a city street while she, two hundred miles away, is coming over the top of the last dune and seeing the swell lines. I'm staring at chewing gum soldered into pavements while she looks down at the rockpools you have to step in to get to the water's edge. I'm turning into that dead-end alley of all that's ill, as Alys walks barefoot onto that shingle bank that pushes out, horseshoe shaped, into the sea. And it only diverges more from there. Me with the beep-beep-beep of that van in my ear, her drifting into position. Me, Noah, seeing my life's plans and ambitions mean fuck all in the face of death, blood, power. Her going through that reverse awakening when you catch your first proper peeler.

I can see it in my mind. A neat line of water surging through the smooth ocean surface, rising upwards, pronounced, as it drags against the seabed. Alys with the momentum, pulling water through her fingers, palms pushing against cool, sunlit saline. Then the point when the wave's energy takes over. Bet she'll have got it all right too, all the stages; feet in place, back leg kinked in and a raised front knee. It's instinct to her already. That girl has the ocean in her now.

I trudge to the Whiteout offices the next morning and all her rides, even though I wasn't there, are replaying to me over and over again. I hear up close the water cutting off the bottom edge of her board, like I was paddling right in front myself. It flicks out from the edge of her nine-footer as she trims along a racing row of folding ocean – always just far enough ahead.

Then I'm sitting down to try and write my logs up – logs I stopped keeping pretty quickly into that last day's observations – and there's her hair flailing as she flies through the warm sea air. I'm wondering the purpose of it, as she times a quick jump-off at the shoreline and turns round to paddle out and get another one.

So I'm turning in a report. For the client. It's gonna read like a professional job. Coz that's all it is. This is my plan. Say what I saw. Nothing more. No reading between any lines – leave that to Alys.

How does she end up taking over my space like that? How's she catching the swell, getting priorities in order while I'm the one getting lost in a job, getting spun out on wildly unreal shit and maybe even believing some of it. Time to right that fucked up balance.

Alys sits up, out back, looking at the horizon to choose her next wave.

And I start to type. Dates, facts, details. Recommendations.

9

Whiteout Agent Report

Client:	Miss A Clare
Subject:	Haydn GREGGS & related businesses
Wh Ref:	24/4506
Result:	Positive
Agent:	Noah

Customer Ref: N/A

We thank you for your instructions in relation to both Haydn GREGGS Dir HIDEOUS CnC and Brian Godfrey LOVELL Dir HIDEOUS CnC, and in relation to the whereabouts and currently known business activities of both subjects.

As you may now be aware, both of these subjects are known to trade in the financial services industry from the registered offices of the above named company. Both of these subjects have proved difficult to locate, and we are now of the opinion that Mr Brian Godfrey LOVELL is no longer present in either of his known abodes in London or South Wales, and that he is unlikely to have any further relations with either of these locations at all. We do not believe, furthermore that he and Haydn GREGGS are in contact, following extensive surveillance of the principal subject.

Due to the exceptional circumstances of these two cases relating to each other, we have written one report and copied it onto both files, which will now carry the above title, Haydn GREGGS. A detailed log of these is attached.

Haydn GREGGS is certainly still active with the company HIDEOUS CnC, and there have been no changes to the directorship. There are eight other officers of the company, namely Clayton SPILLER, Steven BALZER, Paul PANG, Adam HARFOOT, Adam WILSON, Douglas HILL-JONES, Richard

FROST and Graham JOHNS. All have London addresses which we have verified and can confirm have no links to Brian Godfrey LOVELL. It is our understanding these people have no legal ability to change or affect boardroom decisions in the company, but have all been involved as investors at various points. County Court Judgments are registered against three of the above named officers of HIDEOUS CnC at their home addresses in London, each time for significant amounts of money (all in excess of £400,000). Six of them have addresses elsewhere, two in Jersey, three in the Home Counties and one in Northern Spain. There is also a Jersey office address for the company itself (in St Helier), although we infer from previous understanding of how financial companies operate that this address it is not the centre of operations. All addresses are now verified, with the exception of Spain. Appendices detail this.

In the past four years, all eight elected officers have lodged joint applications for finance, using nine separate addresses in the Greater London area. The likelihood that this is to dissuade significant investigation or credit searching of their affairs is high. In 2001 three of these officers obtained credit for another unrelated company and supplied a well known financial institution with a home address that led to a hotel in Margate, Kent.

Haydn GREGGS, Brian Godfrey LOVELL and his wife (deceased) have never been involved in any of these transactions, and we have found very limited credit information on them. The company is solvent, and we can purchase further accounting information on your instruction.

HIDEOUS CnC does not advertise. There is no marketing information for the company, and discreet consultation within London financial circles has not led to anyone who knows of the company or its purpose. It may be possible to contact one or more of the eight elected officers, but we would advise against this for reasons of client safety (consider the reasons outlined for instructing us in the first place). Such avenues of inquiry would certainly alert members of HIDEOUS CnC to our presence.

Our covert surveillance of the principal subject, we must now report, has led to no observations of suspicious behaviour, and we have not seen him relate to or meet with any of the other officers of HIDEOUS CnC. He attends the registered office in Kinsella House (address in appendices) on average two or three times a week, rarely staying for more than half a day. We have not been able to observe or locate any other occupations, companies or addresses than those already known at the commencement of the instruction.

We understand you may wish to consult our opinions on other matters related to these subjects, and suggest this is better done in a formal meeting at a location arranged by you. We regret that our investigations have not led to anything further and remain in a position to assist you in any further capacity required.

WHITEOUT LEGAL INVESTIGATIONS SERVICES
SURVEILLANCE LOGS TO FOLLOW

→

Yeah, I know. We feed her just a load of watered down shit. But what else can be done? Sure, Miss Clare, your sister's death is grim, but can't you just take the safest interpretation possible and decide she was off her rocker and maybe just bought it by accidentally knowing the wrong psychopath? Come on, Miss Clare, don't go on believing that letter you had. You don't need to run with this anymore, do you? The police found nothing so how did you expect us to? Let it lie – if there's anything else, let the authorities deal with it all as they can and should...

I stick the report on a copied Whiteout form, and even think of coming clean to Starsky, telling him what we did but swearing affidavit on this version only. If I can say it enough times, write it even more, get it official, registered in our company diaries and wherever else, then maybe this version can become the truth.

Of course bits of it are fine. Those dodgy co-directors and elected officers – bunch of wankers by the looks of it – are in the financial mire and Greggs is clearly the one shafting them all. Looks like he's had Mr Lovell's help too at some point because they're the only two with any say in this fucked up company, Hideous CnC, and the only ones without debt and blacklistings. Come to think of it, the pair barely exist. And it's also true I never saw Haydn Greggs using his home address.

So what is this gig of theirs? Greggs, Lovell, all those other names? People are paying in, getting shafted? Then there's the fact one of the main two directors from that list is gone, missing, probably forever after his wife got sacrificed in their own garden. Could easily have been for revenge over some lost investment or a threat from someone influential he pissed off – husband conned the wrong powerbroker so they slash up a family member? There you go, Miss Clare, grab that as your closure theory.

But then this other guy, Greggs, the one connection left has led me to...

Shit, man, there's only gonna be a finite number of times I can say that, now. And definitely none of those few remaining occasions are going to be to the fuckin client. That bit I *have* got right. The less people sucked into this the better. Yeah, we're doing Miss Clare a favour by keeping the alley pictures to ourselves.

So there you have it. My professional opinion. It goes no further than that.

And there is no more, anyway.

Until Alys gets her say.

→

'I've got it Noah,' she's telling me. 'I can see why you all call it a bug.' She means surfing. 'I caught some really long ones at the shingle bar. Really got the feel for that board.'

Listening to this, I wonder what I've done. There's gonna be no escape now. Alys is hooked on *my* thing. Complete role-reversal, this. Suddenly she's seems to be the one who gets it – gets that there's no point playing along so why care in the first place.

I was late waking. Somehow sleep came, early hours, and it held me right through to mid morning. She's already been up the beaches to check today's conditions but the waves aren't doing anything great so let's have brekkie in Noah's flat. Typical how a sweet summer swell pulses through while I'm gone, only for the high-pressure doldrums to drop back over the ocean for my return.

Alys is topped up on the surf stoke though. She's so eager to tell me all about this, something so new to her but taken for granted by me, that I have to demand my chance to explain what happened in the City yesterday. It's like she's totally forgotten this job we've been on, as if she's simply aware of me arriving back without really thinking about where from.

But then I start to talk more about where from, and these changes all drop off her. Alys's shoulders rise slightly, the neck muscles tighten – but more than anything else I see the way something falls out from behind those eyes. And, that easily, the depth from the first time I ever saw her is back. The sense there's stuff behind the scenes in Alys's world, driving her places you don't really want to go but can't help feeling drawn in by. Now my mind has lost for good that picture of her taking a high-line over a clean wall of water. I've re-infected her with my problems. Or so I think.

As always though, she wrests control of that straight back.

'Of course,' she's saying.

It takes me a while to get out what exactly I think I remember I saw.

I've been holding off scrolling through the photos – didn't even take as much as a quick peek last night. I kind of wanted someone there when I do. Problem shared, problem halved and all that. I haven't doubted what's gonna be there at any point. Ever since I got on the late Paddington-to-Swansea train I've hoped against hope they won't be there on that memory card – who wouldn't? – but they will be. I know it. You know it. She probably does too.

'Of course,' she's repeating in response. To herself. Or me? It's hard to tell.

I don't want to interrupt her, but my whole tale sounds so silly that it seems kind of wrong to just leave off without trying to dig out explanations I can't really offer.

I saw a carcass. It matched the thing Mrs Lovell wrote about. Of course. Of course. It's not meant to go like that. This isn't how you respond to things that don't exist.

But then there's my pictures. Photons, light waves, whatever you want to call them, have bounced through a lens, been turned into pixels, they've cut their image into my camera. If the camera has it stored, then it happened that way, right?

My laptop takes a breath, its fan turning over as the lights come on. Cables attach, while I fetch us both a glass of water. I'm still trying not to be sure what we're about to see. But I am.

The file opens and, shot after shot, popping into view, row after row, the sequence is there, and it is what it seemed. The lens saw it too. It did happen. I'm not going the way of Mrs Lovell. My mind is holding up.

That means something even worse, though. It means this shit is actually going on. I've still tried to hold some denial, but here it is, all quashed in one go.

'Of course.'

The tiles finish filling in. Payload transferred over and a duplicate of every image is complete inside two minutes. One more set of these pics that would need to be erased before any of this can be denied existence. I hit one of the central shots in which I can see, standing out, that horrible pinky yellow of the dead flesh. The first one to open fully has it right there. I zoom. The outline of a thigh, the unmistakeable base of a spine and edge of a hip. With my fingertips heavy and prickling, blood running to the furthest reaches, I move the cursor along towards the dead thing's shoulders, neck, and head.

'Of course,' she says. There's no emotion in this reaction. Once more, it's just work to her. So I let her lean over and drive the mouse instead. She's close to me again. The tingling in my fingers almost involuntarily reaches over to her. I'm a bit-part again. Have I done her a favour here? Has she anything else to say?

She zooms back out, and hits 'next'. Another shot, same angle, carcass just above the camera's eye line but everything perfectly lit and no doubting what this appears to be. You can see the reddening smear on both men's shirts as it's brushing their midriffs. The next few slides all show near identical frames, before a wider angle that gets Haydn Greggs's mugshot into the same picture as well.

Alys stops, there's a slight quickening of her breath. She's been calmly drawing in air through her nose, mouth closed – but now she jabs one short puff inwards in which her lips open with a hint of a tremble. She flicks the cursor over the '+' sign and pulls us in closer to the subject's face. The first zoom she makes is a miss, as the picture swells and takes him out the side of the frame, but quickly she finds the arrow keys and pans right until his squinty eyes and soft face fill our view. And she stops breathing altogether.

It's got to be nearly a full minute. I can't say anything.

Then she draws a sharp, full lung of air and swiftly stifles a groan.

'Shi...' The word stays unfinished. She tries to say something again: 'Shi... oh my... fuu...'

'What?'

'Noah...' a tear arrives on her face.

'You OK?'

'Oh my Go...' she's whimpering rather than speaking. And then nothing intelligible is left, just a whining, extended cry; someone who's just learnt a piece of news more horrible and devastating than most of us will ever get in our lives. She covers her face. This isn't like the last time she was upset. This is someone who's right on the edge. No, this is someone falling over that edge.

'Alys?'

'Aaah,' she cries, soft but sharp.

'What is it?'

'Aaah,' it comes again, as if she doesn't have any control over her words.

But then, through her hands, she manages half a phrase that tells me where we're going with this.

'Noah... Noah... It's *him*!'

Looking at the floor – coz it's as good a place as anywhere right now – I see Alys's bare feet. I track my sight along the wooden blocks towards where she's left a pair of flip-flops just inside the door. It's cool inside here, with shade and surfaces that don't hold the heat, but beyond the window I can see a bright day where it's hot already and that heat will soon bring the sea breeze. *We need to hold on to those rhythms around us right now, Alys*, I think. There's stuff out there bigger than this. Things that are on our side.

I leave her inert on my couch, and carry out the meaningless gesture of taking the glasses of water away and filling a kettle. Any extra noise is welcome distraction, and before it's even bubbling I'm back on the couch and I'm taking Alys into my arms. She doesn't react at all, so I move away again as the water boils, and leave her to work it through. No pressure, no pushing from me.

It's not needed anyway, because *I will be the one who hears*.

And now the story she has only ever half begun, is going to fill in.

It's nearly two hours later, during which I make her cups of tea, toast and a scrambled egg, before putting kitchen plants out into the yard behind and flicking through a surf mag which I fetch from the shop opposite. The only thing I leave alone completely is the set of photos that has caused this. Two hours in which she's gaining strength and making herself at home, but not talking or thinking. Two hours that move quickly, marked out by the steady shifting of sunlight across the windowsill behind her, as a long, summer day revels in its powerful pulse.

Two hours later, she's sitting upright and speaking clear. And I hear.

'This person you've been following Noah. This "Greggs". I know him. I've never met him, but I've known him for years.'

Having got this first bit out – the headline – she looks downwards for a moment before going on.

'I'm not really sure how I didn't see this coming,' she explains. 'There have been plenty of other hints I should really have picked up on. This is a really, really bad person, Noah. People shouldn't get involved unless they're really sure of their role.'

I want to ask what on earth she means by *role* but this is only one of millions of questions I'm gonna want to ask, so it stays just a flicker of thought inside my head as Alys continues.

'You know, when my parents met, my mother didn't ask any questions of who my dad was or where he'd come from. My grandma hated it. But it wasn't really my mum's style – she was too trusting. She learnt the hard way, mind. You know I've told you he died before I was born?'

'Yeah.'

'I never told you exactly how, though, did I?'

'You said he was murdered.'

'Yes, but you didn't get the methods though, did you…'

No, and I wasn't going to ask.

'Well, it was *violent*.'

'Didn't you say you hadn't found out?'

'About who he was,' she says.

I make sounds of some kind, to show I'm with her, but you'd hardly call it words.

'It doesn't really affect me to think about it,' she says. 'It's just one of those things you, sort of, grow up with. I don't think I've ever been afraid of physical violence or death, and it's probably because of that. Funny, because things should really be the other way round. But for me the idea of death, and the fact some people can smash at a human head with all the venom in their power – well, they're things that just *are*. Truths. You know, same as the sun coming up or the tide coming in. Facts of life…'

She almost smiles in irony, before adding '…and Death.'

I just listen – not wanting to break her stride in any way.

'Baddies in stories when I was a kid were, well, I suppose just simpler, symbolic representations of the baddies in real life. That's why I can work in that area today. My Dad had been hit straight on, right *through* the head, several times – his face caved in. Stabbed too – eight times, all around the trunk and vital organs – and his throat had been slashed at. That bit wouldn't have killed him though. Same for the fractured neck, or the other marks.'

Other marks?

'The head wounds were the only fatal ones,' she adds. 'It was the last night of autumn, six in the morning. He was twenty yards from my grandma's front door.'

Now she's the one making sure I have space to respond. I don't think of anything in time though – would you? – and before I can speak she's answering the question that's more important than the one from earlier that I've already forgot.

'How did I know about it? Is that what you're thinking? My mother only told me bits of it, Noah. Of course she's not gonna fill me in on stuff like that if she doesn't have to – and she wasn't up to it anyway. I know through my work with the police. They have loads of unsolved and closed murder files waiting to be reopened when the right information comes to light – or once DNA and forensics catch up with evidence collected at the time. After a few cases with them, I persuaded a friend I'd made there to find it all out for me. So I've got hundreds of pieces of tiny, probably useless, little stats and details stored in my head.' She taps her temple with her index finger as if it might change something in her memories.

'He was coming back from sea again, a three-night trip, the attack was definitely the work of one person. That was something they were really sure of, apparently. As close as proof could take them. To do with the reach and height. Same height as him, they reckoned. Short knife – too short for its wounds to have proved fatal without the other traumas – and a blunt bat. "Effort rather than skill had finished off the victim." What a verdict, hey? That's actually what someone had written in a police notepad after interviewing the coroner.'

One person with no apparent reason. One person whose existence remains only a theory.

Alys has lived in the lee of this theory – the shadow of it – and I'm finding out why. Shaking with adrenaline, and trying to hide it from her, I force back the part of me warning this confidence will bring with it consequence.

She knows Noah, *she knows what you're thinking.*

She doesn't show it though, and I wonder if the concentration required to tell this stuff is keeping her from tapping into me.

'So that's me,' she says. 'As a kid they made sure I grew up with it... just... there in my mind. D'you know what something like that does to your... *interpretations*? And like I said, neither of them ever told me the details.'

But somehow it was planted. It was in her mind from the start. From before the first chance she ever had to imagine anything.

Morbid dreams, the knowledge of good and evil, responsibility, reality – aren't these things a 5-year-old should be protected from?

Her mum ignored the biggest questions as almost anyone would. When you think about it, I can't easily imagine I'd be itching to tell a kid that kind of thing. But it looks like life's found its own ways of answering them anyway.

How do you raise a child into a legacy like that? When do you tell them? *What* do you tell them? *How* do you tell them? There's probably no right or wrong way. No way at all, in fact.

Grandma did her bit, but it was Alys's sleep – disturbed, turgid, dreaded – that was able to reveal, one shadow at a time, the background story more than anything else – right up until she was able to get the contents of the police file itself.

Imagine that. Finding out things *in your sleep*. Nights broken up by fragments, where deep swirling reds and greens poured out the backs of her shut eyelids, faces forming, voices calling. Crying for Mum, but only getting Grandma.

'A man's sitting in the window!' she'd shriek, before the adults in her life rushed to get the lights on. Then the sun would come up again, and the pains of the night would drop away. Almost.

It went on every night, for years.

'The man's in the window again!'

And always, the same ending – back to the real world and her guardian adults telling Alys to snap out of it. It's a dream. They happen. There's no man in any window. *Look, here's the light. Look. Nothing.*

'It only got worse though,' today's Alys is telling me, with hindsight. In the here-and-now she talks, Noah listens. And on it goes…

Back to the history. Another night, two decades ago – the words and plight of child Alys, long after bedtime: 'The man! He was here again, just now, Grandma.'

Right after the first instance, her grandma and mother tried asking her the important questions. What did this man look like? What did he say? And Alys would respond in wails, with words too jumbled to make sense. All her grandma could ever make out was the first bit. His whereabouts.

'He's looking through the window again!'

'He was sitting by there!'

And then, two in the morning, twenty-plus years ago with the nearby tide right out and a moon so full the world could have still gone to work by night, Alys, much calmer, called them to the usual nocturnal duty, with one alteration:

'He's in the street below.'

Alys's imagination started getting in the way of everything soon after. Friendship groups, fashion, trends and possessions, identifying the demons that haunted her mother – these were of surface interest to a kid who in the day seemed pretty much content to just stand and stare, before going round the bend at night.

Then, no warning, the world in her head started going after the real one she lived in, and it wasn't long before she started feeling these connections between her nightmares and bits of the life around her that were *meant* to stay unknown.

Dad? She asked herself – now there was one of them: Had he been...? The notion that froze her mother, which arrested the progress of the adults in her life, didn't scare Alys at all. *Aren't we all light and dark in little bits?* Good and bad? Isn't that how to be interesting?

The grown-ups were years behind.

Regular, repetitive, the man in the dream started to develop a spirit, and Alys was losing the fear. Twelve years old, then thirteen, and she hadn't mentioned to anyone the real details that were emerging.

OK, so photos tucked away from her mother's hidden past showed it wasn't her father who'd first appeared in Alys's dreams a decade earlier. But the visitor to her sleep did have his ties. For Alys, it was a certainty. Enough staring into those old pictures would find this man reflected in the wet parts of her dad's eyes. Yes, she told herself, her dad *must* have known this figure.

That 'family portrait'. The one I saw in her apartment of her parents, shot by a forgotten friend – a beach on a dark day, fisherman father for once ignorant of the ruthless grey sea behind, looking beyond the lens instead. Alys stared for hours and years at that image of them perched against a low-tide rock – long enough to see something else. A look in her father that seemed to see even further than beyond. What had he known? In those eyes – that she shared – Alys reckoned there was a message, or a hint.

And, as that gaze falsely promised to allow her dad's story to form, so did the man on the windowsill continue to reveal his own face.

She wrote it down in a notebook, sketched him, pencil versions of photo-fit mugshots – never to be shared with anyone, ever. At first too sharp, this spectre of Alys's nights gradually softened to clear features; a pompous, fleshy smirk. She began to see well enough to capture more than just the outline of eyes. Pin-like pupils that never dilated, with greys and greens fighting around their edges, skin that had never suffered weather nor worry, and thin, light hair – always cropped too short to do anything more than sit, unattended on the top of his head.

He was always dressed the same, too. A white shirt with cufflinks under a smaller, grey jacket. Shoulders pinned back, but not broad, the top half of his body was just starting to grow round, but his legs were slender and strong; there was power behind the short, slow movements that he made. Above the open top button of his shirt, the neck had room to swell, as he moved his jaw towards a smile that Alys would always prevent by jolting herself awake.

There it was. From then on Alys had a purpose. It was at the age of fifteen, she reckons, when it became certain her dreams had found the power of prediction.

'It was a fight with my mother that just opened the valve,' she says to me. 'This day, one spring, it was just so, you know, so beautiful and in bloom, and she was so grumpy and just couldn't see anything. I yelled at her – only time in my whole life I'd lost it with anyone. I told her to shape up, to take responsibility for her life and then, like that, it all started. I had to run inside and sit in the backroom while some kind of sleep just came and sucked me in. And this time it wasn't like any of the stuff before.'

She tells me how faces began to move through her vision.

How, years ago, Alys was wandering, still in the room but moving. Sounds – crackling, stretching and popping – raced across her mind. And most importantly of all, in the sets of eyes that passed in her mind, there was one important absence. No sign of that returning man with the white shirt and glinting cufflinks who'd sat in her dreams. No place in these images for the soft chin, light cropped hair, fixed stare.

'For some reason, Noah, he was out of his depth.'

When as a teenager Alys begun to match faces from that last dream to people who then showed up in real life there wasn't any surprise. She knew it was something she could work with and control. She'd hear a comment or see a line of newsprint and then it would show up in her day – sometimes miles away, to start with – in situations she hadn't planned or foreseen.

Fears concentrate to a single point, Alys, came a piece of advice, a voice she couldn't identify but which she knew was friendly. *That's what they always do*. And then you can crush them. Why couldn't everyone see this? It really was that easy. Channel them, pull them in, *then cut away*. As soon as Alys had begun thinking about controlling it, she knew. It was simple: the world, its responsibilities, her *role*.

Role. There's that word again, I think, ominous as fuck. And I'm right. Watch out for this Noah. You'll be the one who hears. You won't like it but then you kind of might.

Back then Alys had one theory, basic and, for all she cared, proven. Logic held this as a truth. As other faces arrived by the hour, there could only be one reason for that first ever figure no longer showing up in her dreams.

'He must exist too,' she says. 'That's what I decided. In *reality*. There wasn't any doubt.'

And now she pauses. She still has to say this last bit, even though I know what's coming. My insides turn, beyond my control, as if my whole body is resisting the news.

'Noah. *It's him.* Our man. Greggs. *He's the face I used to see.* That's how I know him. And he probably knows me, too.'

If it wasn't for the mad shit that I've seen and heard around this girl, and the clients-turned-subjects-turned-whatever-else-now that have brought us to this stage and state of affairs, I'd be fine with this. But I'm not.

I'm not fine with it, because it's impossible, like it is for Alys too, not to see something in it. She's right. This is a job that's holding some profound significance for us both. Of course she's right. She has to be.

I think about her half-naked form under the skylight of her studio bedroom, asleep next to me, and the way I was ready to take any order of any kind that next morning. She made me feel as if they were my decisions then – but were they really? And I'm having myself on if things are any different now. See it for what it is, Noah. You must.

So Haydn Greggs is real. Well, that much I knew, but that she's *seen him before in a vision?*

A thousand visions, I'm reminded. Maybe more. A vision a day for years. Great.

'I'm ready for all of this though, Noah,' she's telling me, as I gulp for air before it's back under for another freedive through the world according to Alys.

And, with every word she says, it's a place I want less and less involvement in. But I'm locked. Tied to it now. *I may not like it but then I kind of might.*

The books, the years of studying occult and rumour and superstition and myth. It's all built a mighty mountain for this to just sit atop of.

This, she's saying, pointing at the starting sentences of my

187

surveillance logs, is the basic thread of a Peruvian virility tale. I don't look. Don't read the lines. Don't want to know. Just hearing is enough for now. The noises, she goes on, are accounted for often. Greek Roman, Celt, Norse, Navajo – wherever you need to hear. Even the night-time sounds of the fuckin fairies in Shakespeare. Stories come from myth... come from truth... come from life, she tells me. 'No,' I reply.

In a flash she's on to Africa and warriors eating each other's hearts. I'm hearing about chiefs in the old Americas assuming figures or casting their enemies into shapes before defeat. Antlers, but still walking, with human legs. And then they devour. She's throwing up words I don't like. Animism, Noah; *cannibalism*, Noah. She's directing her own way through the pictures I've loaded, showing me how they match a lifetime of obsessions. And it's all leaning in a direction she simply isn't going to get me moving in.

Look at the shapes. Mrs Lovell carved at, cut up with the sharpest of blades. But bite marks too. Like my father had.

Ugh. I want to groan but it won't come out.

Rituals, Noah. Think about what she saw. What we *know* she saw, because *we're seeing it too*.

This man, Noah, she's telling me as that screen on my laptop settles back on Haydn Greggs. 'He knows things I need to know.'

Of course, he does. Of course. And not only that, Noah has a role in all of this. Noah has to stay put. The story's coming around again. The start of its next cycle. Our turn to fall into its ecliptic. The tide's coming back in. Things she needs to know. *Even if we die discovering.*

'So what are you saying Alys? Who is this guy?'

'*What* is he,' she corrects me.

And now, with her calm and in her element, me frozen and listening, she asks me.

'Have you ever come across the story of Ack-tee-yon?'

'Who? How do I spell that?'

'A-C-T-A-E-O-N. Pronounced "ack-tee-yon".'

'No.'

'Really?'

'Er, should I have?'

'Yes,' she says. 'You're in it.'

And not long later, I run. *Hang on*, says Noah, *sod this*. I break and am out the door before I can reconsider.

She doesn't even call back.

First thing I do is drive – she stays at my place, but she'll leave. I head to the beach where, despite the lifeguards' dashboard claiming it's flat, there are actually some tiny, pencil-drawn lines of swell trickling ashore. Not really rideable but worth a go in desperation. It takes twenty minutes of floating and ducking my hair through the breaking peaks to gain clarity. The waves are weak, but just about precise enough to glide along a few. There's no storm anywhere in this hemisphere right now – only cloying heat-waves that have just begun breaking with a sea breeze. Cold fronts are out there, but they won't bring more surf yet.

I stay out long enough to be sure that the message is loud and clear.

When I get back there's no sign of Alys – and I've ducked the call of duty. She's gone. It didn't need words. She was only ever stooping to that level to be polite. She can think whatever she wants about Noah now. Noah won't come round to this stuff – and her quick, no-frills way of sliding out, of making herself absent, tells me that's one message she's definitely receiving loud and clear.

So what is it? Ack-tee-yon? Actaeon. Well, it doesn't really matter, coz that's only a piece of *nomenclature*, she reckoned. Only from word of mouth. Doesn't make any difference. That's just the first recorded version – Greek. It was in Rome too, then Persia – only the transfiguration was to something more like a dog or a big cat. Ireland has the story, much later, and so does Wales. At the same time, oceans apart, native people of the Americas saw it. It's the world over. She's strapped it to all sorts of stuff.

Including us, today.

Main thread of it, so she says, goes along the lines of some guy trying to get in with the gods, trying to seduce a woman he can't have, and then getting ripped to pieces and eaten – after undergoing a change. In the Greek version he's a hunter who pervs on this goddess he stumbles across when she's bathing naked in the woods – Diana, apparently, although there's nothing to say the goddess can't be called Michelle or Alys or Jane or Jill or anything else you want her to be called. Anyway, she finds out and turns him into a stag, so he gets mistaken for a target and devoured by his own hunting hounds. Usually about punishing greed, getting your comeuppance for pushing it too far, not knowing when you've taken enough. Either that or it's a warning not to look when you shouldn't.

'Mr Lovell has done something horribly wrong,' the now absent Alys is still saying, in my head, for longer than I want her to. And then, over and over, comes the breakdown:

Mrs Lovell – then herself a *Miss Clare* – and the tree she cut down, before getting slapped with psychiatric tags all those years ago. But there was nothing the matter with her. She saw what she saw. The man in the window, a voyeur, her future husband, filling the role. Actaeon peeping on the bathing goddess. He made money whereas she *was* money.

The Celtic versions have links through some beast Arthur allegedly couldn't slay, which also made the noises of hounds baying for the chase. That one also gets ripped apart – from within – by its own pups. 'Forests still ring with the cries today,' she says, 'if you can hear them.' Minging stuff that seems too disjointed for me to link anything up.

But to hear Alys go for it, I'd fuckin defy *you* not to flip out.

The letter Mrs Lovell wrote, the noises she heard. All there, all valid. The figure on the lawn – just as it should be, almost. Yes, that's what it was: the last hours of the transfigured victim in the next rise of Actaeon. Almost.

According to Alys's theory, that was the night when something finished going horribly wrong. And it's something that started going horribly wrong *on my watch*.

'I meant it, Noah. Do not, under any circumstances attempt discreet observations of that woman!'

It's mutated, she reckons. Those last minutes when Alys was still in my flat, still present, are flitting through my head as I try to put things in order. These things come around in cycles, she says. Her time with druids and other *people in touch* has taught her to see.

What can you say to any of that when it comes at you?

And before you think telling the person to fuck off is the best way, how does that predicament change when you've got *these photos* in front of your eyes?

'Thing is,' she says, 'when this happens' – and she's learning to see the cycle, to know when the story's next due to recur – 'there's *always a lesson to be learnt*.' It's part of the revolving sequence of human society. Civilisation taking a message from the primeval, from the atavistic. From its source.

Always a lesson, she says, over and over. And it's the duty of whoever picks it up to learn that lesson. And to try and pass it on. It's fate, Noah. Can't be moved. Or changed.

'Noah,' looking me right in the eye, one of the last things she said before I couldn't take any more of it. 'Noah. Mr Lovell killed his own wife. And Mrs Lovell always knew he would.

They've tried to escape the cycle. Instead of being the only victim, he's attacked her as if going after the source. He's been punished for it, too. Punished for the hunt.'

Torn by his own hounds. Eaten.

'So the noises – they were being made by someone?'

Maybe. Not definite. There are bits still filling in. Could be her senses warning her. Telling her what he'd done. Possibly a symbol. Her choice of motif.

But the damage done to the cycle – by annihilating her like that. It could be immense.

Then I'm sneering, and she's racing ahead. Why do you think Mrs Lovell contacted Whiteout? She brought us into it. Nothing held back now, Alys is telling me the whole theory laid bare. I'm like her. I looked into that house when I wasn't allowed. Out of me and Starsky, one of us was gonna get drawn in, and since it looks like I can see it, then I now have to act. Have to do something about what I can hear happening. Because Haydn Greggs is already doing that. And he might not be the only one, so she says.

And you don't always survive it either, she reckons. 'From my experience,' says Alys, 'being able to see this happen can even mean violence for the person who picks up the trail.'

I'm telling her to stop. But she doesn't give a shit for that anymore. All those other guys, everyone from the company reports. Every single soul that helped to torment and spy on that woman in the run-in to her last night. They could all be in line for whatever the rising tide wants to do with them.

Could even be Greggs, though, who'll get it. He's clearly been tuned in for longer. *But that is what's going on, no doubt at all, Noah.* It's what happened to someone else she knew, too. *Or someone she didn't quite get to know...*

I cut her off before too much is said, and it's gonna become even harder to tell her what I need to tell her.

So you're involved, she says. *Along with me. You have to be now.*

Not if we don't accept it, I tell her.

You're not like that, Noah.

How do you know?

I know.

What if I've changed?

She looks squarely at me, and I can see right away there's no friendship in her mind now, nothing that could dilute how she's expecting me to just take this all on. My value to her has only ever been this.

'If I'm supposed to be understanding something here, then I'm not,' I tell her.

You will.

She says it with no sentiment. It's not even an order. It's just conveying something she says I can't do anything about.

Really? Alys? Challenging *me* – to be what I don't want?

So, yes, I run.

Fuck it, I'm happy with that. It's the right thing to do. Just can't see why I didn't make that decision sooner. Whiteout Investigations Ltd, Hideous Whateveritis Ltd, these games, mutations, these dependencies, the lot. All got to go. What was that about not pushing it too far? Yeah, I know. Tell it to someone else.

What with these big jobs, expenses, advances and all that, I might have got my fund together, see. Miss Clare – she paid what it was worth. So like you say, better not take too much more. No one's gonna be punishing *my* greed. Somewhere else is flying up my list of priorities. *That* is what it was worth, and yes, Alys, I do know what to do next. And it's not anything you're ever going to ask of me.

He knows it's been coming, so it's official notice to Starsky, time to look for a new apprentice. It was always the arrangement. When your brain pops that's all there is, he used to say. You know when you're out and no one should ever tune you back from that.

It takes no time at all – just a day. Cash-in everything people owe, including my second retainer from Miss Clare – bollocks to her, eh? – and almost before the thought train is done I'm facing up to the one bit that's hard.

Little Josie is gonna say her goodbye without knowing it. That's the plan, but when I wave her off, on the road with Mum again, she can tell something's up. My mum's not fretting it at all – she's been told where I'm headed, that I want to be gone before they get back, and she kind of doubts my resolve. Either that or she's not attached enough. So she leaves for a four-day stint of sales meetings the same way she usually does – going back into the house to fetch extra things she's forgotten and to make a phone call. But Josie, belted into the passenger seat is questioning why her big brother on the pavement isn't walking off until the car they're in pulls away. That's not normal and she knows it. Scarface is out in the street and hasn't done a runner, and I give him no attention because I just keep waving at her. It's all taking too long. When Mum gets behind the wheel and starts pulling out into the traffic the girl's mouth trembles just enough for me to see.

Why's Noah gonna watch us right out into the traffic and off around the corner? She knows why. It's printed on her face – like it must have been on mine.

Josie asked, so now I wonder, almost enough for doubt to creep in, where Alys is right now. But I have to toughen up here. The stakes are too high now. People have to look after themselves or they'll have nothing. And I'm only gonna be this bullshit *one who hears* if I want to. You know... the Alys thing... maybe there will be consequences of the total let down

I've sent her way. But again, I don't think about it for long enough to feel perturbed. What else did she expect I would do? Some intuition she had if she thought *Noah* would fit into a nasty recurrent game of life and death. Would be laughable if it wasn't being said, thought and acted out by a real person. Or someone who tries to be a real person, anyway.

Clouds draw over the town a day later, and then a front finally comes in. Night falls – my last in the Crawl. I'm back in the office at my nearly empty desk, wrapping up the last of the Whiteout papers.

'Lift back?' asks Starsky. But it's cold out – first time in months – so I decide to walk home and punish myself.

'Noah, mate,' he says as I'm passing over my keys and ID card. 'I've always said it. Do whatever you have to. There's never gonna be any hard feelings here.'

But I know a caveat is coming up: 'You should take a minute, though,' he goes on. 'Just one minute, to think about the other people besides me. Don't get me wrong, matey, I ain't sayin for a second that you don't make good judgements, alright? I know you think things over. But trust me, I've seen boys think they want one thing when they really want something else.'

'It's not about what I want,' I snap back to him. 'It's about what I need.'

'Alright matey,' he says raising his hand in peace. 'That's all. You even said it. Needs. We all have em. And most require us to build things in the end. With the other people in our lives – and I ain't talkin about Whiteout – you know that. I know I often tell ya something completely different. Right?' He raises an eyebrow, and then adds, 'It ain't that simple though, matey. If it was I'd be a lot happier and life would be a lot easier for me than it is.'

He thinks his words back over, as if checking whether to take them back, then he says, 'Keep in touch'.

I nod, and head out into the clear air.

Summer? It's gone already, coz this is a proper chill. It nearly reminds me of the frosty nights the Crawl will have in a few more months – air that stings your windpipe as you breathe it in. Makes you really *feel* the deep, colourless precipice of blank universe all around you. Sun tucked round the other side of the planet, you're staring straight at emptiness and absolute zero when looking into a winter sky in Wales.

Now though, high-season Swansea begins to glitter at me from across the bay, through the thinning, night atmosphere. I love how you see it like that – quite easily as rows of lights, only fifteen miles away. You're an onlooker, but yet kind of connected to the place. Whatever happens there you're seeing in real time. And over the way, those cliffside towns where Alys's mystery father came from. There's specks of flickering light there too. Stories set by true-life people who are going about their thing in the exact present.

But stretch your eyesight up to the stars, I think. Wait for the steam from your breath to fade, and it's another story.

I do it now, as the realisation of where I'm going arrives.

Just the tiniest tilt of the neck upwards, and there it all is, overhead; more real places, but fucking light years away, and yet they look the same. Out front... Streetlamps on Townhill. *Twinkle-twinkle.* Look back up... Uber-massive-epic nebula of some kind. *Twinkle-twinkle* just as much. Or little.

My mind moves. Really, this is all over a few utterly minute shots of a man and some dead flesh in a London alley. Come on, Noah, compare its significance in our jumped up little world to what must go on elsewhere in the *universe*. What does it mean against all that? Against all that we don't know? Fuck all, that's what, and yet those still, digital frames of some insignificant moment, frozen as if they were the be-all and end-all, are telling me how to act.

I pick one point of diamond starlight in the blackness overhead. Probably a blast that could easily puff out not only Planet Earth but our entire galaxy and a million like it. Cities like Lynmouth or Swansea or London a million, grillion times over.

The ocean pushes its scent all around, and its sound. There's this sweet frustration in it. The doldrums of late summer, early autumn. It wants to bust out, to come to life again with the freedom and violence of our journey back away from the sun.

The day I leave there's that cloud outside my window again. And, like before, two magpies – or that's what they look like at least – are perched right on it, no different. I watch them wade gently along to the edge again, before one flies off. When I look again just before dark it's landed back there – along with two more. It meant something last time, I think.

This time though, it's not getting another moment. I'm gone. Whatever wants me to dance to its little beat can forget it. Noah's *out*.

AUTUMN

10

Pointbreak at the end of the road

Ashes from fires lit in the huts overnight smoulder through clear air. Wood smoke carries hints of cooking oil and some spice I don't yet know the name of. Dawn is just swelling into the horizon beyond the dry hills inland, and cold air is made colder still by the offshore wind pulled up from the valley overnight. A rooster breaks the silence, soon echoed from across the sand and brush, as I tread over uneven ground, across walls of buildings half-finished, towards the warm ocean which in a few hours' time will be deep blue and ready to help the sun heat the land.

I've been here long enough to have arrived. At the edge is the sound of sea gnawing away at shore.

Suck, lift... thump, dredge. The routine swishes its way into your head. Rhythms of waves tick time away, monotone, comforting, dissipating. As good a master as any.

I remember how out of place I was arriving a month ago to these same smells and cycles. Red-eyed from days of overland travel, everyone else looking so fresh and with it. The bus dropped me at the little metal post on the outskirts, painted white with red letters: *Fortinoume*. End of the road for Noah.

Long old journey too, and tough. I've left my car with a mate who lives two days' of dusty driving up the coast. He ran off this way years ago, well ahead of his time. What were the rest of us thinking? This is how to deal with modern life. He's halfway between Rabat and Casablanca, and can hold my stuff for as long as it takes me to set up base further down here. Perfect arrangement. It would be hard enough pegging me down to his address in a country like this. But here? Well, I'm off that radar for good.

And guess what else? Only rented for now, but I've done it – that orange-tiled roof and sea view. And yes, it overlooks a pointbreak. So I'm set.

The thing that really amuses me though is the way my own mind speaks to itself here. *You'll have to give this up some day, Noah*, it says, *it doesn't work to just stay away.*

Wanna bet? I'll make it work. It's why I did what I did for so long. I was always coming here. Don't be disappointed in me. It's all I ever promised to do.

A month in, and not even missing the car. No need yet.

Ever wanted to see if you really could disappear? As in go somewhere, without a trace?

I can take a morning bus trip somewhere wonky to draw my travellers' cheques, hide cash under a tile, live it simple and wait for whatever's gonna become me in the next life.

Of course it's gonna work. Watch me. No one goes after Noah.

Fortinoume, nestled down here towards the lines that matter if you like it warm, gets its swells from the angry waters off Greenland and Canada, thousands of miles away. Here it is; the place that shouldn't exist – serenity that draws from somewhere else's anger. There's a crew of about twenty foreigners living here and everyone else is only just realising what surfing is.

I'm out every morning, and this place has been tapping my soul already. Even if I've never been one of those guys who properly *rips*, that doesn't mean I can't love the glide as much as anyone else.

And, out at the point in Fortinoume it's the purest music. The ocean seems to tell you how to ride these waves – when to run high, when to hook your weight back.

Shimmering through the glassy surface, daily swell lines wrap in from the miles of cliff-faced coast to the north, bending into the bay as stretched-out gold. If you look from up in the mountains behind, as I have already, the whole thing is a slow-motion machine – each cog turning and churning, celestially slow yet certain in its cycle. The point has drawn us all because it does what so many others don't. Each wave rises mechanically, then jacks over a little slab of rock. And then they reel, silt-patched and cylindrical, down towards an expanse of flat sands filled with beached fishing boats, cooled ash piles and thin round trees that shouldn't be there.

When you're down below, and in it, it's a movement that consumes you, whole. Which is exactly what you'll want it to do.

It's late September now, when the Crawl would be getting chilly even in the day time, when you'd get that feeling the sun has turned away for good. But, here, we're still getting days when even the wind carries a heat dry enough to tighten the skin on your face as you drift off on a veranda. As was the plan, my body stays warm, while the mind is cooled only by that same *suck, lift… thump* and the faint piping of a pair of wooden wind chimes. It's my space. I'm simple at heart see, but hey, this is Noah's happily-ever-after, now. And I'm gonna rinse it for all I can.

That warm ocean out front is going to pipe a tune back at us any day soon, too. Because now is the time when the balance shifts, the stability fades away – when those early season tasters of winter rage will start.

It doesn't matter whether I've got one more of those revolutions left in me, or sixty-one. Which is exactly the idea.

Nothing to lose, nothing to gain. Neutral. Ticking time off. Going through the motions until my end. Nobody could tire of this existence.

Next door is a pad that belongs to some middle-aged couple from Florida, who no one in the village has ever seen – but their kids come here about half the year and are real mellow people – even if they're obviously stinkin rich. The son, Pat, has to be about my age, and he's got a twin sister, Sarah, who's half an hour older – and it shows. Both of them are pretty switched on to the local psyche too… well, as switched on as you can be buying sea-front land with American dollars in a fishing village that's hardly changed for hundreds of years. Mind you, I can't really talk either. I might only be renting so far, but the dilemma will come.

'Learn a bit of Berber,' Sarah keeps telling me.

'*Insha'Allah.*'

It's all I know so far – means God willing. And it's Arabic, although I'm working on understanding what the difference is.

Both Sarah and Pat have got this open-eyed, freckly blond look that you can only really get if you're raised around warm beaches, and seem to be able to take an interest in anything. Sarah sees the good side of everybody she knows, and Pat is pretty helpful too – each time they introduce you to someone it's along with about five reasons why you're gonna like the person. Both these two are here for the winter now, mainly because they're hopelessly hooked on surfing. That's all you need to connect with people in a place like this. Plus, Sarah and Pat are all about face value. They never ask who I was before, or why I'm here – mainly because they know how simple the answer probably is.

But the best thing of all about them is they have this pet monkey, which is some kind of orangey thing that I've never seen before – 'Roy', its name is. He hangs off the cover to my veranda late morning every day, one handed, casting this crazy simian silhouette across the climbing sun. His appearance serves to tell me Pat and Sarah are back from a dawn session in the point for breakfast. Decent enough routine for an animal – although that must all change for the worse when the twins are away and their mate Lyndon house-sits. Because he is a first-class tosser.

Yes, there is one here too. The place had to have them, eh? It keeps life interesting anyway – maintains a balance, an equilibrium. The thing that baffles me is how they can't see it – but then maybe it's actually the other way round. Maybe he sees through me in a way my new neighbours don't.

Judge for yourself. When I asked the prick where he came from he replied, all cagey, 'Why does it matter?'

'Well, just interested,' I said, diffusive but not backing down.

And then he paused, and replied, slow and deliberate, 'British *passport.*'

I fire back 'God's Land' to the same question from him, and once he finds out that means Wales he sneers and turns away.

Lyndon doesn't get called Lyndon either. He gets called… wait for it… 'GWS'. Again, what the fuck? Well, apparently it means Great White Shark. As in he tops the food chain in Fortinoume. Well, the surfy bit of it anyway. In other words he likes to think there's a pecking order at the point, and that it's his show to conduct. Came out with some quality bollocks when I first met him, too. 'Living things have different value,' he reckons. 'One shark can swallow up any smaller creature to sustain itself and it's no biggie. Thousands of smaller fish… and they all won't ever come close to the value of keeping the bigger one going.'

Then he looked at me and said, 'But it never works the other way. That's important. You can't revolt against nature, bro.'

Quite why that bit had to be aimed at newbie little Noah… well, who gives a shit anyway?

He *might* have taken against me though, I'm thinking, coz of Sarah. You can see the way the prick looks at her. There's no doubt he's wildly mistaken, but her inability to spot it lets him think there's something there. Twin brother is easy going and of the same bloodline, so Noah is the only or main threat. You can hear him grinding the idea around.

Only other time I spoke to 'GWS' with no one around he started telling me how he peeps on her showering out in the back garden, and that she knows he's doing it.

'She's into me, see, Noah, so don't get any ideas there, small fish. The one thing not to be in this town is on the edge of the bait ball. Stay in the middle, and you'll swim for as long as you want.'

None of this really matters though. We're all on the same agenda. Waiting for the seasons to flip, the serious swells to show up. It always happens in surf towns like this – you get plenty of time to over-think stuff, sussing each other out in the small world that exists on land before the call comes in, and forces beyond us are going to lay out their own order. Or *dis*order, even.

Like clockwork, day after solstice, the first of those deep oceanic depressions shows up, spiralling across the Atlantic and word is about in Fortinoume that the shift is going to take place. Swell is on the way.

I'm paddling out one morning, from alongside this old wall that used to be some kind of mooring quay just inside a little inlet. And it's all the voices around me are talking about.

'Eight to ten foot at fifteen seconds, man. Can't wait to see how the inside section will drain once those waves start running down it.'

'Yeah, and we've got low tides too. Shallow banks down there. Fast takeoffs too.'

The butterflies are everywhere, and I'm starting to see it. This is gonna be the new challenge in Noah's life. And it can take all the time I've got left. Even then, that's the beauty of chasing waves – you'll never quite get there. But as long as you realise it, as long as you know your place, the harmony will find a role for you.

'Ah, lookout! Hey, GWS, where d'you get that done?' Someone's calling across, where Lyndon's arriving with a freshly shaved mohawk in the middle of his head.

'Yeah. My new hairdo for the swell, when it gets here.'

Faces growing more familiar to me, I drift towards where this little current will pull us to the top of the point. Pat's telling me about another spot ten minutes north that can sometimes break in huge conditions – says we can go there one morning if it happens. One day of calm before the pulse kicks in. High-angle sunlight raises the colour out of everything. Looking back from out here I see the way the great hills behind Fortinoume drop so suddenly down to sea level. Ridges of rock and scree run across, and then down, chiselling angles into a landscape dreamt up by some cartoonist.

'The mountain range is insane, huh?' says Pat, watching my gaze. 'Jacked up some time before all of us, man. When water and fire shaped things for themselves.'

Dainty and grateful, the buildings of the town hug in close to the incline. Dark oranges and dry greens of the land contrast the bright pastels of the tall buildings that sit improbably on top of each other. A chance deposit, clinging precariously between extremes of mountain and brooding ocean. The beauty of it, the symmetry and order. And all just chance and happenstance. No design or fate in this. Makes me want to pinch myself.

We get a day of it, warm still, with waves like I've never seen in my life. Before dawn breaks I can tell the energy is here.

Big day starts like all the others – call of the roosters, fading wood-flavoured smoke from huts on the edge of the beach. But this time walls of water are marching, with constant, consistent pace, to the top of the point. Rising sunlight begins to bleach the horizon a lighter shade of orange, until the spectrum breaks into daytime and I see waves, a few hundred yards out, starting to feel the seabed. Contours beneath the ocean coax the swell out of its unthinking, plodding journey across deep water, awakening the energy. Waves queue, one after the other, to unload – each grinding its way with uniform power from the rounded boulders and ledges at the top of the point, right through to the horseshoe bay. Even dry sand, under the fishing ribs dragged ashore for their own safety, can feel the seismic leftovers as rolls of whitewater explode up the shoreline.

When you ride one of these it *charges* you. It's all I can do to draw a line straight enough and quick enough to stay ahead. I'm in the storm, even if it's continents away, and no longer extant. This is how to live forever. A moment in which you're locked to the surface, yet lost in freefall. *This* is what I was willing to hear. I'm lost in it now, I think to myself, and nothing will find me unless I want it to.

But then, day two of the swell, the weather turns, and with it, as if dragged down by the howling, salty winds that follow, is the odour of all I've left behind. That easily, the flick of a switch, and it's back. It can't be Alys's doing – she wouldn't – but just as I'm pumping up to take on the really serious end of this surging pulse, the crap comes calling. Exactly like I said it couldn't.

→

It starts in the night. After hours in the water, straining every drop of energy from myself, I'm asleep deep and early – plunging fast and helpless into a horrible, satanic dream. Another one, yeah. Ages since anything like this has happened, but it drags up the visions I've had before. Not for the first time I'm fighting again. It's not Greggs, not any person I've ever served or had aggro off before, not those coppers, not this GWS bellend with the stupid mohawk – yet some or all of the above are there somewhere. I can feel them. Some prick – who's an embodiment of everything wrong – is just beyond my sight and I'm clawing at him through wet mist, darkness and then rain that never falls but hangs in the air around, bouncing off my fists. It's violent as fuck. I can feel my knuckles caving in as I slam away at someone who's still in total control. Then blows come back at me, and a streetlamp catches my eyes dead on, just before I'm about to see who this is.

Still asleep, still in my furious slumber, someone else cracks me across the shoulder blades, and as I fall I do glimpse a face – through the blackening blood that's running over my vision from split eyebrows – and it *is* Haydn Greggs, but then when I stumble up again it's not. I swing, and there's no one there but a voice laughing and saying 'You think you know me?' and then I'm awake.

It's half an hour before dawn and the door's knocking.

This is fucked, I think.

And it thuds again. Someone who isn't going away.

'Waves are pumping. Let's get out there before sunrise,' GWS says to me once I decide there isn't gonna be some Ghost of Noah Past at the door and actually pluck up the sack to open it.

He's flexing his shoulders, and has his gear all ready to go – a thin, short-arm wetsuit slung over his shoulder and a round-pintail board that will hold an edge on anything the point can throw at us.

'The twins are over it,' he says to me. 'They're waiting for the tide to drop back.'

Probably the right decision, I think, tuning my ear to the whacking of a deep-water backwash against the soaking rocks just out front. But it's not what I opt to do. So what if GWS is calling on me to be his dawn patrol wingman just because his usual accomplices are out of action? This is a chance to learn – to get a read on the fucker.

And he's obviously seeing the same thing. The moment I say OK he's through my door, spreading his stuff around.

'Wetsuits on indoors, I reckon,' he says, wrapping a towel round his waist and not waiting for any cue. He's got neoprene up to his waist before I've even found mine. As he pulls his top half on I see rows of rib-muscles and the sinews of his shoulders twitching. This guy has the strength of someone who's fought the sea every day for a decade.

We jump off the point as the orangey yellow of imminent sunlight starts to stain the horizon and each get on a frothy, bumpy, high-tide set-wave straight away. It doesn't get far down the point before I want to kick off, so it's a paddle back up – whereas all day yesterday I was walking it.

Sunrise never quite shows, coz dark, soaking clouds are everywhere, and with them an uneven, whipping breeze that scuffs the sea surface and makes the waves irritable.

GWS is just behind me as we arrive out back again, together. No conversation, because the need isn't there.

When the tide starts pulling back I look to land and can see Roy the monkey, swinging one-handed off my porch – meaning Pat and Sarah are about. Before long the lineup has filled with all the regulars, but the ocean's mood is in all of us and nobody talks. Not a word from anyone – no room for anything but contemplation.

And that's when it starts happening to me by day, too.

I duck-dive a cleanup set, and as I'm underwater and seeing everything in front of me get darker and darker through the deep red of my eyelids, a face, covered in blood suddenly grimaces at me, out of my own head.

Instinct pulls my eyes open and they fill with salt. When I come up my knuckles are feeling the pain of what I did in my sleep. Next time I put my head under, it happens again. It's the face from last night. The face I think I know.

I try to shrug this off, but it's all turned on me now, and next time I ride a wave I can't even register what I'm doing – can't feel any of the bliss I should be lost in by now. It's all shot, lost, interrupted and the ocean wants me out.

GWS's gear has gone when I get back to shore, but this monkey is sitting on a wooden post in front of my window, and I watch his red fur catch and rise in the wind. He looks at me and wraps his spindly, humanoid arms around himself in a hug. It's still not cold, you know, as in Crawl cold, but he looks like he wants to be somewhere else.

You're not the only one Roy, I go to think, but arrest it just in time.

GWS must have let himself in to get his clothes – although I thought he was still in the water.

When the twins get back for lunch they can't lift me at all, and I'm left hoping they won't notice. I try to surf again at dusk, and it's the same. If I duck underwater, the faces flash at me, as if they're encoded into the pull of each wave from under the surface.

And then it gets more fucked still, when I find out the Great White Shark doesn't exist.

Sunset drags peaky shadows back up the valley behind Fourtinoume – same gradual trickle of receding colour that flushes up the opposite slopes most mornings. Striped fronts coming in off the ocean can't cover us all day, so a gap in the atmosphere lets me see the moment when cliffs to the north-east slowly coax the burning ball out of sight, and off towards America and the Caribbean to our west. Then the sky closes again, that roof of suspended water is back over us, and the red light bounces against itself. Rows of ploughed mackerel cloud shine an intermittent purple before, turning indoors, I know night has arrived.

It's when I step round next door to where Pat and Sarah are living – simple invitation, nothing out of the ordinary, a sundown beer and some stew – that a conversation unfolds which makes it pretty obvious what the GWS situation is.

I've simply made this dude up.

It starts with them saying it was odd that I went out so early this morning on my own without the tide being right. 'You must have been super keen for a taste of it to do that,' Pat's saying, as my head reels and, just in the nick of time, I manage to stop myself saying *I wasn't alone. GWS came to get me.*

Then they both tell me again how they saw me go, and it should have been so fuckin clear there was someone with me, and instead they're so fuckin clear that there wasn't. So I start to lead the conversation through things that should make them talk about him directly. *So who's the longest to live here out of all the blow-ins? How do you go about learning Berber? D'you know anyone who's done it?* And it's definite. There's not even a hole left by him. No question. It's not just coincidences, no consecutive flukes of meaning. It's not that he's off topic for any reason. There isn't any mention because the guy doesn't, and never has, existed.

But that's in *their* world. Coz in Noah's he's getting more real by the minute. When I stumble round to my front door again in the dark, wishing I had a torch for the ten-yard hop over uneven walls and boulders, I'm hardly surprised when there's a figure by my gate. That mohawk rises from the head and shoulders of the silhouette leaning against the fencepost two paces away from my front door. He's standing there, arms folded. I walk into him, expecting the outline to phase out as I get nearer, but it doesn't. This is a living, breathing person, tangible and looking at me with victory on his face.

'Think you know me, eh?' he gloats as I change my angle of approach to walk past. I fumble for my key, trying to ignore him, but he takes a step closer and says '*I'm* the only one in the know here. I'm the custodian, man.'

'Get off,' I say back. My words are amplified by the low-visibility and by the fact I don't want to be heard by anyone else. *Yeah, that's Noah talking to himself*, I can hear Pat and Sarah saying any second now. So I whisper it again, 'Fucking get off', and he moves as if to grab me but I try to stand square to him, try to send him away with eyes that mean business. 'Leave me alone, man.'

Once I've locked up I look outside again. The moon has just set, red, so the night can still hide things in shadow – although you can see the lines of whitewater piling down the point, ready to greet us all in the morning. Well – ready to greet those of us who are interested.

Sleep. Something I was getting in abundance forty-eight hours ago now seems a distant concept, like my own childhood – something that must have happened because I'm the evidence, but which is so alien to the here-and-now that it causes all sorts of screwed up ideas of bending space and time to drift through my head.

But I don't want ideas drifting through my head. I want the nothingness I came for. I want out of this cycle.

The door knocks again before dawn and I ignore it.

Thump-thump-thump. Now I'm really off colour.

It repeats in bursts until day is firmly in control, and now I'm thinking it's just me, and I shouldn't give in to nonsense from inside my own head. It always works that way doesn't it? Further you get into daytime and the more distant the horrors of a bad night will seem. Trouble is it also works in reverse – once you're back in those small hours with your eyes wide as saucers staring into nothing, you can't even imagine ever seeing early afternoon again.

At about nine I offer excuses to Pat and Sarah when they come past suited up with boards under arm. Feeling a little creaky, gonna stretch a bit, I'll see them out there. But by mid-morning when Roy's shadow swings over my front window I'm just a mess again. I'm done with seeing – for me now it's all about trying to hear again. I just hope I haven't lost it. The voice that could help in all of this.

Face up to it, comes Alys's advice, as if carried on the salty wind. *Fears concentrate to a single point.*

And then I hear other wisdom that didn't seem anything like it at the time. Do what I have to. No hard feelings. *We think we want one thing when we really want something else.* And anyway, where did 'want' come into this? Coz really it *should be about need* – and not just mine. That way lies peace – I can sniff it somewhere through a deep labyrinth of duty and tribulations yet to be faced.

But face them I will. Noah, *you've come here too soon.*

Emptiness arrives. No thoughts, no voices, and my ear picks up, once more, the soft tones of those wind-chimes. I close my eyes, and feel Fortinoume regress, fall away.

And I'm in *that house*. The Void in the Vale.

It's so quiet in here that any movement gives off sound waves you can feel with every nerve ending. There's something around so heavy it must be more than just air. It's warm too – *lived-in* warm. I can see that long corridor that me and Starsky stood in months ago, and like before there's that light coming from just around the turning. It's got a glow that's weak but deep at the centre – not caused by anything electric. If it's a lamp then it must be flame in there, but it's too steady – no flickering.

As soon as I start tip-toeing towards it I have to stop. Each step pushes noise throughout the hall, noise which lingers. This isn't an echo either, it's as if sounds are soaking into the atmosphere around, as if they can't escape. My skin breaks instantly into a sweat, which throbs up and down from my temples with even, rhythmic surges. If sound can't escape this place what chance have *I* got?

Drop the cautious act, Noah, and keep moving. I listen to my own order, and try again to put one foot in front of the other, steady, careful, certain, without regret. Each step fills the air again, and as I move faster it gets thicker and heavier – to where it seems impossible to push forward the last few paces to that turn in the corridor.

I can see the light now, trembling slightly against some sort of interference. It gets more agitated as I approach closer. And that's when the noises start. First there's a ticking, as if someone's turned a Geiger counter on, but then it turns to a beeping, keeping pace in the background while other vibrations and impacts take their turn to be heard. Between the deep, threatening sounds that wallop off the walls I recognise that whirring, encircling effect that came at me when I watched Greggs and Mr Lovell meet in Ealing, and behind it – yes *behind it* – as if these sound waves were some kind of foot-soldier army pushing ahead for their commanders to exploit space behind, there comes a whisper. I can only hear the hissing parts of its words, but soon those gaps are gonna fill and whatever this place is trying to tell me will come across. Noah, moments from getting the full brunt of it... which is what I think I want.

But I'm learning. I know now that whatever I want is only gonna be a distraction. What I *need* is to put this off for one last time. I will hear – but not here, and now – not on these terms. I'll hear, in the way and time and place that others need me to.

It's gonna take a big push to get through, but I go. I aim for that shaky brightness, focus on a point in its centre and drive forward. The air around tries to grab me, it's humid, then damp. Through steam and something else I shove onwards, as the noises try to force me back. Almost there, intensity rising, Noah breaks through it and out.

It's got to be just before dawn again. I can't see a watch or clock anywhere, but the stillness in the room is matched by stillness outside. I wonder if the swell has dropped already, because even the sea in Fortinoume seems asleep.

Nothing has come for me yet. There's no one here to wake me, nobody at the door. Pretty soon I've got eyes for this darkness and can pick my way around enough to fill up two bags with the things that will keep me me. Cash is ready, passport and driving licence. Rent is paid ahead so that's not gonna bring me any bad karma – if such a thing exists beyond imagined importance that Starsky taught me to overwrite years ago. I don't need to leave messages for the people I've come to like here. Once this has all gone right I can return anyway – if I ever find the need for it.

The first heralding rooster calls must be near, and I think I can see the fading-out stripe of the Milky Way starting to give way in the east. Soon comes the saving light of the one local star that keeps all these circles in motion.

There might just be time. Fortinoume has one road in and one road out. The Berber, its real locals, start their day early. There's gonna be someone around to give me a lift, and from there the main routes north will be easy to get onto.

With my back turned to it, I strain my ears enough to make out a set of three or four long waves grinding down the point in the dissolving dark. Like they have done since before people came here, and like they will long after our importance has run out. I think about how familiar these sounds may or may not be, if and when I ever hear them again, as I lower my shoulders slightly under the weight of two bags and a board, and walk faster the wrong way up the only road in.

11

Offshore

Dust spins off my tyres and fills my mirrors, piling layers between me and what's behind. Or in front. Chasing, waiting – whatever – there's no use ignoring, so I hold a steady pace up through arid landscapes. Scrubland and small palms cling to hills of rock and thinning dust. Pinker shades of irrigated topsoil look as if they've been sprayed on with a paint can – strips masked out by tape to make farmers think it's theirs.

But I'm only looking sideways to stay within the lines of the road, which turns and kinks gradually this way and that. Doesn't bother me, as long as my dot is tracking onwards, ahead.

Southern Spain breaks to Central, breaks to North, and then I'm on the Basque coast. The Pyrenees notice me – hoped to sneak through on the quiet – and throw an hour of rain straight down. Wiper blades push torrents out the way, as Noah's ever-onward slows to a nearly. But still I push ahead; border? What border? I'm out of two countries now, getting across that continent, raising my latitude back to where I belong. The night comes with more rain, and I stop for an hour of sleep in a forest layby. Pines overhead ease the tapping of water from the sky, and soon that single hour becomes four, or five.

Before dawn, I'm moving again. Nothing to be spared here.

Cyberspace, satellites, the systems of the modern world; they know Noah's back by now, less than a hundred seconds on my mobile phone under a canopy of steel and thumping hailstones has given me away to whoever cares. A hundred seconds in which my trajectory tries to resolve itself even more.

It's already mid-morning, fourth day on the move, when Bordeaux's ring road rolls into view, and I'm still pretending to only play with the idea. Even after that it's not really yet a full-on commitment to the cause. The road back to that big, easy, northbound run of Poitiers, Tours, Le Mans etcetera is still just one wrong turn away – as this whole screaming, crawling mess always has been. But then I see signs for La Rochelle, and then Nantes turns to Rennes turns to St Malo and now the path really is clear, and there's no going back.

There's a morning ferry to Jersey, gets in at St Helier, which will have me there before the place is barely waking. It's so close I could fuckin swim it.

'Good afternoon. Reception.' It was that young lad from last time – what was his name... Joel! Yeah, that's it. Joel! And just like last time his tone is helpful, doing his best to come across low-key and pleasant. Not his fault he answers phones and holds guests for the anti-Christ.

'Hi, is that Kinsella House?' I asked, as if the answer was gonna be anything else. I don't get numbers wrong when I dial them, but for some reason you always end up asking the obvious on calls like this.

'It is.'

'OK, cool. Can I speak to Mr Lovell please?'

'I'm sorry, who?'

'Brian Lovell? Hideous CnC?'

You could sense the unease over the line – or could you? Would Joel really have any idea?

'Erm, he's left Hideous,' came the reply. 'I'm afraid I don't have a forwarding number or address to give you.'

'OK then, what about Mr Greggs? Is he about? Haydn's still there, right?'

Back on more comfortable territory. For the receptionist, at least.

'Er, yes, Mr Greggs is still based here, but not today. Can I ask who's calling?'

I was 'Geraint' last time – and since it was pretty likely Joel would remember me from that shit, Noah's voice had to be kept to a minimum. I tried to think of a name that could mean... something.

'GWS & Co.'

'OK. Well I can either take a message, or you could probably reach him at the St Helier office if he hasn't left for the day yet. You've got the number, I'd assume.'

'Yes, of course. Thanks. Will do.'

'No problem Mr...' and I'd hung up.

And then came the doubt. Why did I cut that call off before hearing one word more? *No problem Mr...*

Did I miss the rising intonation of a question then? Was that all it was? Joel, only fishing for my surname – because he didn't know it. I switch off, stop myself from thinking too hard and inventing any other possibility.

Not until I'm there, at least.

It's a calm sea as I cross. The dawn air is thin and sharp. I watch the tide, shifting the ocean from somewhere deep in its soul as the most minute of swell readings rocks gently underneath the boat.

There's hardly any other passengers on board – just a few white-van-men and some middle-aged couple in an old car. I buy the shittest coffee in the universe and try to hide its taste with a wrapped-up biscuit, before wandering back on deck.

Land is all around, but still it's the water that's in charge. The island of Jersey appears, with permission. That's what we all need to remember. I'm arriving offshore, but only at the mercy of all this.

One set, three or four waves, a bit bigger, more spaced out than the others, shifts its way up the channel and lifts me. I feel it, right there, organised, distanced, weary but ready, as the open-ocean disappears and we set up to dock.

Again now, the call I made runs through my mind. So little to work from and so many questions to ask myself. Enjoy it while it lasts, coz here is Noah, for the first time ever, going for it without knowing what he's doing.

Yeah, believe that, I tell myself. *None of us have ever known really, have we?*

I want to contact someone, Starsky, Alys... even Mum and little sis. Touch base. Hear real voices of real people. But that would be giving in. First I have to hear myself.

It's been something like a hundred hours, I've slept for part of one night and some other half hour stints in the spaces next to the petrol pumps, and now here come the turrets and powerhosed promenades of St Helier. It's the same delirious state that dropped me in Fortinoume and I remember how alien that aroma of the woodsmoke was to me then, and the sweet dry air out of the dusty valley. It carried excitement with it – and promise too.

Realisation comes with a groan. I'm back north, up towards the sanitised, wintered top of the continent. There's intermittent autumn light getting through, but the great patches of cloud that keep floating overhead are all that counts. No alluring unfamiliarity, the Atlantic looks like the ocean I've known all my life. No such promises in the landscape now. Architects have done their best, but where I'm going is about more than the bricks and mortar. Glad to be here? One day, maybe, but for now this is about treading water until the current really hits.

Biggest tides in the world here. I remember the famous fact but not who told me it. Doesn't matter if it's true, anyway. From the seafront, I can see the castle that gets cut off at high water. To go back and forth you have to time it for when the moving current allows, else you're caught in the flooding mudflats. You get two windows a day – maybe one in winter when the light is shorter lived.

I make straight for the address I've got. What else is there to do? Need to seize my own window of opportunity.

Past a row of coffee-shops that are just starting to put their chairs out, at the bottom of a lane with a steep downhill, is a four-storey building. It's got thick walls – like three-foot thick – and has been freshly painted a brilliant white. Tree shade is everywhere, hedges and plants lining a front path. The roof is new, and has five Velux windows running along it. There's three addresses here, and each of them has office space for a couple of companies that use a yellow-gravel carpark around the back.

My thighs are just starting to tighten from no sleep and the downhill walk when I reach the flat ground. I look at all the cars here. None of them familiar – but why would they be? Just getting into the role, I suppose. Meticulous, ready for worst-case scenarios.

'Always do it, Noah,' Starsky used to say. 'Imagine the most far-fetched, fucked up thing that can happen to you on any job you ever do. Run it through in your head. Most important thing you'll ever do Noah.'

'Why?'

'One time, matey, it'll happen. Might be only the one time, but when it does you'll be ready. And not just for that, either. You'll be ready for anything short of the worst, too.'

I remember asking him to do it for me a few times, and he'd always pluck crazy shit out of the air. Trust no one, respect all targets, assume they're a million times more clever and more involved than you'd ever guess. But Haydn Greggs? What unimagined situations would Starsky have me rehearsing now, if he was here, with me, on a recce for this one?

Still. I try it. Who might drive each of these cars? Where could I run to from here? Where could I hide? What would I say if…

Thing is, I'm gonna know what to do anyway.

So is he, Noah.

Early, early doors still. I go to each of the entrances, look below the hanging baskets and scroll through the doorbells.

Not me who should be feeling out of place here anyway, I tell myself as I read through the trading names emblazoned alongside the entrances. Then I find the one I'm after and all the blood in my head suddenly drops straight into the pit of my stomach. I flush fever hot, then my skin hits back with a cold that instantly condenses sweat into the palms of my hands. What they've got written on their plaque can't possibly get you anywhere in the lines of business these fuckers purport to go after.

'Don't matter what companies call themselves, Noah,' comes Starsky's voice back from the days he used to know everything that I'd ever need. 'Just letters on a page to get reg'd. The big dodgy ones, the proper arseholes, go for names that ain't anything to do with who they really are or what they sell and buy.'

I stare at this supposedly meaningless alphabetical combo and wish that was the case now.

'Most of 'em are the missus's initials or the bloody kids. Or just a pair of letters that sound cool or might bring 'em to the top, middle or bottom of a list they want or don't want to stand out on. Don't read anything into it Noah.'

I try to recall what I may have thought when I first saw this name back in London – or rather its abbreviation – when I didn't know what would follow or where it would lead.

'One time,' says Starsky in my head, 'there was this con artist who'd called his company Smartarse Holdings,' and then he laughs – at his own memory. 'Clever bastard. So clever he had to rub our faces in it.'

Nothing clever about this, though.

I need to move. Yes, Noah. It says what it says. Now walk away. Re-adjust. Go and invent more possible scenarios before you take this any further.

Floor 2: Hideous Carcharodon Carcharias

Fucking Latin. And fucking abbreviations.

It's not my scene, all that Classics shit – I only know the odd legal term I've been forced to deal with over the years.

And this.

I know this. The only other phrase I could translate. You kind of can't miss knowing it if you live like me. Nothing to do with the law. It's my other life that means I know these words straight away.

It's the name of something.

Carcharodon carcharias. More commonly known, in lay terms, as the Great White Shark.

I've run from something that existed without me, to something that can't be allowed to exist at all – whatever I do, whatever *anyone* does.

12

The exchange

I'm in too close. Pull back. Widen the perspective. It's the only way to see or hear anything now. My legs, hardly my own anymore, are stepping me backwards, away, out of the heavy air. The words on the plaque retreat, and with them their importance, or my reverence for it.

The voice of logic is back. I'm thirty-plus paces away from that door now under a roof of gently falling leaves, and the pull has weakened again.

There has to be an angle from which I'll see and hear – maybe just a few arcseconds – but it must exist. An angle from which I can slip out of this orbit and be the one pulling instead.

It's crystal clear. *That's why you're here.*

So just wait, Noah. Hold yourself out of motion, and everything else has to adjust – if it wants to keep moving.

Back doing what I know best. I shouldn't be proud, but you can't unlearn these instincts.

Observations post established. Plan of the area in my mind. Only way in and out is under my watch. It's a waiting game that I'll play all day.

Greggs arrives mid-morning, on foot. Either he's staying nearby, or someone's dropped him at the top of the sloping lane. There were the sounds of motors just before he appeared, but it's a pretty well-used through-road, so could be anything.

Even with the toes and gait adjusted for the sharp downhill, you can see his walk. That slight bowing of the legs, deliberate and ingrained. Nice shoes – always watch the shoes! – and an importance in his swagger. Manages to look like he's in a rush and crazy busy, as well as casual; total master of his own day. He does what he wants, and so do you if you want to matter.

I realise it's never left me – not in any place or any time of day – the look of his eyes, tight together and sunken back. His smooth, pinky face and shiny hair, as he waits in that alleyway with the lorry approaching. It's in my head even further back than memory. Along with the sight of his shirt buttons tightening around his midriff as he carries that carcass of whatever or whoever out of a freezer van and into... Fuck, I don't even want to think what happened to that flesh next.

And yet, despite all that I know about this guy, here I am, on his case again.

This time though, there's no camera. No recording equipment. This period of obs is only about the experience.

↗

There's another system out there, you know. I mean *out to sea*. This time of year the ocean will roar an end to every flat spell. Swell has to be coming soon. I can tell.

We're south-facing here and protected by more headlands to the west, but on the seaward side of this island there's probably a few breaking already. Those three long-period waves that lifted and lowered the ferry at dawn probably peaked up nicely somewhere along that coast.

Same three waves are probably gonna roll down the point at Fortinoume in a day or two. Nice thought. I try to work it out – open ocean speed, distance from here to North Africa, what the fetch between those shores and the origin of the low pressure must have been, the convex curve of the swell line across the Atlantic basin.

And then I wonder again why we attach such importance to the here and now. D'you know, most of the waves that have ever broken here, in the entire natural history of the planet, have probably broken in Fortinoume too – and in the Crawl. Before those places were called anything. Before people even went there. Same then, same now. Doesn't matter where you hop on or off, these swells think beyond borders, beyond continents, beyond ages, generations.

Somewhere over that horizon, past more water than you can get your head around, is the twisting torque of the next autumn storm – and when those waves start to march, as their circles grow and shiver across the saltwater swathes, the same thing will happen here, there and *there*. It's inevitable. And it's the source of my comfort.

Swell has to be coming soon. Wherever and whenever Noah is lost, that's the one certainty it can all come back to.

'Carcharodon fuckin carcharias,' I repeat under my breath. G-W-S. Who calls *themselves* something like that? I'm back in the game again now, and searching out the mindset that's helped me rinse these kind of jumped-up tossers over the years.

So let me take a good look at your perfect LINE, I hum to myself, as I have so many hundreds of times before. Less different I can make this feel, less different it's going to be. *So I know just exactly how I don't want mine.*

Mid-afternoon is all I have to wait before Haydn Greggs goes on the move. A couple of hours, tops, after he first enters the building. Sweet.

And it gets better – no car, no buses – he's on foot. Exactly where I want him.

Tunes familiar and important are ticking over in my head as

I slip out of my shadow and feel the thrill of the chase begin. Great White Shark... yeah, OK, mate – if you want to be, suit yourself. We'll just see what that makes *me*.

He needs to be allowed over the incline and around the corner before being picked up – so first off I have to sprint uphill to be sure of tailing him for the rest of his journey. He's walking pretty slowly though, and is still dangerously near when I reach the street and try to hide my thumping breath from passers-by. Falling in quickly to the flow, I start peering, distracted, through the coffee shop windows as I make my way along the same pavement. But my real vision is occupied by one thing only, one ambling figure just in front. Wherever he goes now, he's gonna be taking Noah with him.

Far end of the same street, about five minutes on, and next it's a right turn down another slight slope and we're heading towards the ocean. Late lunch? Could be. Either that or he just likes to take in the sea air with his little carcharodon nostrils.

The tide has pushed water in so far and tight to the island that the whole horizon seems a few inches loftier. Either directly beneath us, or directly above but blinded out by the waning sun, is our planet's moon, bulging this water up. The weight and volume of it all is so much more imposing when it's this blue, and this still. No breeze of any kind has ruffled the surface for days, but Noah knows it's out there – as it always will be, beyond when any of this shit matters.

Greggs is walking quickly towards the end of a seafront block, opposite a marina which has a small construction site at its far corner. Tall boards have been erected to mask out what's inside the plot of land. Whoever's investing in this prime venture is more than happy to advertise what's going up here, though: Luxury apartments that will look out over the moorings; ready soon and sold out to the last one.

In Wales, Starsky made about half his income a few years

back from twats who tried to build one luxury apartment too many near the waterfronts of Cardiff, Swansea, the Crawl and other towns west. Small players. Didn't know when they were out of their league.

Why should that ever stop someone, though?

Greggs slips into a thin gap between the hoardings and with nowhere else obvious to go I have to just walk by.

I try to get a glance in as I pass, but there's another board behind where he entered that hides what's beyond. I keep going and turn the corner, heading back away from the ocean. There's a pub on the opposite side of a swerve in the road. It's been burnt down and is also boarded up, both across its windows and around what must be the property's perimeter.

From here, there needs to be a round-the-block route, somehow, to getting back to the other side of the road and posting up in a credible location. Just stopping or backtracking is not an option. Sussing my surroundings, I can see that next to the marina is a bench from where I'd be able to sit and see the gap Haydn Greggs used to get into the building site. Dashing the long way round is the only sensible way to get there and I'll have to move really fast to be sure he couldn't have slipped out again without being seen.

There's a minute – maybe two at most – in which losing him can't be prevented, but all good foot pursuits need a bit of luck anyway. So as I'm coming round to go over the same bit of promenade again, I have to work on the likely premise he's still in there.

That bench is a hundred metres away now, and it couldn't be more ideal for this purpose. I think of trying to sneak in somewhere to buy a paper – otherwise I'm gonna have to pretend to play with my phone to avoid standing out.

But those details don't end up mattering at all, because when I do get back onto the bit of pavement where I first lost him,

Greggs is standing right there, a stone's throw away, shoulders square, waiting for someone.

And that someone is me.

'Let's go for a drink,' he says.

'Sorry?'

'Let me buy you a beer.'

'Er,' I mumble and fumble for something convincing. 'I, er, think you've got me mistaken for someone else, buddy. I'm lost. D'you know how to get to the main carpark here?'

I'm close, but he steps closer. A proper space-invader. I'm holding on to a shred of hope it's just his manner and not something deliberate, when he takes a handful of the front neck of my t-shirt, and pushes me against the hoardings so hard the knuckle of his index finger smashes into my throat. The back of my head hits against what's behind me and starts to rebound towards him but never gets there. With me pinned against the wood, he lifts his arm up further, taking just enough of my weight to make me light on my feet. My clothes, clenched in his fist, rise to meet my chin which he holds steadily in place with the same hand. Immediately I start needing air.

'We're going somewhere to talk,' he says, 'and you can choose where.' His voice is quiet and all around me – supreme in its confidence.

Behind him the swollen sea is starting to dull and lose definition. I'm so desperate to breathe, so angry at what's happening that the helplessness is guaranteed to win out. I think of biting him, of kicking, of throwing myself at him, but with no firm ground to push off, and no plan, the fainting sensation only grows. I try to breathe through my nose but as soon as the air reaches my windpipe the pain is too much. I've got less than a minute.

'So come on then,' he says. 'Decide. Where are we going?'

◤

In darkness, there's a low-tide, perfectly moonlit wave. About waist high, it keeps running across a sandbank. This could be the Crawl. It's a warm night though, and I'm stepping barefoot towards the water's edge.

We're far enough down now that the sand is soaking. If you stayed too long your feet would sink until only your ankles were left. A creeping band of foamy shoreline washes over and pulls my feet further under. The cool of the wet sand and the moving water soothes away the big worry that I won't get there in time.

Alys's voice comes out of the darkness.

This is the right place, Noah, she says.

Sunrise could be any moment, or maybe never at all, and I know what she's gonna say next:

You're safe, but you'll have to do the right things. Even if you don't know what they are.

Or if I don't want to?

'Even then, Noah. You know that.'

'OK, OK,' I'm telling her. 'But you're stronger. This is *your* fight.'

A little peak peels across the sand bar. I see its edged form deepen and then explode white in beautiful symmetry.

No, Noah. It's ours. It's everyone's. I've done my bit. It's your turn now.

To start with it's like a confessional. Only totally one-way. I'm sharing with this fucker all the things I wouldn't want Starsky or Alys or my mother to know. Or at least I think I am, because there's this urgent desire in me to trust this man – like when you see a doctor or a surgeon and they just nod and listen and get you to tell them everything.

Trouble is, I don't know what I have and haven't said.

Sitting opposite me, his stare can seem kind. He sits still, so still you could hardly tell he's there, and then when he moves or shuffles it's with these mechanical motions. And yet everything he does is smooth, instant and gradual, calculated but natural. 'Simple questions, one-word answers,' he's instructed me.

That's not what's happening though. He's got me doing all the work.

'D'you like it here?' he says.

It's a café that probably doubles as a wine bar later in the evening and there's a coffee in front of me. We're in a booth-style table towards the back and warmth is coming through an overhead window. Natural light everywhere, and only a few other people in here – but enough space that this conversation is private.

'It's a nice place,' I tell him. I can't see the street outside, so the blanks aren't filling in. 'I like how it's...' I'm just looking for words to glue the gaps instead. 'Yeah, those beams, they're nice. Someone's done a lot of work on them. Wonder if it was a belt-sander or... well... they're high up so must have needed some scaffolding, but indoors? That roof's new isn't it? Must have cost a lot.'

He smiles warmly, with pride, as if I'm saying the right things. And he asks:

'So where have you been before here?'

I start blabbing about the boat, and about the French forests and how the trees fluttered past me in rows as I drove up, and about the mountains and the dry air and the other boat before that. I'm talking so much I can't even focus on listening to all of it, but he's sitting there, nodding, smiling, getting closer inch by inch. I must be telling him things he already thinks he knows. His face glows, taking reward from hearing me say everything he expects, as and when he knows I'm going to.

Noah's still talking away, all valves open, when I clutch half an idea and manage to eject a question for him instead.

'You like it here too, don't you?'

He nods, says 'yes' without quite finishing the word. Did I say this guy was like talking to a doctor? Scrap that. He's way more engaged. Now it's like meeting with a priest or a fucking counsellor. But there is some kind of initiative coming back to me now, and I try more questions. 'One word answers,' I say back to him.

And that's what I get. One word on every bit of nothing.

'What do you eat here?'

'Risotto,' he says.

'What's the time?'

'Four.'

'Is that too early?'

'Yes.'

'Can we wait?'

'Yes.'

'Was it far to get here?'

'No.'

These simple questions go on and I'm getting so little it's wearing me out more than when I was doing the talking. That's coz I still am.

But then, out of nowhere, I manage to fire in a deeper one, and it begins.

'Where's Mr Lovell?'

'Absolutely no reason for you to care.'

'But I do.'

'Well don't then.'

'That's not possible though. You know it's not.'

'Once you're in on it, you're in on it,' he says.

'I'll decide that.'

He looks square at me and it fuckin bores a hole through

somewhere just behind my chest. Which is when I realise he hasn't once glared at me full-on until now. Every part of his face is hummingly taught like twisted rope – stored energy waiting to go off on someone.

'Will you?' he says – voice has no rise in intonation but it has to be a question.

'Yes.'

'Fine then.' The stare is eased, saved for when it's next needed, and he answers with a shrug and a puff of air: 'Mr Lovell. He's where you think he is.'

'I think,' I say, and falter. 'I think...'

His shoulders relax and I see his neck and throat loosen. I'm allowed to take my time.

'In London...' I mumble. 'He went into that restaurant. He was taken in. I think you've...'

Greggs laughs. 'I love it. I knew you'd say that.'

'Well, was he?'

Replies come fast, without tone or cadence: 'Like I said, once you know about that, you're going to be in on it. Can you commit?' I've heard just enough now to pick up the accentless absence of all emotion in his voice.

'I've always known anyway,' I say, and in a sliding, unpinned moment he looks like he's losing that hypnotic patience that's been getting me to talk so freely. I've got his attention – but it's a different part of him that's listening now.

'You mean *she's* always known,' he says. Again I get that instant warming of the blood that zaps my fingertips, and the relish in his face sends me in search of anger.

'What do you mean "she"?' I ask.

'Nothing. Go on. You say you've both known about me for a while?'

'Both? Who else are we on about? This is between you and me.'

'Not that it means anything,' he says. 'Let's not slow ourselves with the small print. You were telling me about what you know?'

When he threatened to bring Alys up – *did* he just threaten to do that? – it got me straight on edge. But then the relief when he seems ready to drop the mention…

'You… and me,' I carry on, trying to control the pitch of my voice, straining to keep it steady. 'I'm asking about Mr Lovell.'

'Call him Brian.'

'OK. *Brian*. What I want to know is how he ended up the way he was… you know… just before you, well, before you did what you did to him.'

Hunted by his own hounds.

This feels like it's going to be hard again. I look at him, as if I can't hear very well.

'They all end up that way,' he says. 'His wife too.'

'No. Your handiwork. Both times. And it's nothing special. Nothing to be proud of. Anyone could have done that, as long as they wanted to – or were sick enough.'

'Hold there,' he says. 'They did that to themselves. Both of them. And they were more than happy to do it. They knew how it could have been different. You could, too. It's the most amazing thing in the world.'

'You were there, though, weren't you?'

He looks at me, and I can almost see him fighting off the need to lick his lips.

'She used to look good in the mornings, asleep,' he says, definitively, moving us on.

'You what?'

'Yeah, you'd love it, too. To watch her lying there.'

'Who?'

'You know who. We can do it all again if you like? I told you, it's easy when you've got the script.'

'Watch *who* in the mornings?'

'Your client,' he tells me. 'Why, who else are you thinking I might watch?' Then he holds back another knowing smile – just. 'Oh,' he says, slowly. 'I see. You thought I meant... Ha! Great. No. Not *her*. Watching *her* stopped being necessary in the end. No, I mean your client. I mean watch *your client*.'

Still, neither of us has mentioned Alys, but he knows what I was just thinking. Which also means those crazy childhood dreams of hers were...

I have to ask him more. We're so far beyond any codes I know. So I go after the links:

'My client then,' I say. 'Did you make the noises she heard? In the house.'

And he smiles, like he's my friend. Or like I'm his friend. '*Make* them?'

'So there is kit in the walls of that place – like she thought?'

He's got his tongue just scratching at the edge of his mouth again. 'No. She made them. Every sound. She chose them all. She heard what she wanted to hear. All I had to do was change a few of the details for her – just one or two noises of my own. It's so easy. We could do it to anyone – they'll go wherever you want, then.'

'What she *wanted* to hear?'

'Yeah,' he says, in a big, drawn-out exhalation. 'Yeah. She knew what she wanted. She wanted to be someone. Like we are – you and I. But you don't get to hear it like she did, unless you choose. And she did. She chose the role. You're just the same, you listen when you want, Mr Lloyd.'

'Stop! Alright! Shut it off!' I'm yelling at him, and he looks around tentatively as if I'm going to embarrass us. No one else in the building bats an eyelid our way.

'Too late now,' he says. 'Since you do know, you're tied in completely.'

'What?'

He delays, gives me breathing space, lets me think I have a chance in this conversation again. So I think of the water nearby. Where it might be moving, and when. Yes, it's nearby. The pull is still on us.

'Only if I choose to see what you tell me to,' I say.

'You will.' The grin of someone who's never been wrong.

'What if I don't pay in?' I ask. 'What if I don't recognise your currency?'

'Never going to happen.'

'Only coz it hasn't yet.'

'We'll involve the other people that matter if you can't make this instalment.'

That shock of whizzing pulse knocks at my temple again. *He can't mean this*, comes a voice – a voice I can't connect to. And then *Fears concentrate to a single…*

I look up across the table, and for the first time since I've been watching him, there's an inkling of some kind of doubt. And as soon as I see it, and he realises, my own mind starts to cloud all over again. Dread pours over me. Yes. I actually am about to try and stir this thing up.

'Do you have any idea what we're talking about?' he asks me.

'I know what you *want* us to be on about.'

'Well then, you'll know – last time I'll say it – that what happened to the Lovells was what had to happen. Don't worry, she made enough noise back at us. Enough noise to last a generation. Enough to get us through to the cycle's next turn.'

'What were you doing there, anyway?'

'Never said I was,' he says, stern eyes again threatening to catch me dead on. 'I didn't need to be. Brian did a beautiful job. He played his part.'

'I know he killed her,' I say – Alys's theory. 'But he wasn't meant to, was he?'

I'm reckoning that showing him what I know will help, now – even if I haven't believed it until far too recently. So I add, 'He did it because he thought it would stop you from dragging them into that tale we're all meant to be acting out. And he took your purpose away. He broke the rules – deviated from the story. Did it work? I reckon so. Your cycle. It's gone, isn't it?'

'He did what I told him to,' says Greggs, 'My idea. And he did it perfectly. She didn't mind at all – even when it hurt.'

'Neither of you had to do *shit*,' I say. 'Actaeon *bollocks*. There you go, mate. I said it. Made up story; that's all it is. Nothing to neither you nor me if we don't want it to be.'

'Right about one of us,' he grins. 'Yeah. But I'm the one who owns it now. It's registered to my name as of this year and season. *Hideous*. Oh, yes. The mutation in the cycle, it's *my* mutation. Wanna know where I got it from? How I took control?'

He leans towards me.

'Go on, take a guess,' he says, and then, before I can speak, 'Good work. Correct. Absolutely spot on. Nail on the head.'

One person with no apparent reason. One person whose existence remains only a theory. Alys's father? There it is. Now I get it. That killer. This killer. Are they both... Did he... Did Greggs... Am I staring at that very person, right now?

Without it even being spoken, the question sends him into a tiny jolt of pleasure. And after I ask it he takes relish in his own turn at the confessional: 'Kill's such a simple term, Noah. When it's time to play your part there's no other option,' he says. 'Try to go against the grain and that's what can happen. We could call what happened to him "punishment", a warning – or both if we like?'

'So it was you?' I say. '*That's* how you "took control"?'

'If I wanted to,' he says, completely ready for the question. 'But d'you know what? I could just as easily point out how you did it, and, if I wanted, that would become every bit as true.'

'Would it fuck.'

'It's what I do. It's my job. You're right. I put the threads back in place. In any way I want to.'

'It was his story first, wasn't it?'

Yes. Alys's father. I'm buying it all now. He was the first bit of this whole push in the tide. That's why she's so drawn to it all. *Got to find out*, *Noah*, got to get the answers. Even though she's probably known them all along. *That's* why she's been so obsessed with the sea, with its rhythms. She thinks that stuff is how to be told the rest of the tale.

'Go on then,' I say. 'Let's go there. Alys's father. How did he get to be, you know, where he was?'

'In the role?'

'If that's what you call it.'

'A voyeur,' he says.

'Actaeon.'

'No need for the name,' Greggs snaps – words that almost sound like Alys. 'Doesn't mean anything. It's the *meaning* we need to follow.'

'Fine. Call him whatever. We'll agree on that. Come on, how did...'

'He peeped, didn't he. Naughty, naughty. Spied what he shouldn't have.'

'But he could do what he wanted, though. Her mum? She wasn't out of bounds. They could both do what they wanted.'

Greggs ushers me on. 'Good boy,' he says. 'Keep going.'

'So he didn't peep. She wanted to be with him.'

'Good... and then...'

'They were having a *child*,' I say. And then choke on my next words.

'Slipped through, didn't he?' says Greggs. 'He's not meant to get to the goddess is he? He was marked anyway. But look at how wrong it can go if you let them meet!'

239

The skin on the sides of my head pulls back, as if I'm being dragged through high winds. 'So you're saying…' I have to take the subject directly on to her now. There's no choice. 'Alys is… Alys… she's the…'

'Descended *from*, Noah. Descended *from*. Her mother still passed the role on – that girl escaped it. But you know who it was passed to, eh? Catch a mutating myth why don't you? It'll fuel you forever.'

The brutality of that moment, this man's first murder runs through my imagination. A killing he thought was going to be some divine act that placed him up there with the legends. And I remember how Alys told me her mother had seemed hollowed out, empty, hadn't ever recovered that grip on life. Of course she hadn't.

'The bit I'm enjoying, is what that makes *you*,' Greggs laughs.

For a moment, I'm too heavy to move any part of me. Not even to sit up. We're here, at the all-of-it. It's what Alys most wants to know, and yet if I push it more the whole thing will slip through my fingers. And that's when I hear. She was right all along – I *am* involved. That's what she meant. *You won't need too many more directions once we get there*. She said that, didn't she? How could I miss it? I'll know what to do when I'm there.

And now I am. Alys! *There's* the person who was spot-on, nail-on-the-head. Of course she was.

He starts up with another attempt to explain, and this is where I've got to get control for good. 'It goes the way I want it,' he's saying. 'It always will. I made my move first. You should have listened to Alys.'

'I have been,' I tell him. 'Now I *know* you're off track.'

The air around us – no, not the air, the weight of the air – turns and shifts. High tide, Haydn. There it was.

'You prop me up,' he says back.

'How?' I say.

'Tell me what you do.'

'What I do?'

'Yes. Do.'

'Nothing special.' I shuffle back in my seat and lift my chin to meet his.

'Wrong, and you know you are,' he says.

'I'm nothing special,' I tell him, again.

'But you're ready to be. The harder you work for us, the more you become.'

'For you? I haven't decided if you exist yet.'

He laughs. 'I love that. Another one who thinks the same thing. Listen to Alys.'

'I just said to you. I have been.'

'I'm *fact*,' he says. 'Tell anything over and over enough times, my friend, and it's true anyway. Here it is. You've done it – all of you. And there's nothing you can do to reverse...'

'Alright, I'm bored now,' I tell him. 'I'm not interested. I'm nothing special. *We're* nothing special. You should try seeing things that way sometimes. It might help.'

And as if a switch flicks in him, he changes tone to a faster, deeper voice.

'Right, you little shit,' he says. 'What I have is what everyone wants. You chase my grace, my...' he pauses, and again his tongue just pushes out of his mouth before he adds, 'My manna.'

'Yeah, OK,' I cut him off, because I want to tell him so badly, and if there's any chance of getting anywhere it's going to be through taking the lead. 'Shall I tell you what you want to tell me?' I say. 'Coz I can hear it, right now.'

He looks through me. Fuck, this is going to be hard. But then I realise it's coz he's actually got decisions to make here, and he might not actually know which ones to take.

'Fine,' he says 'Go on.'

'I know this story,' I tell him. 'I know what everyone's meant to do. But it's only the *lesson* that matters. The ending is irrelevant – and that's the bit you can't handle. You're empty. That's why. And empty people are empty people. They don't mean anything. They might as well... I dunno... burn ants through magnifying glasses to feel like they can make a difference. It's all the same, just petulance. But you...'

'OK, what do I do then?'

'Who cares? Bollocks to your addresses and your aliases and your clients and the coffee I'm drinking,' I tell him.

'You are bold,' he says.

'It's easy when I don't subscribe.'

'No it's not. You might not be going back. You know that, don't you?'

'I fuckin am.'

'Not without something from me. Do what you want,' he says, 'but first I've got something to give you.'

'Who are you to say anything?'

'I'm the choice you'll make.'

And he's smiling again. 'I am what you don't want me to be,' he grins. 'I tell you what to think.'

I fold my arms, raise my eyebrows, look sideways. 'OK.'

'I tell you what to see. Whatever you do, you're feeding me. Go any direction. You'll just make me stronger. I pull the strings.'

'Or what?'

He laughs again. 'That's all there is, Noah. Do what you want, because really it's just what *I* want. You might think things move for you, but really you all move for *me*. I'm there, whenever you don't want me to be. I always will be. Push back, I'll grow. Pull away, I'll grow. Watch my size. I'm dangerous.'

'I'm not trying to deny you that,' I tell him. 'I just don't care for it. It's that simple. I'm opting out. You've passed the baton to the wrong one!'

And her words begin falling together. I'm *meant* to have run. Because I wasn't really running – I was hoping it would come for me. It made this idiot need me. I was *meant* not to want to know. The ditching, the let-down, the I'm-not-playing-along. That's all we needed. She's not playing along either, now. Go on, Greggs, keep trying. You're fighting receding waters here.

'Everything you do is a reaction to me,' he squawks, and you can hear his dilemma. 'Everything you'll ever be, everything you ever were. Go against me... and I'm still shaping you. Come with me and at least you'll like the sense of choice.'

'No,' I say, sure it's got to happen now or never. 'You really, really aren't getting it. I won't. I'm listening, because you've brought me to listen. But then I leave you here, just like you know I will.'

He pushes his chair away and to the side in a single, swift movement and as he stands the fear that gripped me earlier is back. Thrilling, violent, nasty fear. The fear of an animal outnumbered, the fear that makes life cheap, and allows you to throw everything you've got back at trying to raise its value again for one last desperate fling against your own limits.

'Look in the mirror,' he tells me. 'I'll make you seem whatever I want you to seem. You want horns and hooves and to be frozen and salted and served up to the people you owe... I'll do it for you.'

'You'll do it for yourself,' I say. 'And that's about it.'

I go to stand up and his shoulders part and rise back, giving him a few more inches over me.

'What ever made Mrs Lovell listen to you?'

'I did,' he says. 'That one wasn't your doing. I can't let you take any credit there. She wanted to go that way.'

'OK,' I say. 'Good for her.' And I do stand this time.

'I'm out of here now,' I tell him. 'You keep convincing yourself that anyone's gonna give a flying fuck about what you want from now on.'

'Push all you want,' he says, but there's feeling in his voice. This is new.

'I don't need to. No one does. I'll just hop off, thanks.'

'You'll lose the chase,' he says.

'Not if I'm not running.'

'You will.'

'OK then, it's time,' I say and he presses himself towards me, but from just the wrong side. The door is right there. What's outside of it is starting to be visible. I call back to him, loud enough for others to hear me: 'Dream on. I can dip in and out, buddy. There's millions like me, and your say is over.'

He's moving into my path once more as I pass through the doorway. He follows me outdoors, in no particular rush, and we're in another of those little sloping lanes. There's only pavement on one side – the opposite one to us, and a handrail next to a high wall with ivy running down it. I cross the road and he moves sideways in front of me, growing, swelling. He's taller than me.

'Where are you going,' he says. Again no intonation.

'I'm going back. There's gonna be another swell soon. I'm going beyond low water. Where you can't be heard.'

'Fine,' he says. 'But like I said, you need to take something with you.'

And he's on me. He pushes me, and I fall backwards to a sitting position against the kerb. The fuckin speed on this guy… it's like when you see a spider shoot out to wrap a trapped fly. Five paces are covered without even a shuffle and he's swinging a kick for my head. It connects and with a *whomp* that sound is between my ears in stereo – a pinging reverb that's throwing my own thoughts around in elliptical loops that speed up and up and up as they race around the back of my head and find the soreness in my neck from the impact I've just absorbed. My temples throb, and the anger tries to rise.

He has the energy to keep doing this until I'm gone. The only thing holding him back is the pleasure of it. He wants me to know what's being done to me.

So I get up, and charge at him which at least gets it underway. He starts smashing at me, and it's a blur, and there's blood, and there's fury, and there's something unbelievably right about it all because before I have time to feel the sadness that it's come to this, my own hands are in front of me and Haydn Greggs is mine for the taking. Hunted by his own hounds. I'm watching myself, Noah, go for it, as if from above, and I'm crying to stop but we're trading impact for impact for impact, and the boundaries are slipping. There's a knife, and it's his, or is it mine, or is it there at all? Then the same spike is made of bone, or antler, or some other element altogether and I know the damage being done – it's gonna be so much further to return, but on we go. Darkness is pressing in – not sunset, but that wintery snap-to-night-time that makes me think weeks are passing by. I'm crying for what's happened to me, for what I'm going to have to live with when I finish – but then I'm also crying with the fear of what happens if I stop too soon.

He has to be dead. I've found his rage and hurled it at him, but now it's going to be mine. Forever. There can't be any way to reverse this. I'm thumping and thumping at something that's no longer animate and getting colder by the second. My mouth opens to plead for this to be undone, but my throat is mobilising drying blood from my gums and tongue.

I'm walking away – fresh, bright red drops and tears filling my torn eyelids and I'm both terrified and fascinated by the face-down lump of raw victim that something from within me has made of my attacker. The stillness in the air has seen it all.

Moon, from somewhere directly above or directly below, slides out of alignment and the huge weight of cold water continues to pull away from the land.

Noah has to get off this island, away from what's going to be behind me. The rest of the hounds can't be far, wanting me as one of their own. I make for the water's edge, but it's getting darker and I won't reach it in time. Shame, I think, smiling at what I should be screaming to prevent. I'm not going to leave, so there we are... Maybe it really will still follow me, forever. The pack is nearly with me, baying for a lifetime of hunts. No point running, it's going to be here.

Yes there is. Heave, Noah, heave.

Alys's voice is almost coming through. I'm straining to listen coz now I don't know what she's going to say. I don't know anything anymore.

'That's how it happens,' she's telling me. 'Just stay with it. Almost there.'

'Your dad was only a deep-sea fisherman,' I try to tell her. 'Nothing special. No role. Same as the rest of us. That's how we're getting out. We're handing it all back.'

And my legs are giving up the way you can't run in a dream. Only I'm trying to run *to* one.

Zero +/- One

Dust

It's the time of year when we see less. Daytimes turn in on themselves as we swing away from the source. Sea-facing windows gather salt residue, and mask the ocean's fightback as I think of heading out. The Crawl is always here. It's where you'll end up. This time, anyway.

So that was how it went. She was right. I wasn't. And I *am* still Noah. Nothing more.

Except for the way that, sitting right here, in front of that expanse, I can try to look over the lot. The logic Alys pushed on me was what got me back.

For the last time now, I'm looking over my shoulder at where it led. Here we go. I'm there… Alys walking towards the headland, west end of town, sea shaking beneath the rocks in front of us, just after I made it home.

There it is. I'm following her out to the edge, and she's telling me my cuts look terrible – hideous – that I'm gonna scare the living shit out of Josie and my mum when they see it. She's telling me I look like I've been in a plane crash, or dragged along a road face down. I'm sore from head to toe, and don't want to go anywhere near anyone medical. Alys has tried to suss my condition, but she says she can't.

'Noah!'

It slips away again, as little sis calls to me.

'Alright? What is it?'

'Mum says someone's on the phone for you.'

'Really?'

'No.'

'Oh – OK. Why d'you say it then, Josie?'

'It's funny. You looked excited.'

'Good work. Didn't fall for it though. You know no one phones me here!'

'Mr White does.'

'Yeah – but he doesn't count.'

Good old Starsky, eh? There's another one I had to hide from for nearly a month. And even then he knew. When I turned up my mother said he'd already rung and told her to expect me back any day.

'Yeah – well if he phones again, Josie, you can tell him I'll speak to him.'

'OK.' She bounds off to another room.

And I'm back on the edge again, listening to the last bits.

Loud wind and thick rain are drowning out the decaying past as we try to piece it together.

'It doesn't matter,' says Alys. 'There's no need.'

But I have to know. Or to measure the blanks at least. The many gaps in the who and why of this thing that I'm about to forget for good – along with the *how*. How I made it back from the Channel Islands, bleeding and blinded by tears. Sitting at the water's edge plunging my face into the sea to try and drown out the events before. Towelling my face with force before passing officials on the ferry ramp. Then hours behind the wheel back on British soil desperate to pass out – which I did, but only after arriving at Alys's place, where she seemed unsurprised to see me.

The memory of it fades somewhere around there, or stops mattering. I'm not sure of the difference.

'It did all come around, then,' she's saying. 'But it won't again. We're OK.'

'What?' I'm asking, as the lights fade.

'It's happened, Noah. It's passed.'

There's never anything in the papers, or online, or anywhere, about a body – no suggestion Haydn Greggs turned up anywhere else. Nothing in the news and nobody matching his description in the hospital in St Helier – I know coz a few days on we make some calls on a pretext.

'There was never going to be,' says Alys, before she tells me how yes, I had to run – even though it wasn't the right thing to do. 'You were always going to be called back anyway,' she almost laughs.

Doesn't change my wrongs, though.

I haven't even told her how it happened either. 'No need,' she says. 'Someone else will know the way it ended, next time.'

'How far ahead is that?' I find the clarity to ask.

Further than you.

Yes, further than any of us. Or the Lovells, the Clares, or Starsky – who Alys hopes I'm going to contact as soon as I'm alright to go out and about. 'Further ahead than you can fathom. So don't try,' she says. 'Coz *I'm* not going to anymore.'

I try to ask her why. I only get a 'Because,' and then she changes tack.

'Doesn't matter if the roads ahead fork from now on, Noah. It's what's behind that nobody must change.' Not easy listening – not when you almost wish you could change it.

I'm learning, though. Her behind-us is my in-front-of-us, or someone else's here-and-now.

'I'm not going to do this for much longer,' she says, enough times to really mean it. 'I'm going away, too.'

'Where?'

'Somewhere that lets me hear all the things I've never noticed.' Then she laughs, 'Over the rainbow.' But in a way, she's serious. 'Too much to enjoy in this world – and not enough behind me. The sea will be still close by, but it can't be *this* sea anymore. We all have to change sometimes.'

And her story moves on, too.

So, with her last piece of advice echoing in my mind, I've realised – properly thought it through – and identified, once and for all, what we all really like to do most: To look ahead and know that what you're seeing is something that can actually happen.

I will not like it. But then I might. Then I'll love. Then I'll hate. And I'll run.

More time pushes through. She's right. The inevitable things do indeed change; rhythms alter, cycles keep turning. And we grow into it. I ran. OK – wasn't hard to foresee. I'll always run, but now I run towards.

Noah's drifting to the corner of these pictures now, if you please, and it's gonna feel great. After all, that's what was always meant to happen. The only thing that matters is that the picture is there at all.

I will not like it. But then I might.

I thought she sounded clever at the time. But she was only saying the obvious. Still, I wasn't hearing it.

So when I look, what is there to see? Everything important.

Summer – any one of the many to come: it's warm again and we're pushing my little sis into a wave – maybe with help from someone else, maybe not. Not a big concern. It's happening anyway – and the detail can fill in at the time. Doesn't matter what I'm doing to pay bills. These exact scenes are what we're here for. Rhythms kept before, rhythms kept during, and whatever else. Even what we don't know is still comfortably spread out in front of us.

Rage will come in from the ocean too. Months of it, and we'll love the whole thing. There's going to be those crisp, thin-aired days when grass turns crystal and ground feels brittle-hard.

Then will come the power of sun to warm once you escape the shade. Days drawing back out again – any year, every time. Growth and renewal – but never once repetition.

A little peak rises, out of a sparkling sea surface. It's got my name on it, or yours, or hers, or his. Watch it lift, as the pulse ticks its way across the ocean floor. Feel the weight of water pulling you in, the draw, the rise – and know that somewhere there's coming a moment where that pull can fling you forward. Here it is. Eye the line it draws, tap in and choose yours. Don't think too hard. It has to be anything but perfect.

Acknowledgements

Thanks to the band Face to Face for granting the use of a lyric from their song 'Velocity' (*Everything is Everything*, Kung Fu Records, 2001) in this novel.

The author also wishes to acknowledge the support and advice of the following: Chelsey Fox, Richard Davies, Susie Wild, Cerys Jones, Anne Gallagher, Tim Kevan, Jim, Noel and Paul Anderson, Cathy Hutcheon, Jon Gower, Daniel Morden and John Howells. Thanks, sorry for dragging you in, and hope you manage to free yourselves of the Tide in time.